ASSASSINS?

They came out of the cedars on horseback. Both riders wore masks. They were armed with pistols, but he didn't wait for them to shoot. He put heels to the roan and bent low. As he fumbled with his coat buttons to get to his .44 and urged the roan to go faster, a cold chill of fear swept over him. Expecting one of their wild shots to strike him at any moment, he reined the roan off into the tall cedars. At last, with the gun butt in his right hand, he reined to a halt, looking back for sight of any pursuit. Nothing.

Damn. Where in the hell had they gone? He turned the roan back. All he could hear was the rain on his hat and wind in the cedar tops. His heart still thumped hard under his breastbone and he breathed hard to get enough air. Who were they and why were they on this road? Worse, why did they want him? Were they headed for his place to get him?

He'd not recognized them or their wet horses in his haste to get away. Daylight was fading fast. He holstered the pistol and swung the roan eastward. Who wanted him dead?

Ralph Compton

Trail to
Cottonwood Falls

A Ralph Compton Novel
by Dusty Richards

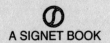
A SIGNET BOOK

SIGNET
Published by New American Library, a division of
Penguin Group (USA) Inc., 375 Hudson Street,
New York, New York 10014, USA
Penguin Group (Canada), 90 Eglinton Avenue East, Suite 700, Toronto,
Ontario M4P 2Y3, Canada (a division of Pearson Penguin Canada Inc.)
Penguin Books Ltd., 80 Strand, London WC2R 0RL, England
Penguin Ireland, 25 St. Stephen's Green, Dublin 2,
Ireland (a division of Penguin Books Ltd.)
Penguin Group (Australia), 250 Camberwell Road, Camberwell, Victoria 3124,
Australia (a division of Pearson Australia Group Pty. Ltd.)
Penguin Books India Pvt. Ltd., 11 Community Centre, Panchsheel Park,
New Delhi - 110 017, India
Penguin Group (NZ), 67 Apollo Drive, Mairangi Bay,
Auckland 1311, New Zealand (a division of Pearson New Zealand Ltd.)
Penguin Books (South Africa) (Pty.) Ltd., 24 Sturdee Avenue,
Rosebank, Johannesburg 2196, South Africa

Penguin Books Ltd, Registered Offices:
80 Strand, London WC2R 0RL, England

First published by Signet, an imprint of New American Library,
a division of Penguin Group (USA) Inc.

First Printing, April 2007
10 9 8 7 6 5 4 3 2 1

 REGISTERED TRADEMARK—MARCA REGISTRADA

Printed in the United States of America

PUBLISHER'S NOTE
This is a work of fiction. Names, characters, places, and incidents either are
the product of the author's imagination or are used fictitiously, and any resem-
blance to actual persons, living or dead, business establishments, events, or
locales is entirely coincidental.

The publisher does not have any control over and does not assume any
responsibility for author or third-party Web sites or their content.

THE IMMORTAL COWBOY

This is respectfully dedicated to the "American Cowboy." His was the saga sparked by the turmoil that followed the Civil War, and the passing of more than a century has by no means diminished the flame.

True, the old days and the old ways are but treasured memories, and the old trails have grown dim with the ravages of time, but the spirit of the cowboy lives on.

In my travels—to Texas, Oklahoma, Kansas, Nebraska, Colorado, Wyoming, New Mexico, and Arizona—I always find something that reminds me of the Old West. While I am walking these plains and mountains for the first time, there is this feeling that a part of me is eternal, that I have known these old trails before. I believe it is the undying spirit of the frontier calling, allowing me, through the mind's eye, to step back into time. What is the appeal of the Old West of the American frontier?

It has been epitomized by some as the dark and bloody period in American history. Its heroes—Crockett, Bowie, Hickok, Earp—have been reviled and criticized. Yet the Old West lives on, larger than life.

It has become a symbol of freedom, when there was always another mountain to climb and another river to cross; when a dispute between two men was settled not with expensive lawyers, but with fists, knives, or guns. Barbaric? Maybe. But some things never change. When the cowboy rode into the pages of American history, he left behind a legacy that lives within the hearts of us all.

—*Ralph Compton*

Prologue

Big Mike Donaho polished glasses with a Turkish towel back of the mahogany bar in Rosie's Shamrock Saloon. His only customer was a regular, the ex-drover Ed Wright. Wright's six-foot frame was hunched up over the bar and he was well into his purpose of the day—to get stone blind drunk. Same as Ed did every day—got soused. He came in about nine in the morning, still hung over from the day before, and he passed out in the afternoon or evening. Then Mike had him hauled to one of the empty cribs in back to sleep it off. Big shame; Ed'd been successful and made some big money driving Texas cattle to Kansas. He owned several sections in the hill country and had some Mexicans looking after his place.

Six men filed in the door and Mike stopped polishing to watch them headed for Ed. He recognized their homemade shirts and dress, they were those same small ranchers—again. Filled with dread, he shook his head over their reappearance in the bar. They were back to try to change Ed's mind.

"Ed," the leader said. "It's me. Frank Hogan."

Shaking his head, Ed raised his unsteady gaze to

the man. "I know who you are. I know who all of you are. What're you doing here?"

"Ed, we've all got cattle—we need 'em taken to Kansas and sold. They'd rob us blind if we sold them around here."

He agreed with them, bobbing his head. "They damn sure would. Cattle ain't worth nothing around here." He turned and looked in the mirror behind the bar, and closed his eyes. "I can't help."

"Ed, we all owe money. You know ranching is a corn bread living at its best. If we can sell two hundred, two hundred fifty head each up there we can hold on."

"Just take 'em north. You'll find it." He waved an unsteady arm in that direction.

"Can I help you gents?" Mike asked, wiping off the bar top in front of them.

"You sure can. Convince Ed to make another drive."

Mike shook his head. "Can't do that, boys."

Ed twisted around so his elbows hung on the bar and looked at the floor. "I don't care if hell freezes over and polar bears move to south Texas—I ain't taking another herd of cattle north." He swung his left arm out as if to clear the air. "Any of you boys ever take a war widow the news her only son was killed on the trail, and give her sixty bucks of wages for his life insurance?

"No, no, you ain't done it. Buried some kid that died of pneumonia at the Red River crossing. What was his name, Mike?" He scrubbed the side of his beard-stubbled face on his palm.

"Lars Kyle."

"That's the one." Ed shook his head warily and then raised up some. "Jesse Collier's boy—damn gambler shot him in Abilene. Hell, that boy was no gunfighter. Lucky Earl was the gambler's name—I tracked him to Salina and called him out in the street. Blew him in half with damn buckshot. But Ethel Mae won't never see her boy's grave up there on the prairie— bad deal."

"We know you're upset. I mean about them pirates killing your partner, Dave Ivy, on the riverboat—"

"Marsh and Corley Brady—I trailed them bastards plumb to Fort Smith and lost 'em. I'll get 'em."

"Ed, we know losing Dave Ivy was a big loss to you. But we don't know the way to Kansas. Ain't got the slightest idea how to ever get them there. Folks lose everything they've got on them drives that go bad. You—you could get them there."

"Go find you someone else. I ain't the man . . ." He whirled around. " 'Nother beer and two shots of whiskey, Mike. They've got my mind churning up all that crap and I can't stand it."

"You boys better leave," Mike said. "He's not going to Abilene ever again."

"That's right," Ed said. "Besides, it's Newton where Joe McCoy's setting up the new pens. Newton, Kansas."

"Ed," the shortest man in the group said as he stepped up. "Billie Miller. You remember me? We fought them Yankees together."

"Yes. Known you all my life."

"I'm asking—no, I'm begging. Take our cattle to this Newton for us?"

With a pendulum shake of his head, Ed dropped

his gaze to the brass rail at the foot of the bar. "I can't—can't go through it ever again. I can't even forget it! Now get the hell out of here. All of you!"

Mike watched them leave, crestfallen, then he came out and guided Ed to a table, and set him in a chair. "They're gone." He put a new beer in front of Ed and patted him on the shoulder. "I won't let them bother you."

Ed nodded and looked close to crying. "They don't know how hard it is. Don't know . . ."

"I know. Take it easy pard," Big Mike said. Why did they keep hounding him? Didn't they see how upset it made him?

"Thanks," Ed said to dismiss him, and put his elbows on the table to support himself.

Things had quieted down in the almost empty barroom so Mike busied himself polishing glasses. He never served a drink in a water-spotted glass. At a rumbling sound, he looked up. Someone out front had a pushcart on the boardwalk. Then, to his shock, a fine-looking lady stuck her head in the batwing doors and looked around. She was a handsome, respectable-appearing woman in her early thirties, and she shocked him even more by walking right into the place.

She had a well-proportioned figure that would make men's heads turn when she strolled down the boardwalk. Her tight lips and the glare in her blue eyes told him she was headed for one thing—Ed. At least there was one good thing; she didn't have an ax to chop up his bar like they were doing in Kansas. Then Mike frowned at the next sight. Why in hell was that swamper coming in with the damn wheelbarrow?

"Lady, you can't be in here." He came around the bar to run her off, and waved his rag at the swamper to get out. Whores were one thing, but decent women weren't allowed.

She looked around in an unimpressed gathering of what she could see and then met his gaze. "I'm here to get him."

"But that's Ed Wright and he's drunk. He's also sleeping."

"I know who he is. Now help Charlie get him in the wheelbarrow. He's going to my place."

"But he's Ed Wright—"

"One of the best cattle drovers in Texas. Now help me." She had Ed by one arm.

Mike took the other and Charlie picked up his feet. They sprawled Wright's six-foot frame into the wheelbarrow.

"But you don't know—"

"The livery, Charlie," she said to the grizzly old man, then opened the drawstrings on her purse. "Does he owe you a bar bill?"

"No, ma'am. What's your name?"

"Unita Nance. I'm the Bar U owner."

"Lady, I sure hope you know what you're doing, ah, Mrs. Nance."

"Two bottles of your whiskey." She motioned him toward the bar. "He'll need some when he comes around."

"He'll need lots," Mike said, throwing the towel over his shoulder as he slipped in back of the bar. He set two fifths on the bar. "Want it on his account?"

"No, I'm paying for it."

Pained by what he was doing, he considered taking

the two bottles back. "I don't think I'm supposed to sell whiskey to a woman like you."

Not to be put aside, her words sounded sharp. "How much is it?"

"Oh—eight dollars."

She fished out the money and put it on the bar. "This might be like the farmer who's mule died."

"How's that."

"He said he'd never done that before either."

Mike laughed. She was not only fine-looking, but she had a good sense of humor. She'd sure need one— in a few days she'd bring Ed Wright back and dump him off there. Her obvious plan was to sober him up. It would never work.

After she left, Mike went to the batwing doors to watch her stalk up the street for the livery. There was one helluva lot of fine woman packed in that blue getup. He closed his eyes. Fine or not, she was making a big mistake hauling Ed out of there. Unita Nance had kidnapped that poor old drunk Ed Wright in a wheelbarrow, with that wino Charlie as her cohort in crime. Mike chuckled over her absolute poor judgment. Might ought to report it to the Bexar County Sheriff. Ramon Gittez would laugh too.

Chapter 1

Where in the hell was he at? Ed woke up on a cot in some shed, with cobwebs in his brain and hardly able to open his eyes, which were matted shut. He sure wasn't in a crib in the back of the Shamrock. Aw, where in the devil was he at? His eyes rubbed open at last, he tried the door and it opened. It was dark outside, quarter moon shining, and he wasn't in San Antonio, either. Damn, how did he ever get to this place?

Made no good sense at all. He tucked in his shirt and headed for the corral. Maybe his saddle pony was there. How did he get there anyway? Whew, he needed a drink, and badly. His teeth were about to float out of his jaw. In the starlight, he surveyed the corral of sleeping horses, all hipshot and grunting. No sign of one of his ponies. Must not have ridden there. Had he drunk himself into something? He was used to waking up in a crib in the back of the Shamrock. Most times by himself. Sometimes he had company, like when one of the doves got cold—she'd come over for the warmth off his body and climbed in to sleep against him. Or if one got too drunk and thought it was her room. This wasn't one of those deals—there wasn't a dove around. Besides, it was too cold to be out in the dark in only a shirt. He rubbed his arms for more circulation. He was so cold, he'd begun shaking all over. It was hard to swallow. Freezing to death and he was taking the damn d.t.'s. Then he noticed the light on at the main house. Whose place was this? Hugging his arms to stop the quaking, he headed for the lighted window in the house.

He managed to open the door and fell to his knees inside. Blinking against the bright light in the room, he finally managed to stagger to his feet. The room was empty save for a long table and chairs. But he could smell ham frying and the sweet aroma threatened to make him vomit. Then he blinked his eyes at the sight of a woman framed in the lighted doorway.

"You finally wake up?" she asked.

"Where—in—the—hell—am—I?" he managed, shivering all over until his skin felt ready to crawl off of him. His jaw even clinched until his teeth felt ready to come unhinged.

She nodded to the table. "There's some whiskey in that glass."

"There—there is?"

"There is." She turned on her heel and went back into the kitchen that was emitting all those damn food smells. He could hear her and a Mexican woman talking and laughing back there. Probably about him—he didn't give a damn.

He dropped down on the chair before the whiskey. For a long moment he looked at the glass. His trembling hand slid across the tabletop to clutch it. Better not spill it—there might not be any more. Still uncontrollably shuddering, he bent over, with some of the sharp vapors going up his nose. Then, sip by sip, he began to recover.

A loud bell ringing outside jarred him up. In minutes, the door came open and several ranch hands came bursting into the room.

"Oh, hi, Ed."

"See you got up."

A clap on his shoulder. "Glad you're better. You were in bad shape when she brought you out here."

He knew most of the hands—Rusty Keyes, Sparky and Don Don—all taking their places around the table and nodding to him, all of them busy with the morning's small talk of an outfit. A busted girth, a horse that needed to be shod, a ranny cow that didn't appreciate being snaked out of a bog. Ranch-hand conversation, and with a little chiding throwed in about some chubby German girl having her blue eyes set on Keyes.

The boss woman, the good-looking one, brought in platters heaped high with food and began serving them. Eggs, ham, big biscuits, fried mush and flour gravy—workingman food. An older, short Mexican woman began filling their pottery cups with coffee.

"You want some food?" she asked him in an accented voice, holding the pot.

He nodded and the boss woman put one of the plates in front of him at the same time.

"Eat up. Be a long time till supper," the woman warned.

Ed looked hard at the food, undecided. The enticing aroma made him nauseated.

"Ed? You still got that crop-eared Injun stud

horse?'' Rusty asked. The grinning freckle-faced red-
head looked past two of the others at him for the
answer.

Ed bobbed his head. "Ten Bears. Yeah, he's Comanche bred. Got him with some mares at the ranch."

"How did you ever get him?"

"Rangering—" Ed, afraid he was drooling, wiped
his mouth on the side of his hand. "Couple of us
chased down a band of them. I got the horse."

"Way I heard it, you boys had a big firefight with 'em."

"Oh, just part of rangering back then."

Rusty nodded at the others. They hadn't heard stories like the E ranger company digging Ranger Wylie
Sherman's grave with their rifle butts. Everywhere he
turned people, people that he really liked, kept getting
killed. Stampedes, river crossings, gunfights, horse
wrecks—and that damn bitch Lady Fate left him there
every time to bury them.

He began eating and figured that with his mouth full
he wouldn't have to tell any more stories. The food did
flood his mouth with saliva. He wasn't risking sounding
stupid about how he got there. He'd been drunk. He'd
been like he wanted to be. Then he didn't have to
think about them—those he had planted between there
and the Illano Estacado, as well as between there and
the whorehouses in Abilene. He kept his head down.

She, the tall voluptuous woman, crossed the room
and stood in the open doorway as the first golden light
came across the Texas hill country. "I guess today you
boys better push some of those steers that's down on
Florence Creek back north. Crabtree'll be up here telling us we're eating up his range."

"Ma'am. It ain't his land."

"I know Rusty. But I'm not Sam, and I can't stand in his face and shout at him till he backs down."

"Us boys—"

"You boys are getting twenty a month and found to work my cattle, not be enforcers. We've got range and feed. Move them north."

"Yes, ma'am."

"More coffee?" she asked, swishing past Ed on her way to the kitchen.

He nodded. He must have been really starved to have eaten all that food on his plate, though he wasn't sure when he did eat last.

Her hands had left for the day to go move steers, after saying their good-byes, and Ed pushed the empty plate away. Despite the goodness of the food, it wasn't setting that well in his stomach.

She came out and took a chair opposite him at the long table. She was pretty—wavy shoulder-length, light brown hair, the suntanned face of an angel and a full lower lip that looked ripe as a peach for kissing. Most women avoided tanning their faces, but on her it looked like rich cinnamon sugar. But it was her blue eyes that locked in on him.

"Get enough to eat?"

"Too much."

"Guess you figured why I brought you here."

Things began to fall in place. She was Sam Nance's widow. He was killed in the war. Her name was—

"I'm Unita Nance."

"I knowed who you were." Every cowhand between there and San Antonio had a crush on her.

"Good." She folded and unfolded her hands on top of the table. "You know why you're here?"

"I've got a notion—" He caught the first surge with his hand clamped over his mouth. Turned over the chair, getting up and rushing outside. On the porch at last, he upchucked it all over the edge, and then, using a porch post for support, had debilitating waves of the dry heaves.

"You've been trying to kill yourself, Ed Wright."

He wiped his mouth on his kerchief and turned to look at her in the doorway in anger to cover his embarrassment. "What're you? My new mother?"

"You could use one." Arms folded, she stood and squinted against the glare at something. "That's probably Crabtree."

Ed looked to the dust and then backed up to put his butt against the stucco. "He give you much trouble?"

"All mouth—so far."

He shook his head and his hand went to his hip out of habit. No gun. He'd not worn one in months. He straightened, feeling naked as two riders galloped in. No love in his heart for Terrrance Crabtree. He considered the rancher a blowhard and a bully. Biff Tyler, his right-hand man, was swarthy-faced with a little mustache—a ladies' man. Crabtree, with a big gut and loud mouth in his forties, was no pretty sight. He wore his clothes slovenly and spat tobacco in rapid-fire fashion. The right corner of his mouth was usually stained brown. This day was no exception, but he needed to shave as well.

Ed watched her shoulders stiffen, standing on the porch and telling the stock dog that had been left behind to hush. Wonder the dog hadn't bit him when he was wandering around in the dark earlier.

"Unita, them damn steers of yours—" Crabtree spat sideways and brushed his mouth on the back of his hand.

"The boys are moving them, today. You may have passed them on the way."

Crabtree shook his head like that wasn't enough. "I ain't warning you again, bitch. Keep them cattle off my land."

Ed stepped forward. "My mother would have washed your filthy mouth out with soap."

She tried to contain him with her arm held out, but he shoved it aside. Anger raged through his body, and he wanted to slam his fist down Crabtree's throat and shut him up permanently.

"Where I come from insulting a woman is—" Ed started off the porch for him.

Tyler bound off his horse and met Ed halfway to his boss's horse. His fists flew like lightning. Ed's guard up, Tyler's fist still slammed him in the jaw. Then three more into his gut and ribs and he staggered backward. Ed found himself on his butt and blinking his eyes in disbelief up at the dandy.

"Unita—" Crabtree laughed doubled over in the saddle. "You better hire you somebody besides that damn drunk if you aim to go up against me. He couldn't wipe his ass, let alone fight. Come on, Biff. She's got our message."

"Terrance Crabtree, I'll fill you full of buckshot you ever come back up that lane again."

"Big talk. Big talk."

She was on her knees beside Ed as he tried to clear his head and rub his sore jaw. The sumbitch about loosened all of his teeth. A concerned look on her face, she ran her hand over his cheek and put his mussed hair back in place. "You all right?"

He closed his eyes and then nodded. "I'll be fine."

Not really, but the next time they meet he'd have a gun on his hip. That dandy wouldn't get a second chance at him and live to talk about it.

She helped him up. "I didn't bring you out here to fight my wars. I'm sorry about this happening."

"I'll be all right." On his feet, he brushed himself off and glared after the pair. The bitter sourness kept burping up his throat and he needed another drink.

What was with this woman, anyway? He closed his eyes. When he reached for the porch post, a sharp pain in his side felt like a mule'd kicked him. Damn, that dandy must have broken a rib or two. He tucked his right arm to his side and winced.

"You all right?"

"Sure."

"Then why did you wince so when you reached for that post?"

"Damn it, I can wince if I want to."

"He's cracked your ribs?" She scowled at him, standing in the doorway with a know-it-all smirk.

"Might have."

"Get in here and take that shirt off."

"I'll be fine."

"No, we'll fix you a hot bath and I'll bind you up. I've done that before."

"I don't need a bath."

"That's a matter of opinion. Get those clothes off."

He felt his face heating up. "I don't feel like it."

"Rosa and I have both been around enough—we

won't peek, anyway." She took him by the left arm and dragged him inside. "Rosie, fill the bathtub."

"I don't need a bath."

Unita narrowed her blue eyes. "I can tackle you and win. He cracked your ribs; you'll be a pushover. Now take off those clothes."

"I don't need a nursemaid."

"Shape you're in, you may need two."

He toed off his boots. Damn, she was tough. He'd never seen the likes. He needed a drink, not a bath. Damned if she wasn't in his face, unbuttoning his shirt. If it didn't hurt so bad to do it, he'd shove her away.

She hauled him back in the kitchen and that little Mexican woman was pouring steaming water in a big tub. He was down to his one-piece underwear and they were gathering his clothes up. Maybe, like a chicken, they'd scald him in hot water, then pick his feathers. Why hadn't she just left him at the Shamrock Saloon?

Chapter 2

She issued him a pair of bib overalls to wear while they washed his things. They left him alone to get out of the tub and dry himself on feed-sack towels. Then, with him seated backward on a chair, she used some sheeting to bind his chest so tight he could hardly breathe.

"What can you keep down?" she asked when she finished and he had managed to put the suspenders up.

"Keep down?"

"You have to eat something and keep it inside."

He sat backward on a straight-back chair and rested his forehead on the top rung. All he needed was something to drink. His molars were about to float out for a good shot of whiskey. He didn't want any more fussing over him or meddling in his business. Besides, she was holding him captive there—especially in them bib overalls. Lands, he'd never go to San Antonio in them. When his clothes got dry . . . And he'd find that Biff Tyler and even that deal up too.

"I'm dead serious. Look at yourself. You're skin

and bones, not eating and all that drinking like you've been doing."

"I eat." He'd never thought he'd see the day a dandy like Tyler could whip his ass—but he had. And he did it all in the shake of a lamb's tail, too.

"Why didn't you keep breakfast down?"

"I ate too much."

"Ed Wright—" Her blue eyes narrowed to slits. "If I have to tie you up in a shed and force-feed you, I'm going to sober you up until you can see what a mess you've made of yourself."

"Pretty damn strong words coming from—coming from a lady."

"You're going to think strong words. Now, Rosa made you some chicken soup. I want you to eat a small bowl of it."

"I don't need no—"

She reached over and put a finger on his lips. "I need a guide to show me the way to Kansas."

He shook his head and started to fold his arms over his chest. That hurt so bad that he kept his elbows at his side. "No, you don't need me. I've done that."

"You afraid you'll fail?"

"Fail? No, I've never failed. Oh, I did, and I buried those mistakes beside rivers I can't name and pounded crude crosses on prairie graves where no kin will ever find 'em. What do you tell folks looking for a son or husband to return, and all they got is you to look at and cry with? Goddammit, woman. I'm not going back."

"Ed Wright, you're the biggest coward I ever met."

"I don't care."

She dropped her gaze to the tabletop and shook her head. "Yes, you do. 'Cause deep inside you're a lion. Why, you left that porch mad enough to whip an army over Crabtree's comments to me."

"Got my ass whipped too."

"That's because you're still drunk."

"I'm too damn sober right now."

She looked at him hard and slow, and shook her head. "I'm going to dry you out, and you can hate me, cuss me, fight me, but if I have to hog-tie you, I can."

"You get your mind set you can act plenty tough."

"I don't ever act, Ed Wright. I do it for keeps." She nodded to Rosa. "Bring the soup."

No need in him arguing. He'd eat her damn soup, and when his ribs healed he'd rustle a horse. *Big Mike, I'll be coming back soon. Ugh.* He made a face at the first teaspoon of the hot liquid. Chickens were for honyockers to eat—went right along with the baggy bib overalls he had on.

All he wanted was a bottle and enough damn liquor to slip off—get out of this world. But she wasn't serving any, just chicken soup—ugh. But to save having to argue with a hard-headed woman he sipped it off the spoon. She never left till he had finished it all.

"Is it going to stay down?" she asked.

"How should I know? I didn't bring up the last. It just came up."

"Rosa, your soup worked I think."

The Mexican woman appeared in the doorway and nodded in approval, then looked at him. "You drink goat milk?"

"No!"

"Be good for you belly." She smiled and went back.

"Goat's milk. I ain't no baby."

"No, but you've been colicky and nothing is better than goat's milk for that."

"I'll be fine."

"You've said that ten times. You aren't. Tyler cracked your ribs. And you aren't sober yet."

"All right. I'll go take a nap."

She nodded. "That'll be fine. Nothing more should happen here. We've had our chewing out from Crabtree and the rest of the day should be peaceful."

Ed frowned at her. "He do that often?"

"He asked me to marry him as soon as he heard Sam was dead. I wasn't interested and told him so. Then he tried to buy me out. Now he just complains about all I do."

"Complains? I'd shut his mouth permanently."

She shook her head. "He's a windbag, and every time he rides up, I say, 'Thank you, Lord. I almost accepted his proposal.'"

Ed nodded like he understood her. "I'll see you later."

"Your clothes will be dry and ironed by then."

"Sure—thanks." He headed for the door feeling foolish in the loose-fitting overalls. The shed was across the open yard of dirt. He went inside and opened the small windows and door for some air. Warm day for fall. Lying on the bed dressed, he looked at the underside of the dark shingles and tried to plan his escape. He needed to get back to San Antonio and Big Mike. A pesky fly buzzed him. Finally he fell asleep.

When he awoke the boys were back—he could hear

them and their horses. His clothes, all clean and
pressed, were on the old chair beside his bed. He fixed
his hair with an old comb he found and studied his
face in a worn-out mirror with most of the silver stuff
off the back. Man, he did look bad in a bad mirror.
But who cared? A shave might help; he appeared to
be kinda wooly and his hair was long enough that it
might need to be braided in another week. He'd fix
that when he got back to San Antone.

For supper, the crew had fire-braised beef, frijoles,
biscuits, and peach pie. He had more chicken soup.
But it stayed down. Unita never mentioned Crabtree
coming by. Ed figured that was on purpose; her hands
would have ridden over and thrashed him for talking
to her like he did. They'd driven most of Bar U cattle
back north to suit their neighbor, Rusty said between bites.

"How did your day go?" Rusty asked him.

With a new stack of biscuits to set on the table
Unita fired him a look. *Don't tell.* Ed simply nodded.
"All right."

"Ed, tell us about how it was going up the trail
sometime. None of us ever been up there and we'd
sure like to hear what it was like." Don Don looked
to the others and they all agreed.

With a bob of his head, Ed said, "Sometime I'll
do that." He busied himself eating more soup. It did
stay down.

Day two on the Bar U. The d.t.'s woke him up
before dawn. He'd wrestled with horrible nightmares
all night, and woke up screaming, "No!" On top of
that he wasn't sure what it had been about. He found

a glass of whiskey poured and set on the table, and the women busy talking in the kitchen. With little fanfare, he downed it and gave a long sigh. Besides the shaking and lost feeling, he had a fire in his belly that was setting him ablaze.

"I bring you some goat milk," Rosa said, and set it down before him on the oilcloth.

He thanked her and looked at the glass. If it cured babies, maybe it would cure him. It tasted too sweet, but he forced it past his tongue. Finished, he put down the glass and looked up at Unita.

"We made you some oatmeal."

"Oatmeal? Goat's milk? Think I'm a baby?"

She looked hard at him. "I thought Tyler showed you that yesterday."

He started to point his finger at her and the action of his right arm caused a catch in his side. The pain made him crouch over. "Fine—I'll eat it."

Rosa rang the bell and the crew came busting in. They made him nauseated eating stacks of pancakes, butter, sorghum syrup, fried eggs, and pork sausage balls.

Rusty split them up for the day, sending some to clean a spring and tank, and the rest to scatter a couple of her new Durham bulls who liked each other's company better than being out alone with another bunch of longhorn cows. Nothing wrong with them; they just liked their own kind better.

After they rode out, Ed had Unita shave his face. She never mentioned his shaky hands, but deftly scraped the soap-lathered whiskers off with a sharp razor and showed him his shaven face in a small mirror when she had finished.

"A haircut wouldn't hurt." She laughed, light-hearted. "Get out on the porch. I'll get a sheet."

"You have lots of things to do—"

"I'll carry the chair. Go on."

He frowned and did what she asked. Cleaning himself up didn't hurt.

"How is your belly?" Rosa asked from the kitchen.

He blinked, then recalled why she asked. "Goat milk and oatmeal is setting good."

She smiled smugly as if to say I could have told you that.

He went outside and waited for Unita's return with sheet, scissors, and comb. He'd need to go by and check on Jorge and his own ranch. Good man, but it was still his place. Jorge and them boys could run it for months while he was gone on drives, so they'd make it for another week. Then he'd be strong enough to ride over there. Ride over and get his own damn horse.

His belly was doing better—not on fire, either. Maybe Rosa knew what to do.

"You have any Durham bulls?" Unita asked as she set down the chair for him.

"No, but I have some half bloods."

"More beef on these longhorns wouldn't hurt."

He agreed. Two hundred apiece for those purebred bulls sounded like highway robbery—but he might have to consider buying some of them.

"How many big steers you have?" he asked, to make conversation as she nipped away at his hair.

She stopped as if considering his words. "Close to a thousand."

"Whew, that's a lot."

"Too many?"

"No, but that's lots of steers."

"I sent four hundred up last year with Jim Bob McGregor. He got there with two hundred seventy three and split the proceeds fifty-fifty."

"Fifty-fifty?"

"That was after his expenses."

"So you got?"

"Thirty-two bucks a head."

He nodded. McGregor was a crook. He closed his eyes and thought about being drunk.

"What do you think?" She broke into his emptiness.

"He ever say what happened to the ones he lost?"

"Drowned crossing rivers, stampedes, rustlers. He'd had it all, he said."

"How many of his cattle made it, since he lost a third of yours?"

She tapped the closed scissors on his shoulder, which was covered in hair clippings, and looked deep in thought. "I never asked. Why?"

"Sounds like you might have taken all the loss and little of the gain."

She shrugged and went back to work. "I at least had money to pay the help and my bills."

"Sure, but he made a damn killing."

"You mean McGregor? I guess I did good for a woman running a ranch."

He nodded.

"There, you look less like an Injun." She swept off the sheet and shook it on the edge of the porch. He gazed at her backside. He could visualize a shapely woman under that dress.

"What do I owe you?" he asked.

"No charge. How're your ribs?"

"I'll live."

She agreed and went back inside. He ambled around to the stack of wood. Needed something to take his mind off getting drunk. It was all he could see, think about, or consider. His tongue longed for it. His back molars felt ready to float away.

So using his left arm and a hand ax he went to splitting firewood for the cookstove. It was hotter outside than he had thought. Sweat soon began to run down his face. He wasn't as handy with his left arm, but his right he kept tucked to his side to ease the pain. Not satisfied with the sharpness of the ax, he went to the grindstone and found he could not crank and hold it with only his left hand. So, prowling in the shop he found a whetstone and wedged the ax head so he could use the stone on it one-handed.

Sharp enough at last, he went back and split more. At noontime Unita came out and called him in for lunch, and nodded in approval at the large stack of ready stove wood. "Rosa will think you're *muy grande*."

"I may need to borrow a horse," he said, sipping some beef-stock soup.

"Where are you going?"

"Oh, to see about Jorge over at the ranch."

"If it don't blow in a rain, I'll drive you over there."

"I'm not an invalid."

She shook her head like she was his mother. "You split some firewood one-handed. That don't make you well."

"Wasn't nothing wrong with me to start with."

"No, you were simply trying to kill yourself."

"That's my business. I guess that was my right."

She drew her shoulders back and shook her head. "No."

"No, what? I don't have a right to go blow my head off?"

"No." Final word, and she left him at the table by himself. He finished his soup and thanked Rosa from the door. No sign of Unita so he went to the shed. It wasn't any problem to shut his eyes, despite the nagging pain in his side, and he napped all afternoon. The boys coming in woke him up.

If he ever needed a drink it was then. Sitting on the edge of the bed, he scrubbed his smooth-shaven face in his callused hands. Where did Unita keep that whiskey she doled out like it was gold dust every morning? There'd not be a chance of him snooping around and finding where she had it stashed. Either she or Rosa were in that kitchen every waking hour.

He ate chicken soup and drank goat's milk without an argument. His fiery belly and the upset were finally gone. Maybe he could try real food soon—not soon enough for his part, but he was feeling better. Or his stomach felt settled, anyway. Oh, what he'd give for a drink.

The next day he spent at the shop, firing the forge and pounding out some iron bands to hinge the main corral gate, to replace leather straps. Unita came down at noontime.

"You're overdoing it," she announced, looking over his handiwork.

"You a doctor?" he asked, motioning for her to use the bellows.

"I'm yours."

He drew out the last strap and began to shape it over the anvil, with the hammer in his left hand, the sound ringing like a great bell. Then he reinserted it in the red-hot coals and wiped his sweaty face on his sleeve.

"That enough?" she asked, and stopped pumping.

He nodded. His head felt dizzy. He put down the hammer and dropped his butt back against the bench. Things began to swim and his knees buckled. Her shrill scream was the last thing he recalled. He woke up in the shed, on the cot. The boys must be coming in. What had happened to him at the shop? He rolled over and went back to sleep. More bad dreams. Dreams of boys dying in stampedes—trampled to death. Those long horns shining in the bright sun above the muddy, stained river, horses and riders bobbing in the water, crossing another swollen river, and a tornado swept down to drown them all.

"Wake up. Wake up, you're having a bad nightmare."

Seated on the edge of the bed, Unita was holding him up against her firm breasts, real familiar like, and pressing a cup to his mouth. He could smell it— whiskey. *Ah, at last.*

Chapter 3

A week at her place, and his head felt clear anyway. The sore rib hadn't healed but the binding was off. He could eat some real food—not a lot, but half rations anyway, and keep it down. The burning in his belly—the goat's milk worked on it, or he gave it credit for helping improve that condition. Rosa beamed and told him he must keep drinking it. He shook his head—no way was he milking a damned goat every day for the rest of his life.

Unita loaded a picnic lunch and he hitched her buggy horse. He drove and they headed for his place. He'd been two days without a drink of anything, save the dang milk and coffee. He wasn't past wanting it, but he was living without it.

On the drive to his place they made small talk about when they'd have a first frost. She hoped her green beans in the garden made it before the cold killed them.

He found Jorge's wife, Tina, at the jacal with the two toddlers. The short, pregnant woman came out and spoke to Unita. Tina told him Jorge and the boys were cutting firewood in Blanco Canyon, but she could

ring the bell and fetch them. He agreed and they
waited. The two women were busy visiting and he
went around to inspect things. He found nothing
wrong and circled back.

Jorge rode in and they talked about the ranch, the
cattle, and how they were doing. Squatted by the corral, they had a good visit.

"She is some woman," Jorge said as if impressed
by the sight of the widow, and nodded in approval.

Ed sucked on his eyetooth and finally bobbed his
head. "She don't need a man. She's getting on plenty
fine the way she is."

Jorge gave a knowing smile, like he didn't believe
none of it.

"How's my old stud horse, Ten Bears?"

"Fine. Raphael checked on him and the mares a
few days ago."

"Good. We better get back. You need anything, Mr.
Lorain at the store in Banty will fix you up. I don't
know how long I'll be over there."

"We are fine," Jorge assured him.

"Good." Ed's side caught in a sharp pain when he
went to stand, and it reminded him of his beating at
Tyler's hands. He owed that dude a good whipping
the next time they met. He might get a chance to
pound that foulmouthed Crabtree too.

He caught his breath, pushed in on that side, and
tried to hide the pain. But Jorge saw it and nodded
like he understood. They shook hands and walked to
the jacal. Ed hugged Tina, and the two women talked
all the way to the buggy. Loaded, he promised Jorge
he'd see him in a short while.

"You pull something back there?" Unita asked as they drove out the lane.

"It only caught."

"Give me the reins. I can drive."

"I'll be fine."

In the end she won. He sat back in the bench seat in a slight crouch where the pain wasn't bad and took the road bumps with clenched teeth.

"Maybe you need to see Doc."

"All he'll do is bind me up. You've been doing that fine enough."

She looked at the buggy top and about laughed. She'd done all the rest, including dragging him out of the Shamrock when he was passed out. Strange, how he could almost smell the sourness of that old bar and the sawdust on the floor. Be good to be back there drinking with Big Mike. Mike never drank, he just listened.

"Everything was fine at the ranch?" she asked, breaking into his thoughts of getting drunk.

Ed nodded. "Jorge is a good man."

"You're lucky to have him."

"I am. Aren't you about tired of nursemaiding me?"

"Why?"

"My ranch is doing fine. I have a powerful thirst. Why don't we end this whatever and I go back to San Antone?"

She looked over at him with a scowl. "And you have a catch in your side so bad you couldn't ride a horse there."

"Give me a few shots of whiskey. I'll make it."

She flicked the horse to make him keep on single-footing. "I'm not giving you any more whiskey."

"I may need it."

"What for?"

"My side is really hurting."

"It's hurt before. You're tough. Should we stop up here pretty soon and eat the lunch I brought?"

"Suits me."

She halted in the next creek crossing to let Brandy, her buggy horse, drink, and then she drove him up on the flat. He climbed down, stood for a minute to let the pain subside, then put his hands on his hips and strained against the sore right side. Walking back and forth, he hoped to escape some of it, but it felt like he had a hot Comanche arrow in his side.

She spread a fine patch quilt on the ground and began to unpack her things. He watched her, hypnotized by her movements and by the lithe way she turned as she set things out. When she looked up at him he felt his face heat like he'd been caught indecently spying on her. He didn't want her to think that of him. To be truthful with himself, since the war the only females he'd been around were doves. Hadn't been any "woman" in his life in a long time. No one to court—that was all over with him.

The dark-eyed Mexican girl, Margaretia, he had met down on the border after the war and her beauty stole his heart. But when he proposed, she told him she could never leave her family at San Jose on the Rio Grand, or marry someone outside her church. That had been shortly after the war—five years ago, maybe longer? No, seven? After that he'd given up looking for a respectable woman to marry—he sure didn't need one.

"Cold chicken?" she offered, and brought him back to the sunny fall day beside the small creek.

He grinned hugely and sat down on her quilt. He'd never before been on a real picnic with a good-looking woman. Might never happen again. Better savor every minute of it. "I sure will."

"This was my grandmother's quilt. See the wagon-wheel design?"

He nodded and made a face of disapproval at her. "Ain't it awfully nice to just sit on?"

She wrinkled her nose to dismiss his concern. "I have a feeling she won't mind."

He paused before taking another bite of the tasty chicken. "Why's that?"

"My grandparents came from Arkansas to Texas. Grandpa fought with Sam Houston. He came home crippled and never was right again. She ran the Bar U until my father was old enough to take over."

Ed nodded. "Your father was killed by Mexican bandits. I remember that from my ranger days. They never were caught."

"No, never did catch them. So my mother and grandmother ran the ranch. Grandmother hired Sam as the foreman and later we married." She looked off at the cedar- and live oak–clustered hillside. "I almost knew, the day when he rode off to war—he'd not come back."

"Too many didn't come home."

"Yes, and some of the sorry ones made it back unscathed."

"Ain't no justice in this life." He went back to eating cold chicken.

"I want to go over and see a man at Bourne who deals in mules. The trip will take two days—"

"You need mules for what?"

"I wanted to buy a couple of teams to pull the chuck wagon."

"What's that got to do with me?" He tossed the bare chicken bone away and wiped his mouth on the back of his hand. No way he was being any part of that operation.

She wet her lower lip as if uncertain, then spoke. "I wanted to hire you to negotiate a deal on them."

He rubbed his palms on the top of his legs. "Why not just leave me off at San Antone?"

Her blue eyes narrowed with anger. "I'll go by myself."

She began to pick things up. Then, looking furious at him, she handed him a piece of chocolate cake. "I forgot this."

"You can take me back to my place," he said, getting to his knees.

In her fury, she tackled him and he saw stars. Flat on his back, he could barely see her drawn-back fist ready to hit him as the pain from her sitting astraddle him . . . hurt deep. *Damn* . . . He caught his breath from the lightning in his side.

She slipped off and sat on the quilt beside him. Not saying a word.

"I hurt you?"

He made the hard effort to sit up and shake his head. "Hell, I couldn't even whip—"

"Whip me?"

"Right."

She straightened her dress tail over her bare calves and never looked at him. "Can I help you up?"

"No, I'll make it." He rolled over and pushed off his knees to stand. He took what was left of the piece of cake in his right hand. For a long moment he looked down at the blue circle pattern in the quilt—they called them wagon wheels. Then, all businesslike, she swept it up, shook out the dry grass and dirt, and folded it.

The sweet cake gummed in his mouth, but it tasted delicious. He hobbled to the buggy while she loaded the blanket and the basket. On the seat he let the hurting subside and looked up into her worried gaze as she sat beside him.

"I didn't hurt you on purpose."

"I know." They never said another word all the way back to her place.

It gave him plenty of time to think. If he didn't get well enough to pull out soon, he'd crawl away on his belly. What she had on her mind for him to do, he couldn't—wouldn't—didn't want to and wasn't going to do. He wasn't about to go on no damn cattle drive to Kansas.

Jarred by every bump of the buggy seat as she hurried the horse homeward, he held himself with his arms and clenched his teeth. Her tackle had sure tore his ribs up again. He needed a drink.

Chapter 4

Ed watched her drive away the next morning without a word to him. He guessed she was going after mules. In fact, they had not said more than a few words to each other since the picnic episode. The trip to his place had sapped his energy and so after their return he slept through supper. Rosa woke him in the dark and brought him some food. She lit a candle.

"You must eat," she scolded, and he sat up and ate for her.

The sight of Unita's buggy disappearing the next morning gave him a twinge of guilt. It wouldn't have hurt him to have gone along with her and helped her dicker for the mules. It was a matter of who was the most stubborn one. He still couldn't get over the fury in her when she tackled him. She was a lot more powerful than he ever imagined she was. Why, she could have whipped Tyler and Crabtree by herself.

The boys rode out after breakfast, and he drank another cup of coffee. Wondering where she kept the whiskey, he ambled out to the woodpile to take his mind off of it and tried to split firewood, but even busting up the small pieces jarred him. He went up to

the bunkhouse and found some *Police Gazette* maga-
zines and read about some Ohio ax murderer. Maybe
after lunch he'd saddle a ranch horse and try to ride
a few hours. He had to get his strength back . . . A
little whiskey and he wouldn't hurt half so bad. He
dreamed about the stuff at night, and all his day-
dreams drifted back to it. He had to have a drink.

Unita returned late the next day and the boys ran
out to take the four mules on leads that trotted in
behind the buggy. She swept the hair back from her
face and got ready to get off the seat. She looked Ed
in the eye. "You going to see how bad I got took."

"You really want to know?"

"Yes."

He offered her a hand down. His effort made his
side catch, but he never let on. She nodded and he
stepped aside. Lots of woman there. He followed her
over to the mules and wondered if her stony manner
ever melted.

The ranch hands were busy examining her purchases when he mouthed the first one. Don Don held
the lead.

"How old is he, Ed?" Don Don asked.

"Six."

The cowboy nodded in agreement. "He stands good
on his feet."

The third one was smooth-mouthed. Ed looked over
at Unita. "How old's Jude here?"

She looked aloof and nodded. "He said maybe ten.
But he was sound."

"Mules can live forever, but he's older than ten."

She nodded, looking seriously at him. "You don't
think he's worth what the others are?"

"No. He may be fine, but he's an old mule."

"He'll replace him. All I have to do is send him back."

"In that case, if it was up to me, I'd get a younger one."

When he finished and nodded his approval, she said thanks and hurried to the house. He went with the boys and helped them match up a harness from the assortment in the saddle shed. Adjustments were made as he studied the fit, then gave instructions to them to shorten or lengthen straps. He checked each collar until satisfied they fit and would not scald the wearer's shoulders. New buckle holes were bored in the leather straps and, by the time the supper bell rang, the mules had their individual sets of harness.

"You must have worked lots of mules," Sparky said, sounding impressed as they went to wash up.

"I did a little farming before Dave Ivy came by my jacal one rainy fall day." He wet his lips and nodded. "He brought over two bottles of bond whiskey. It was cold and had been raining, so my roof was leaking, of course. I had all these tin cans set around on the floor catching the drips. Sounded like an orchestra he said, all that plunk, plink going on. We made a deal that night—I had to find and break eighty mustangs for a remuda that winter, and he was bringing the cattle and the grub for our first drive to Joe McCoy's pens."

"Eighty horses?"

"Hell, Sparky, I had all winter."

"How did you ever do it?"

"One at a time." He smiled over at the boy, who was hardly out of his teens.

Supper was the usual friendly feast. Talk was about

a dance on Saturday. Unita brought by a platter of extra biscuits and leaned forward to put them on the table in front of him.

"You still dance?" she asked as she straightened.

"I guess . . ."

"Good, you can go too," she said, and just about laughed.

He felt his face light up. Damn, she could get under his skin. He had her permission to go to the dance. By damn, if his ribs were healed, he'd leave her and this bunch. 'Cept he knew riding a horse would make him suck up his breath at the first jar.

Saturday night, the boys put on their *other* shirts. Earlier in the day, Rosa had given him a starched white shirt, a pair of striped pants, and suspenders.

"They were Sam's, but he can't wear them," she said softly.

He nodded and thanked the sweet gray-headed woman. Before supper he put them on and then Sparky helped him harness Unita's buggy horse.

"You're still sore, ain't yah?" the boy asked.

"It shows?"

"I can see it."

Ed thanked him and let him finish the harness business, then he drove the rig around in front and parked it. He dismounted with care. Why was he still there? His brain was so scrambled, maybe he was losing his mind. All he wanted to do was get drunk and stay that way. He hadn't had a drink in over a week. Didn't change his wants and needs. Still, with his sore ribs and all, he hung around the Bar U feeling as worthless as he had ever felt in his entire life.

He sure didn't owe her anything. His foot wasn't

nailed to the floor. She wanted him to drive her herd north to Kansas in the spring, a task that looked so revolting to him that he wanted to throw up at the very notion.

After supper, they climbed in the rig and he drove it to the Plain View Schoolhouse. Neither spoke much, and he caught a faint hint of lavender. She had on a blue checkered dress that must have been her best, and looked very nice. Her shoulder-length hair shone in the setting sun and she'd stir a fire in any man's guts, including Ed's. But he was so far down, thinking how to escape her and finding no good way to get away, that the trip was a grim one for him.

When they came in view of the clapboard-sided building, she motioned for him to stop. "You can turn around here and take me home. I can see you're not going to have any fun. I am concerned about your ribs."

He looked at the reins in his hand. "I think the best thing for me is go back to my own outfit."

"And fall back in the bottle?"

"Yeh. When a man can't stand his own company any longer then he needs a shield from it. Mine's whiskey."

"At least you're honest."

He nodded, not looking at her. "That's cheap— being honest. I know you want those cattle up in Kansas. Drunk or sober, I don't think I can face going back up there. Been too much dying and bad things in my life." He stared off at a tall cottonwood bathed in the bloodred of sundown, the yellow leaves twirling in the wind.

"Could a woman make you forget them—those bad things?"

He turned and blinked at her. "I had no ambition to blackmail you."

"Ed Wright—I must get those steers to Newton. It's not, do I want to. It's not, it would be nice. If I don't get those steers up there, I'll be through—busted. All I have worked for since the war is to hold this ranch together. All I've done to keep the Bar U together will be like sand and sift through my fingers."

"You're a helluva woman, Unita. I respect you, but I don't think—" He chewed on his lower lip.

"Name your terms, Ed Wright."

He closed his eyes and shook his head without an answer for her. There'd been a day he would have given all he had in this world for a woman like her. Looking at the whitewashed schoolhouse bathed in blood, with her beside him on the leather seat, the only thing he could think about was finding a drink. He must be plumb mad.

Chapter 5

She offered to go back home. He agreed. They turned
around and headed back to the Bar U. Crickets
creaked in the warm night. A coyote or two barked
at the rising half moon. Ed felt relieved that they
hadn't gone to the dance. He wouldn't have to explain
to anyone why he was staying at her place, for one
thing. Probably enough rumors and gossip in the country about what he was doing at the Bar U to fill a big
trunk anyway. They must have been the talk of every
tea party. It didn't bother her on the outside, but she
had a hand in what she'd put all her chips on, including her reputation.

When they drove up in the starlight, he noticed a
horse at the rack, and a boy came from the porch
before they could dismount the rig. He recognized
Ramon, who worked on his place.

"Oh, Senor, they said you were at the dance. I
waited for you. Senor, the rustlers, they have taken
your stallion Ten Bears and some of the mares."

Ed dropped his chin. Rustlers had Ten Bears. How
would he ever go after them in his condition?

"I need to borrow a gun, a horse, and some grub. I can pay you." He turned to Unita.

"You won't pay me and I'll go along."

Taken aback, Ed blinked at her. "No. I don't know when I'll be back."

"Or how? I'll get some things. This boy can help you find some horses and a pack animal. There is a star-faced horse with one white sock; he's mine. You know where the rest are. Take a dusty saddle; they're the ones that belong to me. The others are the boys'."

Ed started to protest. "Unita, I can't ask you to go along."

"I asked myself. Go and saddle the horses. What is your name?" she asked the boy as she moved to the front of the seat.

"Ramon."

"Ramon, please help him. He is still very sore," she said, getting down.

"*Sí*, Senora, I can help him."

Then she turned back to look at Ed. "I'll bind you up again when you get the horses. You'll need it to ever ride a horse."

Shaking his head in defeat over her decision to go along, Ed drove the buggy horse up to the corral and they unhitched him. Unharnessing him, he asked the youth all about the discovery and what else he knew. By Ed's calculations, the rustlers had at least a two-day head start. The trail would be cold. Still, he wanted his horses back and the thieves punished. He'd earned Ten Bears from the Comanche—he'd earn the horse back from this outfit.

Ramon carried the harness in the tack room. Ed

lighted a lamp and picked out Unita's saddle, and another for himself. Ramon moved him aside and told him to go find the horses.

"I will carry them."

"Thanks," he said, lighting a second lamp. With it in hand, he headed for the corral in a yellow ring of light.

"I can rope them," Ramon said from behind him.

"You Jorge's cousin?" Ed asked, recalling the young men's relationship.

"*Sí.*"

"You rope them. I'll pick them out."

Ramon agreed, set the saddle down, and took a reata from the corral post. In the deftness of the way he handled the braided leather, Ed knew this boy had the makings of a real one. He pushed open the gate on the new hinges the boys had installed, and smiled. It didn't drag. The gate shut again and he held up the lamp. Awakened by the light and their presence, the spooked horses milled around. Unita's star-faced one was obvious with his dish face. Ramon singled him out and threw a loop over his ears. Caught, he settled down like a real broke horse, and Ed let the two out of the gate.

The youth hurried back, making a new loop in the rope on the run, leaving Unita's bay hitched to a rack.

"Catch that blue roan with all the black mane and tail. He's a desert horse and should be tough." A slight ewe neck from being a stud a while, he was stout and wide set. Not over thirteen hands, he still looked impressive enough for the long haul to Ed. Be easier for him to mount, too. Rope singing over his head, Ramon tossed it, and cinched the deal with a swift backhanded jerk to tighten the noose.

Caught, Blue blew some boogers out of his nose at them and the light. But Ramon ignored him and led him out of the pen. Ed tried to find a horse in the milling bunch that he thought would lead well. He hated a head-slinging packhorse.

"Let's try that black for a packhorse." He held up the lamp and ignored the sharpness in his side. "He leads good, we'll use him."

"Sí, Senor."

The black, on a lead, came on the trot after Ramon. Ed nodded his approval. Those boys might be mad he took horses from their strings, but there wasn't the time to worry about that. With a currycomb, he brushed the dirt and dust off the roan's back. The effort was not easy, but he forced himself. No more baby stuff; he had a situation that needed handling. Pain would not be a consideration, so he hurt. Too damn far from his heart to kill him. But he wasn't certain, as the boy tossed the saddle on the horse he chose, how having Unita along would work. Chasing down rustlers was like his old days as a ranger—tough, hard riding, dry camps, and miserable days spent in the saddle. He didn't know if he was up to it, let alone with a woman tagging along.

"Rosa is packing the food," Unita said, coming from the house dressed in a divided skirt, a long-sleeved man's shirt, and wearing a cowboy hat.

He must have blinked in the starlight at seeing her in that garb.

"Here, you will need this, I can tell." And she shoved a tin cup in his hand.

His left eye shut, he stared at her in disbelief over his gift, and exchanged a nod with her in the lamp-light. He knew what the cup contained even before the vapors reached his nose—whiskey. The holy grail. A man had to be plumb stupid to worship damn juice, but when he raised it to his mouth, his molars were flooded with saliva in anticipation. Just a sip. It slid across his tongue and cut through three days' worth of dust slipping down his throat. Then he felt it disappear and his ears warmed. Damn, that was good.

So involved was he in his present, he hardly noticed that Unita and the boy were busy cinching down saddles. He didn't care. He wanted to savor the experience as long as he could. She broke his solitude.

"Get that shirt off and I'll rebind you," she said.

He tossed the rest down his throat and let out a breath. Then he tied the cup on his saddle for later usage and undid his shirt for her.

"Thanks," he managed.

"Might help you. I figured." Her fingers fumbled with the knots. "Ramon, take the packhorse up to the kitchen. Where the light is. Rosa will have two panniers to put on that pack saddle, plus three bedrolls."

"*Sí, Senora.*"

"Thanks for the whiskey," he said softly and straightened against the sharpness when she drew on the straps.

"You sure you can ride?"

"I'll make it."

"Sure, and fall off your horse somewhere." She pulled harder on the next one. "You can't hardly stand for me to tighten this."

"Damn it, I'll be fine."

"Enough whiskey, you may make it."

He nodded and sucked in his breath. "I will make it—"

"Where you figure they've taken him—this stallion?"

"Lord, I have no idea. Have to find the tracks."

"There; you're bound tight as I can get it. I'm going after some slickers in case it rains." She left him in the cool night air to put on his shirt and button it. She'd thought of everything—he was impressed.

She, Ramon, and the packhorse returned in the starlight. In her arms she carried two long guns. "One's mine. It's a shotgun. The rifle is a .44/40. Figured you'd need it."

He thanked her and jabbed the Winchester in the scabbard. She put the scattergun in a boot under her right stirrup. Then she unslung a holster from her shoulder. "It's an Army .44. It was Sam's. All they brought me back of him. It's been oiled and kept clean."

"You better—"

"No, you wear it. I have bullets, caps, and powder for it in the pack."

He looked at the weapon and nodded, impressed. Unita wasn't leaving any stone unturned. From the packs she took the slickers and tied them on each of their saddles. Slowly he examined the cylinder, and the smooth surfaces shone when he pointed them at the light for his inspection.

When he looked up, ready to strap on Sam's gun, she and the boy already had the tarp over the packs and were tying it down. What was wrong with him? The rest of the world whirled around him and he moved like a tortoise.

She came leading Star and Blue over to him. "Ready?"

He nodded and considered getting on. His teeth clenched, he took the reins and climbed aboard, grateful he'd chosen a short horse. In the saddle, he let the waves of hurt run up both cheeks. Barely aware of her riding in close and putting a blanket over his shoulders, he blinked at her.

"You were shivering," she said, and then reined Star away, ready to ride.

"Thanks." His mind focused on the roan. He wondered what the shaggy horse would try to do when he booted him out. Nothing, just a stiff walk like he was trotting on eggs, but no head hiding. Ed remained on his guard, just in case. He looked around and Ramon nodded at him in approval. They were set to go. Simple enough, but he still dreaded the whole thing—but he wanted Ten Bears back.

At dawn they reached his place. Jorge rushed out to meet them and invited them in to eat some food. The foreman looked concerned at his boss when he stiffly dismounted.

"Yes," Unita said to Jorge. "He's sore, but that don't matter. He has to find the rustlers."

Jorge nodded. "*Sí*, Senora, I know him well. I would have tried to track those men, but I don't know what I would do with them." A pained look on his face, he shook his head.

"Ranger Ed will figure that out," she said, and dismounted.

Ed shook his head. "I haven't been a ranger in years."

"Once a ranger always a ranger, they say." She herded him toward the jacal. "Better eat this woman's food. It will be much better than any you eat on the trail."

"I'm going to borrow Ramon," he said over his shoulder to Jorge.

"*Sí*, he is a good hand to go with you."

Ed agreed and greeted Tina. "Sorry we have busted in on you."

"No, Senor." She blushed and nodded. "You and the grand lady can come any time. This is your casa."

"I know, but we are your guests."

While they ate her beans, scrambled eggs, pork, salsa, and tortillas, Jorge explained that the tracks went west. Maybe four or five riders.

"Were their horses shod?" Ed asked.

"*Sí*."

"What does that mean?" Unita asked from behind the napkin that she wiped her mouth on.

"Shod horse could mean white men, or Indians riding stolen ones. Barefoot I would think they were Indians."

She set down the cloth napkin. "But all the Indians are on reservations."

"They still make raids. Horse stealing is part of an Indian's blood."

"So who stole these?"

"I would think, first, Mexican bandits. Breeding stock like Ten Bears and those ten mares would bring a high price at some hacienda."

Unita raised an eyebrow at him. "I didn't think Indians had such great horses."

"They did before the army shot them all." He clutched a hot cup of coffee in his hands. "They shot every great horse the Indians had and left them the plugs."

"McKensie do that at Palo Duro?"

Ed nodded slow like to answer her. "And—the Comanche have known Ten Bears was here."

"At any price," she said as if she understood.

"They have no price. Imagine returning to their village with such a famous stallion and the mares; that would be the maximum thing. This would be the highest rank that any buck could ever attain."

"He was spoils of war to you?"

Ed smiled and laughed. "He was all the wages I ever got as a ranger. Texas sure never sent me a dime. I found those mares to match him to later, scattered over the land, and bought them. They were among the ones that others had picked out of the Comanche herd before the slaughter. Some were with the Tonka army scouts who took them as their pay before the army shot the rest."

"How will you know who has him?"

"Easy. Someone out there will have seen them driving horses. They will tell us. Once they got away from here they'll move in the daylight."

"Should we rest?" she asked.

Ed shook his head. "It's going to be tough from here on. Jorge can show you home."

Her blue eyes narrowed. "No way."

"Yes, ma'am." He held out the cup and Tina refilled it. "It won't be nice."

"I didn't come for a picnic."

"Good." He combed his hair back and replaced his hat. "It won't be any picnic, I can guarantee you."

Chapter 6

Late that afternoon they found a place where the rustlers had penned the horses in a set of weather-blackened pens that belonged to some ranch and were only used for roundups. The post-walled jacal with the grass roof Ed discovered contained some freshly discarded cans of tomatoes. Built from posts driven in the ground, then roofed, the single room had only some bed frames and crude wooden crates for furniture, and all their cooking had been done outside at a fireplace made of rocks and mortar under a ramada with a shingle roof—one of the few signs of modern man. Ed noted a stack of split firewood and smiled as he stood with his hand on the sturdy corner post holding up the shingle roof.

"Whose place is this?" Unita asked, dismounting.

"I'm not sure. But we won't hurt it."

"What next?" She removed her hat and mopped her face on a kerchief.

"Put the horses up. Make a fire and cook something, sleep a few hours, then head out."

She studied him, and then frowned. "You look tired."

"Cap'n Jack always said to us rangers, 'You boys can sleep all day when this is over.' "

"How old were you then?"

"Fifteen when I helped chase down my first bunch of rustlers." He jerked the latigos free on his saddle, then lifted it and the sweaty pads and held them in his hands. "I'll do that for you."

"I can do it. I saw you wince."

"Oh—" He shrugged his shoulders and lugged the saddle over to the jacal before dumping it on the horn and spreading the blankets out to dry.

"Fifteen?" she asked.

He turned and nodded to her. "I grew up fast on that chase. A week in the saddle and we caught them."

She put down her pack beside his and nodded for him to continue.

"We caught them this side of the Rio Bravo. Four boys, I was the youngest, and a wiry Cap'n Jack who'd fought with Houston at San Jacinto. We took on seven Mexican bandits."

"Was it tough?"

"Cap said, 'Kid, when you see your first man over a gun barrel there is a moment you will hesitate. In that *uno momento* he will kill you—savvy?' "

"And?"

"About fifteen minutes later, when we hit their camp at dawn, this burly bandit came right at me. Roaring like a grizzly and seeing this weak-kneed kid holding a nine-pound Walker Colt pointed with both hands at him, he laughed. That's how he went out of this world—laughing. I blew his head off."

She nodded at Ed as Ramon gathered the horses

and took them to water. "Guess we better make a fire and cook some food. How far ahead are they?"

He looked at the blazing sun dying in the west. "Couple of days, but they'll slow up when they figure that there's no immediate pursuit. Let their guard down. We'll need that."

"I can't believe that a fifteen-year-old boy took on a killer and won." She pushed off her hat, shook loose her hair, and looked away. "You still running from that?"

"No, he was a worthless piece of shit. I never regretted his kind dying. They needed what they got. It was the kids got killed in stampedes, horse wrecks, drowned in swollen rivers, and got themselves shot by some worthless piece of humanity without any respect for life."

She looked at him with a hurt expression. "You can't be the blame for all of that."

He nodded grimly. "I am. I hired 'em."

"You ever taken a herd north you didn't lose someone?"

He looked at his dusty boot toes and shook his head. "No, ma'am."

"But others have?"

"I never was that lucky."

She dropped to her knees and began to build a fire in the structure. The tinder piled, she ignited it with a torpedo match. When the flames began to lick up through it she nodded. He went off to fill the coffeepot and canvas water pail.

A coyote cut down on the ridge, and he smiled at his mournful song. First time in a long time he'd heard one up close and out like this. Ramon began working the hand pump to fill the trough, and Ed filled the pot and pail from the pipe spout.

"Warm evening, huh?" the youth asked.

"Bet in two days we're hugging blankets and wearing slickers."

"Why, Señor?"

"Them thin, high clouds pushing in."

The youth nodded in the twilight and worked the pump harder. Ed washed his face and hands in the tank before going back to camp. The cool water revived him some. Back in camp, he set the pot on the grill. She nodded in approval, busy slivering some ham into a skillet.

He swept up the other canvas pail, and went back to the source for more water for her. He and Ramon returned together. The horses all had on feedbags and were crunching corn over the crickets' slow orchestration.

Her thick ham-flour gravy over some day-old biscuits she'd brought along filled them before they turned in. He had to admit it was better than most makeshift meals he'd gulped down in times past on such pursuits. Before midnight he planned to get them up and on the trail. So far the rustlers had avoided any settlements, or even ranches. He really wanted an ID on them and how many there were. He imagined four from the foot tracks. Three wore moccasins without heels. That didn't mean Indians. Homemade moccasins were easier on your feet than store-bought boots. Ed's came from a man called Hyer in Kansas. The second pair of to-fit boots he'd ever owned.

He awoke close to midnight. He checked the Big Dipper for the time, then dumped out his boots and pulled them on. He squatted close to Unita and looked at her form under the blankets. He hated to wake her but reached out and touched her shoulder. "Time to go again."

"Sure—" She sat up bleary-eyed in the starlight and nodded that she was awake. "I know—we can sleep all day when this is over."

He smiled and went to the fire's ashes to stir up some heat for the coffee and leftovers. Soon he had flames licking up and she joined him under a blanket. "Cold this morning."

"Be a norther in here in a couple of days."

"Time for one. I just hate them."

He agreed with her and, with things cooking, went off to help Ramon saddle the stock. The horses ready, they washed their hands and came back to squat in the fire's reflective heat and eat more of the delicious gravy and biscuits. They soon broke camp and rode south following the dim back road the rustlers had chosen.

The sun came over the horizon with a cold light and found them in a greasewood sea. He huddled under his blanket and noted that the boy had dug out a serape. Unita had her wrap, too. The tracks of the stolen horses began to look familiar to him.

Midday, some pale cottonwoods appeared in the distance. The sight of the trees meant water. They drew near, and signs of inhabitants began to appear around a cluster of jacals: low smoke from cooking fires, the shrill voices of children. Ed made certain the .44 on his hip wore caps on each cylinder, then reholstered it. The revolver felt comfortable in his grasp. One never knew when he'd need it.

A woman pointed in their direction and several dogs barked. A man under a sombrero came out and, arms folded over his chest, looked ready to block their way.

"Go easy," Ed said to Unita and Ramon, appraising the situation. This person looked defiant, and he decided they should stay there while he rode in to check the waiting man out. He swung his right hand aside as a sign for them to stop. "Wait here."

"Be careful," she said.

"I will." He booted the roan ahead and checked the jacals for any sign of a sniper or his horses.

"Buenos dias," the swarthy-faced man said.

"The same to you, Senor." He'd seen from their tracks that the horses had been driven into this place.

"What brings you to my *rancheria*?" The man's left eye had a lazy lid and drooped, so he peered hard out of his right one.

"Oh, someone stole my stallion and ten mares."

The man shook his head. "I have never seen ten head and a stallion."

Ed nodded, rubbed his palms on the tops of his pants legs, and studied the man hard. *"Mi amigo,* perhaps you need to have a doctor check your eyes."

"Why?" he growled. His face turned black with anger.

"Those caballeros came right through here."

"You calling me a liar?"

"I came here in peace." Nodding, Ed looked around as if appraising his place. "You have many women and children about this *rancheria*. I want none of them hurt, but I could kill you in the blink of an eye. Who

were these men who took my horses?" His rising temper made his heart thump under his breastbone. This
bully had better reconsider his lying or he'd be sprout-
ing some cheap sod on his grave.

"I don't know—"

"Cut the crap. I have rode a long ways and my
patience is short."

"Lonzo Alvarez. . . ."

Ed bobbed his head. He had heard of this bandit.
"What's your name?"

"Juan Sanchez."

"Juan, I would buy some food for my *compañeros*.
And a little grain for my horses if you can sell me
some?"

The man swallowed. "Don't tell that hombre I told
you his name."

"He won't learn nothing from me."

Sanchez gave a toss of his head for them to come
in and join Ed. "Tell them to come. Marie, Juanita,
fix some food. We have guests." Turning back, he nodded to Ed. "Your name is?"

"Ed Wright. I live on Red Wolf Creek. That is Senora Nance and the boy is Ramon."

"Gracias," he said. He swept off his hat and bowed
for Unita's passing.

"He has corn for the horses," Ed said to Ramon.

The boy acknowledged his words and took Unita's
horse's reins when she dismounted. Two of the older
women came and talked to her in Spanish, inviting
her in their casa. She took off her hat and looked
back to him, and he motioned it would be all right.

"Alvarez is a killer," Juan said under his breath,

and frowned as if concerned with what he saw. "You have an unarmed boy and a fine lady with you to catch him?"

"I'm an ex-ranger."

The man dropped his gaze to the sandy ground as they walked to the water trough and he let Ed drink his fill.

"I have heard they only send one ranger?"

Ed nodded. "One problem, one ranger."

"But Alvarez has some tough men."

"How many?"

"Two mean ones, as he is, and a boy."

"These men, are they his kin?"

"One is his brother Quatro. The other one, Tigre, is a breed. The boy is yellow-headed and has blue eyes. I think he was a Comanche captive."

Ed frowned and shook his head. There were lots of white captives who grew up to become tribal members. "You learn his name?"

"They call him Blondie. He only speaks bad Spanish. No savvy *el English*."

Ed agreed, loosened the girth and hitched Blue with the others. "Does Alvarez have a place this side of the border?"

"There is a saloon and whorehouse at Sheba. He stops there often to see a *puta*."

"How far?"

"Ten miles."

Ed nodded. By his calculation, they could be at this place called Sheba by dark. Maybe Alvarez would still be there. His hopes rose.

"Come, they will have the food ready."

"Corn for my horses?"

"Bring them. I will get some," Juan said to Ramon and they went toward the jacals.

"How many families live here?" Ed asked, looking around. Several bare-bottomed, dark-eyed children peered hard at them from "safe" places.

"Three—both of my brothers were killed by bandits. So I have a wife and two widows to care for."

"That's a big chore."

"*Sí*, a big chore."

When they joined the women, Unita met him. "These women say that the leader of the ones who took your horses is a very mean man. He has two pistoleros, too."

"Alvarez," he said under his breath.

She nodded, looking very seriously at him. "They say he has killed many men."

"Reckon he's got a funeral suit picked out?"

"It isn't a time to be funny. There are three or four tough men down there."

"We'll see when the time comes."

"They may only be ten miles away."

He pursed his lips and bobbed his head. "You can only cross rivers when you get to them."

"Can you find any help?"

"Doubt it. All these people fear him too much to be any help."

"Maybe a little fear on your part might be in order . . . She has our food ready." Unita indicated the woman bringing them trays piled high with their dinner.

"Yes. Time to eat," he said, grateful to have the diversion. With nothing in concrete, he planned to handle Alvarez and his bunch of cutthroats as things presented themselves. No doubt this would not be Unita's way, but he knew the ground Cap'n Jack would cover—separate them first, disable as many as possible, then put down the rest.

They sat on a blanket and ate. The three women brought them fresh coffee and fussed over them. Two of them were very pregnant, and the third carried a new baby in her arm.

"Who are they?" she asked under her breath.

"One's his wife. The others are his brothers' widows."

"How long've they been widows?"

"He said he had a big job."

Unita smirked and nodded. "Big job."

After the meal, he paid the man and they rode on. In no hurry to reach Sheba in the daylight, Ed set a leisurely pace moving south. So busy thinking about Alvarez, he'd lost track of many things. All the things Cap'n Jack taught him and that they did as rangers filled his thoughts.

"You've ever been to this place?" she asked, breaking into his concentration.

"No, but we can scout it."

"Clouds are coming, like you say." Ramon pointed out the gathering bank in the north.

"You bet, hombre. It may be cold driving them broomtails home."

Ramon smiled. "I have never been so far from home."

"Well, you can see that it ain't worth much."

"Jorge, he says the hills of Texas are as pretty as the world can get."

"He hasn't told you a lie," Unita put in.

"I believed him, Senora. Now I really believe him."

After sundown, they reined up on a rise. The lights in the small community flickered in the darkness. He was satisfied that one source came from the cantina and house of pleasure—the biggest in the settlement. Ed turned his ear. A stud horse was screaming—Ten Bears.

"That's him," Ramon said, excited.

Wright nodded and turned in the saddle toward Unita. "We've caught up with them."

"What now?"

"We go kill us some horse thieves. Get our stock and go home."

"That easy?"

"That easy."

Chapter 7

"How many guards are at the corral?" Unita whispered in the darkness.

"Ramon and I saw two. One's the blond captive boy, and the other a breed. He's the armed one." He glanced over and Ramon nodded.

"I get the drop on the breed. You two can bluff the boy, I think. Remember he only speaks Spanish, and not good. He looks lost with them to me." Ed shook his head. "Where in the hell they got him, I have no idea."

"Can you use the rifle?" she asked.

"Sure. You can take the pistol. It's loaded. But any shot will warn the others and they'll come out shooting, so try not to use it." He looked hard at her. His idea was to prune down the number of rustlers so he could handle the rest.

"I understand," she said, a ring of impatience in her voice.

He frowned at her affront, but went on. "Good. I'll go around and take the breed. You two watch, and get the boy."

The plan set, he started around the rough-sided

shed to circle the pens. This breed, Tigre, might be the one to realize he was coming around at him, but that was a chance he had to take. Breeds could be tough, alert sentries, but others were incompetent and lazy. He'd looked pretty bored when Ed spied on him earlier. Both he and the boy were squatted by a small fire, busy cooking and, except for the breed wearing a cartridge belt slung over his shoulder, neither showed lots of fight in them. Cap'n Jack had said, never underestimate your enemies. Go in prepared for the worst.

Ed stopped and knelt on one knee. The smell of the fire's smoke on the soft night wind filled his nose, and he heard the two talking in Spanish. Ed cocked the hammer back on the rifle and rose to his near six-foot height.

"Grab some sky!" he ordered in Spanish. He walked up on them, the rifle butt stuck hard in his hip, his finger on the trigger.

With his back to Ed, the breed's hand shot to his holster. But when he looked up into the face of the captive, who was putting up his hands, he must have reconsidered because he raised his dark hands in the reflection of the red light of the fire.

Ed moved in swiftly, and nodded as Ramon took the captive's hands down and then tied them behind his back.

"On your knees and prepare to die," Ed ordered the breed.

The breed hurried to the ground, holding his hands on his hat. "Mother of God, who are you?"

"The man owns those ponies."

"How did you find us?"

"Your tracks, stupid. Who's over in the saloon?"

"I don't know."

Ed jammed the muzzle of the rifle to his neck. "That help your memory?"

"Lonzo Alvarez and his brother Quatro."

"They got girls in there?"

"I don't know. They have many girls."

"Where were you going with my horses?"

"Mexico."

Ed shoved him facedown and soon had his hands tied behind his back. Unita handed him a gag. He nodded and bent over to put it on his prisoner. Soon Tigre and Blondie were on the ground, facedown, gagged, and their feet tied up so they couldn't run off. Ed slipped on Tigre's cartridge belt and a Colt that had been refitted to take .44 brass cartridges. He checked the loads in it and, satisfied, replaced it on his hip.

He took off and gave Unita the holster for the Army .44. "Now get that shotgun, and if one of them busts out those front doors shooting, blow him to kingdom come."

She nodded that she understood. "Where are you going?"

"Inside to roust them up." In the twilight he read the upset his words written on her face.

"Is that smart?" she asked.

"I call that fighting on my ground. Out here is their's."

"They come outside shooting, they're in my sights," she said.

"Good deal." He set out across the starlit bare ground to the porch of the saloon, where yellow light streamed from around the batwing doors. With his hand, he tried the Colt in his new holster. It worked easy enough, and fit his grip. His eyes on the double doors and the glare, he reached the porch and stepped up, letting his eyes adjust to the brightness of smoke-clouded candlelight.

He pushed inside the doors, drawing many cold stares from customers sitting around the room. At the almost empty bar, he took a place and ordered some *pulque*. The bartender brought him a large pottery cup of it and nodded. "Ten centavos."

"Which ones are the Alvarez brothers?" he asked in a soft voice, holding a silver dollar and the ten-centavo piece.

The bartender shook his head. "I know no Alvarez in here."

"Take your dime and go to the far end. Where's your shotgun?"

"I don't have—"

"Sumbitch, put it on the counter right up here." Ed used his finger to point at the place on the scarred wood in front of him. "Or you'll be the first to die."

The man swallowed and nodded. He used both hands to carefully place a sawed-off Greener on the bar. "What else?"

"Them boys upstairs?" Ed gave a head toss toward them.

The bartender froze for a long second, then nodded.

The first shot would extinguish the candlelight and plunge the saloon into darkness. Ed wanted the Alvarez brothers out in the open so that he had a clear shot at them when the light quit. Maybe if he went up there on the second landing. The half-dozen men in the cantina looked uneasy, like they were ready to get up and run before the shooting started.

When Ed took the sawed-off shotgun off the bar, they started scraping chairs and getting up. Even the inebriated ones looked sober enough to obey him. He pointed at the rear door with a "be quiet" under his breath. Head nods accompanied their retreat, and soon he and the barkeep were all that were left downstairs.

Ed considered the staircase and the landing rail above the back half of the building, seeing a row of a half-dozen shut doors. Which ones contained the brothers? He met the barkeep's gaze and pointed with his left index finger.

The man looked up at the floor above his head and shrugged. Then he held up two digits and pointed above him. Second on the left—if he wasn't lying. A consideration that Ed considered as a major factor. He put a boot sole on the worn pine board step and started up. The short shotgun was in his hands, loaded, cocked, and ready. He could hear the laughter of a man, the bold, brazen laughter of someone extracting cruel pleasure from a weaker individual. Mad laughter, and as far as Ed could tell it was from the fourth room from the left as he reached eye level with the second floor.

The rightmost door opened, and Ed swung the gun's muzzle menacingly at a wide-eyed man who dropped back in shock at the sight of Ed and the shotgun.

A finger to Ed's lips and the man nodded, looked relieved, and shut the door. With his heart pounding like a trip-hammer, Ed drew a deep breath to settle himself. He moved to the wall and then began to shout, "Alvarez! Alvarez! The horses!"

"What is that?" a voice shouted.

"Quatro, see about them!" came the order from the middle room. "Someone is stealing the damn horses."

Door two opened and a half-dressed, swarthy-faced man emerged cursing with a six-gun in his hand. Ed aimed between the two barrel humps, squeezed the trigger and the lights went out with the billowing black powder. His shot silenced the man's cursing. A second door opened and a dark figure's six-gun began blazing with orange flame. Ed's remaining barrel of shot struck him in the chest and took him down. Shrill screaming from the doves in the rooms hurt Ed's ears, already ringing from the percussion of all the shots

After not seeing any movement from either man in the darkness, he shook his head and started down the stairs. They were on their way to hell, and he'd opened the door. At the bar he set the gun down, then tossed a ten-dollar gold piece on the bar. "Two bottles of something. The rest is to bury them."

The man had lit a candle. The flickering glow shone on the bartender's pale-as-a-ghost face. He brought the bottles and set them on the bar. Then he nodded and faded back to his corner like an obedient dog. Ed took the bottles by the necks and started for the door. He stopped in the doorway and then parted the wings.

"It's me," he said, loud enough for Unita to hear him.

Across the street, she handed Ramon the shotgun and hurried to meet him in the starlight.

"You all right?" she asked, falling in beside him.

"I'm fine," he said, never breaking his stride. "No one else was hurt."

"How—how did it go in there? We heard the shots—"

"They're dead."

"What about those two at the corral?"

"I been thinking we'll take that captive boy with us."

"The breed?"

He merely nodded and went on. "We'll saddle all their horses and take them back with us. They won't need them. Probably stolen anyhow. Ramon started saddling them."

At the corral, he roughly jerked Blondie up by the arm and tore the gag off of him. "You a rustler?"

The youth shook his head and looked bug-eyed at him in the starlight.

"Who are you?" Ed shook him hard.

The boy managed to give him some guttural-sounding combination that made no sense, nor could Ed have repeated it. "Your name Blondie?"

Wide-eyed, he nodded. Fear made him quake all over.

"You will get one chance." He waved his index finger in Blondie's face. "One chance to live. You savvy one?"

"Sí."

"You go help Ramon saddle them horses and help us drive them back. You do one bad thing or run off . . ." Ed drew the side of his hand across his throat. "You savvy?"

"Sí, sí, me work hard."

He spun him around and cut him loose. Then he turned to Unita. "Alvarez may have friends around here. I want the three of you to drive the horses north to Juan's tonight. Rest there and I'll join you there."

"What are you going to do?"

"Make certain they don't follow us and try to take those horses back."

"But Alvarez is dead, isn't he?"

"Will you do as I say?"

"Yes." She turned on her heel and went to the corral.

He came behind her and went in the gate, closing it behind himself. Holding out his hand he went through the horses, talking softly until he saw a light-colored head bob at him.

"Ten Bears," he said softly.

Blowing rollers out his nose, the big horse acted ready to break and run. Instead, he held his ground and acted uncertain, nickering softly. Ed eased himself up close and touched his neck. His soft words soothing the tense horse, he soon clapped him on the neck, wishing this night was over.

"He must know you," Unita said from the corral fencing.

"I don't know if he does or not. He's simply a good horse. No telling how many buffalo he carried his past owners in close enough to shoot."

"He's light-colored."

Ed nodded, busy rubbing the horse's poll and face. "He's almost white now. He was more a red roan when I got him. Boys, get the horses saddled, and you three can ride on."

"I don't understand why we—"

Ed shook his head at her and started back. "I don't want to be followed."

"What about the one tied up here?" she asked, stepping off the rails.

"I'll handle him too."

"Meet you at Juan's?"

"I'll be along. If I don't show up in a couple of days, go on home."

In thirty minutes they left with all the horses. Ed noticed that Blondie made a hand at helping Ramon and this eased his mind about giving the youth a chance. In the saddle, Unita looked down at him, shook her head in disapproval, and rode after them with a soft, "Be careful."

Half sick to his stomach, he listened to Ten Bears's coarse whinny in the distance. The squeal of some mare he'd bitten to make her stay in the herd shattered the darkness, and the hoofbeats soon disappeared in the night.

Cap'n Jack had said never to leave behind anyone that you'd simply have to track down again. Made no sense to let them go and have to spend more precious time redoing the same business all over again. When they tracked down horse thieves, they only brought the horses back. They drew cards from a worn-out deck. High cards meant you were the executioner, or one of them.

The condemned had been caught red-handed—no doubt about their guilt. And except for two young boys, about like Blondie, they released and sent home in two different cases, they tied the rustlers up, made them get on their knees, and then, after letting them make peace with their maker, shot them in the back of the head. Ed knew in this case he had drawn the ace. Didn't make it any easier.

There'd been two young cowboys who stole a handful of ranch horses on a spree—probably drunk—and his ranger company had tracked them down. He never forgot the freckle-faced one of the pair of boys. He was maybe eighteen, and he asked Ed to send his Bible to his mother when Ed was getting ready to execute him.

Ed didn't know which was the worse part— executing him, or riding up to that homestead ten days later and handing the Bible to the woman who was hanging clothes on a line.

She looked up sad-faced at him, the leather-bound black book in both her hands. "He ain't coming home, is he?"

"No, ma'am." Ed had turned his horse around, too upset to stand another moment in her presence.

He found one bottle he'd bought in the cantina and collapsed to a seat in the dust. His butt on the ground he watched people bring out the two bodies and toss them in a two-wheeled *carreta*. Several peered into the night in his direction, and then, with shrugs, they went back inside. At last, the wooden wheels squealing loudly, the dead were hauled away in the night.

With his teeth, he removed the cork and tried the whiskey. Bad stuff, but he gagged some down.

"Senor?"

He turned and looked at the dark form of the tied-down Tigre, who had not said a word until then. "What?"

"If you are going to kill me, be swift."

"You ever pray?"

"Ah, what good is to pray? I can not go to heaven."

Ed nodded, considered the bottle, and then took another jolt from the neck. "You're right, they probably won't let you in up there."

"Right. I have killed many men."

"How many?"

"All together?"

"Yes. How many?"

"Maybe ten?"

"Ten, huh. How many women have you raped?"

"Several, but I am ashamed of the time I raped a real little girl."

"So you have killed ten men and raped many women—even little girls?"

"I was very drunk at the time."

No excuse in his book for such a vile act. Ed took another snort and wiped his mouth on the back of his hand. "How many horses have you rustled?"

"Many—many."

"So if I shoot you, the world won't be out much?"

"I don't savvy *out much*?"

"You will."

Ed set the bottle down and dropped back on his hands behind his back to stare at the thousand stars. A few more drinks and he'd send his worthless piece of shit to hell. His eyes squeezed shut but he could still see the gun smoke cloud from the muzzle of his .44 and the jerk of Freckles's thin shoulders before he spilled facedown in the dust. Ed had holstered his gun and stepped back. Freckles's blood ran over scuffed boots twisting in the last throes of death, his horse-stealing pard likewise on the ground, still next to him, executed by ranger Jimmy Brown who was puking up his guts beside him. He could even smell the sourness of it. The damn Bible—the one he had promised to deliver—why did all this have to come back now?

'Cause he held the ace in this deal too.

Chapter 8

"Oh, Suzanna, don't you cry for me. I'm coming from Alabama with a banjo on my knee—hello," he sang to Unita, who'd come out to meet him. His eyes closed against the bright sun, he gripped the saddle horn in both hands. "See you made it."

She cut him a sharp look. "We were about to go back and find you."

He turned and looked at his back trail through the greasewood, and then twisted around to nod at her. "Nothing back there that you'd want."

She looked about ready to bust. He knew she would be mad about his drinking. What else could he expect? Then Juan came from another jacal, smiling and shouting hello at him.

"*Ah, mi amigo!*" Ed shouted to him, grateful to have an excuse to ignore her motherly ways. "Oh, we can start home in the morning. Get us some sleep and rest here today."

Her blue eyes bored holes in him, but she kept it to

herself as he dismounted and went to hug "his friend." Damn, he felt uncomfortable under her scrutiny. So he was half drunk; that was his business. Besides, she didn't have to live with the things he lived with in his head. If she had them, she'd drink too.

"Ah. Amigo, you killed those bad hombres. No?"

"*Sí, sí,* they are gone to burn in hell."

"Good place for them. You saved that yellow-headed one, huh?"

"He was no killer."

Juan nodded and looked at the ground. "Maybe he lived too long with them Comanches?"

"You figure so?" He went back to the roan horse and drew out a half-empty bottle of mescal.

"Those red devils, they live on blood."

Ed nodded woodenly and held out the bottle to him. "He don't act like that, does he?"

Juan took the bottle with a sly smile. "You bring good stuff, amigo. I don't know, but he must have lived with them for a long time. Some—" Juan held up the bottle as if appraising it. "Some of their bloody ways may have rubbed off." He took a deep draft of it and then sighed deeply.

"*Mi amigo,* that is good." Juan's head bobbed in approval. "This one, he may be like a half wolf–dog I once had. He was a good dog but he never really got over being a wolf either."

Ed indicated he'd heard the man. "I'll watch him."

"You ate today?"

"I don't need anything." Ed held out the bottle and looked hard at the remaining liquor in it. He had more in his saddlebags.

"Come to the women and they will feed you." Juan looked around and then lowered his voice. "Those bastards raped them when they came through here."

Ed nodded that he heard the man. *No one would ever miss them.* "I don't need any food."

"No. *Mi amigo,* you must eat. Hey. Fix my good amigo some food!" Juan shouted, and the women scurried to obey. He smiled hugely when Ed handed him back the bottle for another drink. *"Gracias."*

The next morning, they rode for home in the drizzle. Light, cold rain fell all morning. At noontime, when they reached the corrals and thatched hut they put the horses up and decided to wait out the rain. It was a good rain for winter oats, and this thirsty land always needed it. Still, the small fire on the floor felt good, and Unita cooked some sheep that Juan had donated to them under the roof of the ramada. Her meat broiling, she joined them, sitting in a circle wrapped in blankets against the chill.

"What are your plans?" she asked Ed.

"I guess I'll go home."

"I still need you to take my cattle to Kansas."

Under his blanket, he hunched his shoulders and closed his eyes. "You can't depend on me."

"If you'd show me the way even, I—I—"

He looked over at her as if appraising her. "I suppose I could bury you."

"Ed Wright, everyone doesn't die going to Kansas."

"That's where you're wrong. Plenty of good ones do."

"I'm willing to take my chances." She didn't look at him as she tossed some grass stems on the fire and it consumed them.

"Trouble is, I ain't."

"How will you know? You'll be drinking."

"Right. I tried being dry and don't like it."

"Will you hire me the hands?"

Something on his neck itched, so he scratched it. "Ain't many will work for a woman."

"I can't help what I am. There must be some hands who will."

He chewed on his sun-crusted lower lip. "I bet there are. I just wanted you to know there's going to be prejudice against you."

"There was when my husband went to war. I was even told by my own help to go to the house—*once.*" She raised her face and he saw the strength in her features. He'd have hated like hell to have been the one said that to her. He blinked when a wind shift sent smoke in his eyes. Maybe if he agreed to go as a guide and help her she'd get off his back about the drinking thing.

"All right—I'll go as guide, but don't count on me. It'll be the worst thing I can imagine ever doing again and I'll have hell passing all those places where I've lost boys and buried them."

"Wonderful," she shouted, and hugged him. In her rush, she knocked off his hat and even kissed him on the side of his face. Sitting up on her knees, her face bright with excitement, he decided she was the prettiest woman he'd ever met.

He would be days sorting out why he ever agreed to the job. Didn't matter; he'd never backed out of anything he'd promised anyone and had no plans to start doing it. That trail north was like a mistress. She could be pretty, all broken out in blooms and

waving new grass. In her stormy moods, she was a
black widow and her swollen rivers were webs of
death. She ran the gamut from soft lullaby winds to
tornadoes. Hot sun to freezing hail, and even snow.
Damn her soul anyway!

Chapter 9

He watched the stud horse from the ridgeside seat on a bay horse out of his own remuda. He'd sent Unita's roan home with her. Tina was a good hand to cook, but he kinda missed Unita and Rosa's cooking. Maybe he missed her company—Unita's. He was headed for Willows and Gunterville. He knew a few point riders and he wanted good ones, with experience. Moving a mile-and-a-half-long string of cattle into water to cross a river all depended on them, the two riders, one each on the right and left at the head of the serpentine line. It took real hands to hold down the speed of the herd, or to close in and make them go faster. The rest of the lot could be punchers. Boys that could sit a horse well enough and had few fears. Ones who wouldn't get homesick so bad they'd quit halfway across the Indian Nation and go back.

Ich Strang lived on a small place above Whittaker, married to some German widow with kids who kept Spanish goats. Ed was on his way to see Ich first. He rode through the live oak that crowded a narrow ribbon of wagon tracks in a sandy draw.

He came out in the open to the sounds of goat

bells, bleating, and some border collies barking at his
arrival. A few grown hens scattered from their
scratching at his bay horse's approach. A full-bodied
woman came out of a jacal and swept the dark hair
back from her face. Three thumb-sucking young-uns
hung on her skirt, too bashful to look at him.

"Ich around?" he asked, taking off his hat for her.

She nodded. Her dark brown eyes boring holes in
him. She knew he wasn't there on a social call and
probably did not approve of it either. No matter their
economics, women didn't like their man off and gone
to hell for six to nine months.

"He's up at the corral."

"Good to see you, ma'am," he said and nodded,
then put his hat back on. He booted the bay for the
weathered gray post corral. He could see the lanky
Ich busy sacking out some young horses.

"Hey, Ed. I wasn't expecting you," the lanky, bow-
legged man in his thirties said with a knowing smile.
"Thought you was drinking San Antone dry."

"I was—" He rubbed his rough, callused hand over
his mouth and nodded. "Run them plum out of
good whiskey."

"What a shame. Climb down and jaw a while," Ich
said, coming out of the corral. He already had out a
jackknife and was fixing to sliver off some chewing
tobacco from a plug.

Ed stepped off and undid the cinch. The bay
dropped his head and lifted a hind foot to stand hip-
shot, ground tied where the reins were in the dust.

"You got some work, huh?" Ed tossed his head at
the four horses tied in the corral.

"They ain't mine. Breaking them for a fellow.

Work's been kinda short." Ich rubbed his hands on the front of his wash-worn britches. "Fact is, I was thinking about going to San Antone myself."

"I'll need a point rider."

"You're going back?" Ich frowned at him.

"I am, as the guide for a woman."

"Who's that?"

"Sam Nance's widow."

"You sweet on her?"

Ed closed his eyes and shook his head. "I only agreed to guide her. So if working for a female is against your religion, tell me now."

Ich kept making circles on his upper legs with his palms and finally said, "Well, goddamn, guess I'll go."

"Good. I can issue you a twenty-dollar sign-up bonus." Ed went and got the roster and pencil from his saddlebags. He held the paper on the seat of his saddle and handed Ich the pencil. "You're my first man to sign on."

"I see that."

"I'd also appreciate you not mentioning the bonus. I ain't paying the rest."

Ich nodded and scrawled out his name. "I'll be beholden to you for it."

"Nope, come next March you'll be saying 'That damn Ed Wright bribed me into this and I don't know why.' "

Ich laughed. "I know it would be asking a lot, but if I had a month's wages before we rode out then my wife could get through till I got back."

"You got a deal, Ich. Don't get busted up on them broncs. I'll need you come March. Where's Shorty at?"

Ich made a face. "Crinerville jail."

"What did he do now?"

"Helped himself to some things. They didn't give him hard time, but he's got six months."

"Who's sheriff over there now?"

"Kingfisher, L. T. Kingfisher. You recall him?"

"I think so." The name didn't bring a good picture of anyone, but maybe he'd recall the man when he got there. "Here's the twenty-dollar bonus, and five more for Chrstmas gifts for them young-uns."

Ich spat out some dark black tobacco on the rain-softened ground, wiped his mouth on the back of his hand, and nodded in approval. "Thanks, this'll make Hiedie a little easier to handle when I break the news."

Ed jerked up his latigo to tighten his cinch. "I'd say she knowed when she saw me ride up."

"She's a good woman. I sure won't complain about her."

Ed swung in the saddle and nodded. "They tell me good ones are hard to find." He saluted his longtime acquaintance and hit the trail for Crinerville.

Past dark he reached the settlement and, besides being starved, felt sore-backed from the hours in the saddle. His side still sore, he dismounted under the livery lamp.

"You got a place to sleep tonight?" he asked the fuzzy-faced old man who came out to wait on him.

The old-timer cleared his throat, cut a big hocker, and spit it out, drooling into his beard. "Yeah, you can sleep in the feed room."

Ed thanked him and took his saddle off the bay. He hauled it and the sweaty pads inside and tossed them on a rack. Then he undid the bedroll and tossed it on an empty cot. The old man returned and gave him the bridle. "Best food's at Chin Lee's."

With a nod to show he heard him, Ed put the bridle up before he headed down the street to find a meal. He went past a saloon and the smell of liquor wafted out into his nose. An image of Unita and her disapproving look at him shone in his mind, urging him on to the diner.

He told the Celestial waiter to bring him whatever he had fixed and thought the Chinese man said, "beast and lice." When the plate came it was heaped with rice, gravy, and strips of browned beef. He nodded his approval and decided that had it been anything not alive he'd have eaten it. After the meal and some rich coffee, he paid the man and went across the street to the two-story courthouse.

In the basement he found the jailer in the sheriff's office. "I know it's kinda late, but I understand you have a fella in here I know. Could I speak to him?"

"Which one?"

"Shorty Turner."

"I guess it won't hurt. Leave that six-gun here and go through that steel door. Shorty's in the second cell. No tricks."

"No tricks." He undid the gun belt.

The man nodded and went back to his book work under the lamp. The holster and gun piled on his desk, Ed headed for the door.

"Oh, what's your name?" the jailer asked.

"Ed Wright."

"Good enough." The man gave a toss of his head.

"That you, Ed?" a hoarse voice asked in the cell

block's semidarkness, the only light coming around the half-open steel door.

"It's me, Shorty. When do you get out of here?" The jail smelled of piss and about upset his supper.

"April, they said."

"Reckon I can talk to the sheriff and get it cut down a month?"

"Who knows? You can ask him."

"I get you out, do you want to ride point?"

"Hell, that's a dumb question. Hell, yes. For you?"

"No. For a woman."

Both hands on the bars, the man frowned at him. "Who?"

"Sam Nance's widow. I'm going along as a guide."

Shorty chuckled. "How did she get you to agree to that?"

"Well?"

"Count me in. If you can get me out one day early, I'd sure appreciate it. They won't ever lock me up in one of these hoosegows ever again."

"You got tobacco and the makings?" Ed asked.

Shorty shook his head.

"I'll bring you some in the morning."

"Ed Wright, you're a winner, pard."

"We'll see." Ed stood up, shook Shorty's hand through the bars, and then started to leave.

"Ich on the right?"

"Yeah, signed him up on the way down here." He turned at the door and looked back. "That suit you?"

"Fine. Didn't figure his wife would let him go." Shorty chuckled. "Guess he's tired of confinement too."

"I guess," Ed said, and grinned.

After breakfast the next morning at the diner, he went by the sheriff's office. L. T. Kingfisher wasn't in and the deputy said he expected him about noon. Ed spent the morning whittling on a bench out in front of the general store. His molars floating for a drink, he fought the urge until the sun reached the highest zenith and he went to lunch.

He was halfway through his "beast and lice" dinner when a big man cast a shadow over him.

"Mr. Wright?"

Ed nodded.

"L. T. Kingfisher."

"Have a chair, Sheriff."

"I will. You and Shorty old friends?"

"He's been one of my point riders for the past few years."

The lawman nodded. "I understand from what my deputy told me you need him March first?"

"Yes, I sure will."

"You come down here the end of February and take him out of my county, and make him swear to never come back here—you can have that pilfering damn pack rat."

"Thanks. Can I buy you lunch?"

"Not necessary. You just be sure he don't come under my jurisdiction ever again."

Ed blew the steam off the cup of freshly poured coffee in his hands. "I'll do that."

"Good," Kingfisher said and rose with some effort. "Just so he don't come back."

"Done."

He headed back to the ranch after taking Shorty enough tobacco, paper, and matches to last him a while. It was after sundown when he chose a place off the road to roll out the bedroll and rest the bay. His pony hobbled, and after eating some hard jerky, he laid down to sleep a few hours. He had the two experienced point riders, and needed ten more good cowboys, a horse wrangler, and a cook's helper. Probably needed a cook too—Unita couldn't do that and ramrod. He closed his eyes and went to sleep to some coyote's wailing.

Chapter 10

At noontime, he was in Banty and stopped off at the bank. He drew fifty dollars from his account and shook hands with Wayne Ripple, the banker.

"You're looking good," Ripple said, and smiled.

"I'm fine. You send word to them borrowers of yours. Unita Nance is going up the trail to Kansas March first, and they might put in with her."

Ripple shook his head as if to dismiss the notion. "They won't send any cattle up the trail with a woman."

"They might if I did."

"You're going to send your cattle with her?"

"I am. Thanks. Have a nice day," he said, and left the flabbergasted banker with his mouth open. Ripple was a good man to deposit with, but he always suspected Ripple's loans were made to increase his empire. The word he was shipping about Unita would hit the live oak faster than a dancing dust devil could travel. A smile on his lips, he went across the street for a couple of beers.

He made a trip through the free lunch counter and after getting some German rye bread, sliced sausage, and sharp cheese he took his plate to a side table and ordered a beer from Otto the bartender.

"It is good to see you again, Mr. Wright."

"Good to be here," he told the mustached German, who brought him a tall schooner of beer.

He was halfway through his beer and lunch when a short, familiar man slid into the seat opposite him. "I got two hundred big steers."

"Why tell me, Dean?"

"They said—you said—you were making a drive."

Ed shook his head, and picked up the sandwich to take a bite. "You need to talk to Mrs. Nance."

"But they said you were—"

His mouth full, he pointed the sandwich at the man while he chewed on it. "She's the one taking cattle north."

Dean Morgan wilted in the chair. "I ain't sending no damn cattle to Kansas with a woman ramrod. Hell, if I want to lose them, I can do that right here."

Ed nodded in approval. "I see how you think. Besides, ain't that Jim Bob McGregor coming in? He'll take them north."

Dean frowned. "And rob me blind. No, thanks."

Inside the batwing doors, Jim Bob McGregor pushed an expensive white hat back on his head and smiled like a shit-eating cat. "Well," he said in a rusty voice. "If it ain't Ed Wright. How are you, hoss?"

"Fine."

"Someone said you'd sobered up. Said that Nance woman dried you up. Wish she'd dried me up. You know what I mean?" He gave a nasty smirk.

"Jim Bob—" Ed held his fork like a spear and pointed it at the man. "You say one more derogatory word about that lady and I'll jerk your filthy tongue out by the roots."

The drover blinked at Ed for a moment and his face drained. "Listen, you drunk sumbitch—"

Ed was out of the chair with his hand on his gun butt. "I said—"

"Hold your horses." Jim Bob held his hands out, looking pale, and started backing for the door. "No need losing your temper. I know you was a ranger— I want no part of gunplay with you. I'm leaving. Right now."

"Whew," Dean said, and reslumped in the chair. "I thought you two were fixing to have a gunfight and I was in harm's way."

Too angry to answer him, Ed took a deep swig of beer, still standing and watching the batwing door carefully to be sure Jim Bob didn't bust back into the saloon. Every muscle tensed in his body, ready for any action required. Where did Jim Bob McGregor get the gall to speak about Unita like that?

McGregor was in the same book with Crabtree, and he'd teach both of them better habits when talking about a woman. The beer finished, he ignored Dean, went to the bar, paid Otto, and pushed his way out in the bright sun. Then he cinched up the bay and rode out of town.

Halfway to Unita's place he took the bottle of whiskey out of the saddlebags and began to drink it, still seething mad about the drover's words about as honest a woman as he ever knew. The sun fell in a bloody pool and he rode on, drinking whiskey and thinking about bad things: flooded rivers, a mile wide across the bottoms; swimming cattle milling in the current's whirlpool and needing to bust them up or lose them all, lightning dancing on horns with a blue light he'd never seen anywhere else.

"That you?" she called out from the porch.

"Yeah." He heard himself slur the word. Then he stepped out of the saddle, his sea legs gave way, and he crumpled in a pile on his butt. Taking handfuls of dust and letting them fall out of his fists like an hourglass's sand, he shook his head. "I been—rinking—a little—"

"Rosa. Come help me. . . ." Unita called out.

Chapter 11

His head hurt when he sat up on the cot. The shack was dark, and he wondered how close it was to bell-ringing time. He scrubbed his face on his dirty-smelling hands and wrinkled his nose. Geez, he felt sore and bad. Why in hell did he come back here to her place? He'd never know, he decided, pulling on his boots, then rising to stomp them on. His brain still in a fog, he felt around, found his hat, stuck it on, and pushed outside.

Light was on in the kitchen. He petted the stock dogs darting around him in friendly fashion. Grateful that they liked him, he went to the back door in the cool air and knocked.

"Oh, Senor," Rosa said, and opened the door for him to enter.

He considered not going in, then shrugged it off and went inside anyway, feeling like the tardy boy at school. In the bright light he blinked and met Unita's gaze from the dry sink where she was busy rolling out biscuit dough. Even exasperated-looking, she was pretty. He wanted to be dressed up and clean instead of smelling like horse sweat and booze. Too late for that—she got what she got. There wasn't anything in their deal calling for him to dress up. He was her guide—scout. Not in charge, either.

"Well, what did you find out?"

"I have two point riders, Ich Strang and Shorty Turner, two of the best."

"They'll show up?" She flour-dusted a whiskey jigger and began cutting out the biscuits to go in an oven-blackened pan.

"Ich's set to be here March first. Shorty, I got to go get him."

"Go get him?" Her blue eyes cut him a suspicious glance.

"Oh, he's in the Crinerville jail."

She nodded and busied herself making biscuits. "Give Ed a towel and soap, Rosa. I think tank water should make him sharper."

"Sure, thank you," he said and sucked on his eyetooth, considering what he could do nice for her. She could be as cold as that water would be. All right, he earned all he got, but he'd stayed sober the whole time getting those two hands. A week or two on the trail and she'd see what it was like—bury a few good boys—that goddamn trail . . . He went out the back door and slammed it. Then he realized he didn't have a towel or the soap that Rosa had gone for. He turned and went back like a sheep eating dog, and the door opened as he reached for it.

Rosa handed him the articles with a sad look of pity for him.

"Gracias," he said and headed out.

In the starlight he washed and dried, shivering in

the cold morning air as he got back in his clothing and headed for the house across the dark yard again.

Inside the back door he held out his hands to the tall cooking range and absorbed the heat. His body still shaking, he glanced up when Unita poured steaming water in an enamel basin and then swung out a chair.

"Let's shed some whiskers," she said, and began to strop the razor on a strap.

He went and sat on the chair. Soon she had his face hot lathered with a shaving brush. Then she deftly peeled off the week's growth and gave him a towel to wipe off the extra soap. His face smooth, he ran an index finger over his smooth upper lip, wadded up the cloth, and softly said, "Thanks."

"So we have point riders? What is next?"

"Line up ten punchers, a cook helper—"

"And?"

"If Blondie works out, I'd make him horse wrangler."

"Fine with me."

"Takes a certain sort to do that job."

She nodded, swishing off the razor and then drying it. "What about a cook?"

"You got a notion? Probably the most important job we have to fill."

She shook her head, then went and threw out the water. When she came back from the back door, she set the pan down and took the other chair across to the dry sink. "You have anyone in mind?"

"No, but he needs to be good at cooking, patient with them boys, and a half doctor too."

She frowned. "Where we going to find him?"

"Cooking in some big outfit's cow camp. A busted-up older hand or, Lord, Charlie Hawks had a Frenchman he found in Houston, could make crepes."

"What's that?"

"Fancy little things like fried pancakes in cobweb fashion." Ed laughed and shook his head. "Baked these long loaves of French bread in a sheet-iron oven and served 'em hot with olive oil and spices instead of butter. Lord, them boys loved him."

"What happened to him?"

"Oh, Frenchy got killed in a knife scrape over a dove in Abilene."

"So he's not available?"

"Right, but I'll keep my eye and ear open. One will come along. We've got months to find him."

"Rusty and the boys been driving the mules. They're a little spooky." She looked warily at him about them.

"Then we'll have lots of it out of them by March."

She rose and fetched her first pan of biscuits from the oven with pot holders, and popped another one in to bake. Next she delivered a table knife and a bowl of new butter, and nodded to the pan. "They'll be hot as hades."

Rosa poured him some coffee in a mug and smiled at him. "Good to have you back, Senor Ed."

"You don't know how good it is to be here." Then, shuffling the first hot biscuit from hand to hand, he laughed. *Whew, it was good to be back.*

He ate breakfast with the crew, though he was full of biscuits and butter to start.

"Unita said that you were going to help her," Rusty said, looking up from his breakfast.

Ed nodded.

"Sure good news. She's been fretting about it, especially after McGregor skinned her so bad last year."

"It ain't a free card—folks lose all they've got on a drive gone bad."

"But it's a lot better with someone's been there."

All the hands stopped eating and looked at him for his answer.

"Yes, it can help."

"Thanks," Rusty said, and the rest added theirs.

More people depending on him. Why didn't they depend on someone else? All he could do was get young men killed. And their faces at the table haunted him.

Chapter 12

Ed figured the Bar U came up with eight hundred steers that were solid enough to ship. Jorge and his two hands gathered three hundred three- and four-year-olds wearing his IW brand. That, by Ed's calculation, left room for eight hundred more they could contract to move north with theirs. Word had spread quickly about Unita's drive but few showed up to see her. In fact, no one came by and even asked about sending theirs with them.

When she asked for his help to find others, Ed held up his hands in surrender. "This is your drive. I figure we can take about eight hundred more steers—no junk, no limpers, no bad ones to fight or break 'cause I'll shoot them."

"Fine, but we need those cattle to help share our expenses, right?"

"Sure, but I can't make them join us."

"Ed Wright, all these guys know you."

"All right, I'll ask some of them. Remember I'm the scout. You're the boss."

"Thanks, we can use them. I've already decided this boss business won't be easy."

"I could have told you that months ago."

She shook her head, tossing her shoulder-length curls. "You're impossible at times."

"I have to ride over and see Jorge tomorrow. Anything else you'll need?"

"No, but that was nice of you to ask me."

"I try to be that ever so often." Then he smiled at her. "I owe you something for all the food I eat here."

"You're Rosa's pet. You plan to come back, don't you? I'll have lots of questions to ask."

"In a couple of days. I'm still thinking about those back shooters cut down Dave Ivy. Maybe I can get a line on them."

"You miss him, don't you?"

He nodded and swallowed a knot. They'd made a team. Ivy could do the business thing and cattle buying, and Ed drove them to market. After their first year Ivy left the trail drive to him and took a steamboat upriver and met them at Abilene. No doubt easier on the older man than the drive. It was on a steamboat that the Brady brothers robbed and murdered him.

"You be careful," she said and followed him to the front door.

He stopped on the porch, rubbed his palms on the front of his pants, and looked hard at her. If it had been the decent thing to do, he'd have hugged her—might even kiss her. But it wasn't and he wasn't making any sort of commitment to her, so he'd only be toying with her favors. He considered himself more of a gentleman than that toward an honest woman, so he nodded and headed for the corral to saddle his horse.

Damned if she didn't traipse along.

"You regretting agreeing to be my guide?"

He looked off at the clouds—it might rain. They could use it. "I'll do what I said I would do."

"You know I appreciate it."

He nodded.

"Men are all the same," she said, shaking her head. "Sam was like that. You could ask him and get a short answer, and know good and well he had a thousand things churning over in his head."

"I reckon we're all alike," he said. "I don't reckon I can change much."

"You ever get in the mood of mind to talk, I'd be all ears."

"I'll recall that one day," he promised her.

"Ed, I know you feel pressured by me and the others. Maybe one drive will be enough—"

"And maybe the new calves'll have wings to fly up there."

"Take the roan. He's closer to the ground."

"My ribs ain't that sore now."

"I just wanted it to be easier on you."

If he didn't catch a horse and get the Sam Hill out of there, he'd sure enough be trying to kiss her. Lord, she'd really got to him, and why? No telling about a man's brain. He grabbed the lariat on the fence and waded into the corral letting out rope. The loop whistled over his head and it fell on the shaggy-looking roan's head. Be another reason to come back—he had one of her horses. This place felt like some kind of magnet to him.

He worked on one side of the roan, she on the other, with currycomb and brush to get the dirt off his back and make him ready to saddle. The job complete, he led the horse to the leather oil–scented shed and got down his own saddle. They must have put the bay and his gear up. He hadn't felt all that drunk till it hit him, sitting on the damn ground.

When he turned with the saddle she was facing him down. She reached across it, took his face in both hands, and kissed him hard on the lips. The saddle tumbled from his hands and he stepped over it. *All right—you started it.* He gathered her in his arms and their hungry mouths closed on each other. Her ripe form pressed hard to his body, he savored the sugar of her mouth and the heady feeling of drowning. Things swirled like a dust devil in his mind as he bent her over to reach the deepest pleasure.

When they finally came up for air her face looked pale in the shadowy room and her eyes were wide open in shock. She swallowed hard and said, "I'm glad you didn't tell me all that."

He pushed his hat higher with his thumb and looked down at her. "Some things words can't always explain."

"I understand," she said with a great sigh and moved against him, burying her face in his shoulder. "Sorry if you think I'm too forward to consider, but—"

"Too forward?" He shook his head in disbelief. "Lord, I'd have done that to you on the porch but figured I had no right to do it."

She raised up and forced a grin at him. "Consider it as all right."

"Whew. I won't miss the chance ever again."

"Well—" She bent over and swept up his saddle blankets. "I guess we do have to act decent in public."

"I guess we do," he said, and threw the saddle on his shoulder by the horn to follow her outside.

The saddle on the roan and cinched down, he made sure no one was in sight and kissed her good-bye. "I'll be back in two days."

She nodded in his arms and stepped back. "I'll be looking for you."

Ed rode out singing a cowboy ditty about a lanky girl from Boston that he'd heard night herding. From the gate, he could barely see her on the porch. He waved and then put spurs to the roan. He had miles to cover, but they'd all be long ones going away from her.

Chapter 13

The letter was wrinkled, mud-stained, and worn like it had been through hell to get there. It was date stamped two weeks earlier in Fort Smith, Arkansas, and addressed to Ed Wright, General Delivery, Banty, Texas. Ed stood in the noon sun on the post office stoop and opened it.

Dear Mr. Wright,

In regards to the two men you sought a few months ago in Fort Smith, Mr. Marsh and Corley Brady, two brothers. I have on good authority that the two men are in the northern part of the Cherokee Nation. The two have a gang and reportedly are preying on and robbing returning drovers. However that is hearsay, for no one has reported such theft and robbery to any authority. It is highly suspected at the U.S. Marshal office here in Fort Smith the reason such crimes have gone unreported is the fact that all their victims are dead and buried.

If you would like assistance in bringing these

men to justice, for the standard salary and expenses of a deputy marshal I would be glad to accompany you in your search. That's one dollar a day salary, one dollar a day expenses, ten cents a mile, and a reward of ten dollars a man upon their capture.

Please wire me at the U.S. Federal Courthouse, Fort Smith, Arkansas, if and when you are coming.

Sincerely yours,
Bruce Conway, U.S. Deputy Marshal

How far was Fort Smith? A damn long hoss ride. He'd have to take a stage from San Antone to Fort Worth, then another from there up through the Nation. That would take several days. Chances were he might not find them when they got up there. Still, Conway might know that area well enough. He'd better go by and tell Jorge where he was headed, then the widow Nance. If he got back by Christmas, they'd still have plenty of time to gather the rest of the crew and road brand the cattle. Besides, there was no way they could put all those cattle together until just before they were ready to leave anyway. There wasn't enough feed on anyone's place for that many head. Those two killers needed to be brought to justice or sent to hell; Dave Ivy'd been one swell guy and a hell of a partner.

It was dark when he reached the IW and Jorge came out to greet him. "Ah, Senor Ed. Did the senora run you off?"

"No, but she'd like to." Ed grinned at his chiding

and dismounted heavily. He'd been all over hell that day, getting things set. In the morning he'd go tell her—a thing he really dreaded, but she'd understand what he had to do.

The roan put away in the corral, he threw his arm over the shorter man's shoulder and they went to the house with him explaining the letter and what he must do. "You can handle this place, right?"

"*Si,* we can watch the ranch. We can't make it rain, or the oats to grow."

"I didn't expect that, *mi* amigo. You watch things, don't let them rustle the stock, and we'll make some money out of this drive and there'll be a bonus for you and the boys."

"You are generous man. We like to work here."

"Good, I count on you and those boys." He threw his arms open and hugged Tina. "Tina darling, you ever get tired of that grinning husband of yours, I'll take you."

"Oh, Senor Ed, where is your lady?"

"Home running her ranch."

"Oh, I think maybe—maybe you would marry her."

"She needs a guide, not a husband."

"Oh, I am not so sure."

"I am, and I can smell your good cooking."

"You must really be hungry." She led him in the lighted jacal and Jorge shut out the night chill.

"Starved for some of your good food."

She tapped him on the chest. "I bet you say that to everyone."

"Naw, just you."

She shook her head in disbelief and rushed off to get the meal ready.

"Where are the boys?" he asked, not seeing the pair of ranch hands.

"They are drifting some cattle back to our land. They will spend the night up at the shack."

"Good. When I get back we need to start bunching those big steers. I thought we could get close to four hundred head."

"I think so," Jorge said. "We only counted three hundred ninety."

"I know that. Mrs. Nance's got around nine hundred, plus ours, so we can fill in some of the others need to make a sale."

"Tina's uncle, Benito Salador, has maybe fifty head—"

"They good big steers?" Ed asked.

"Ah, *si*, but Senor McGregor offered him only eight dollars a head for them."

Tina had stopped to listen to their conversation.

"That old crook won't pay nothing for them," Ed said, shaking his head. "But they could die on the way, going with me."

"He knows that. Can we say you will take them?" Tina asked, anxiously wiping her hands on a towel.

"Sure," he said, lowering himself into a chair. He couldn't save every small Mexican rancher, but he could help some close to him.

Tina ran over and clutched his head to her small breasts, rocked him back and forth, then kissed his forehead. *"Gracias."*

Ed smiled at Jorge. "You got any more kinfolk need cattle took north? I liked that." They both laughed at the embarrassed Tina's expense.

"Laugh," she said, sneering at them. "I don't care.

Benito and Marie will celebrate when they get the news their cattle are going to market."

"All them steers die and they may cry, too."

"One steer in Kansas would bring more than fifty here."

Ed filled his first flour tortilla with brown beans, fried onions, and browned meat. "No, but it would take five or six to do that if he sold them here."

"But he has ten times that many."

"I ain't defending Jim Bob. Everyone knows he'll skin you if he gets a chance."

Tina shook a finger at him. "Especially *Mejicanos*."

Ed winked at her. He loved to see fire in her dark eyes. They sizzled when she was mad.

In the morning he drew out three hundred dollars from the bank and shook the banker's hand, promising to be back in a short while and that he had business to settle up north. Then he swung by Unita's place.

She came out on the porch frowning. "What's wrong?"

He looked around behind himself like there might be the devil trailing him and, hat in hand, approached the porch. "I got word those killers are up in the Nation."

"From who?" she asked, opening the door and showing him inside.

"A U.S. marshal in Fort Smith."

"How far away is that?" She indicated that he take a seat, and Rosa smiled at him from the kitchen.

He acknowledged her with a nod as he sat down opposite Unita. "Maybe five days by stagecoach from San Antone."

"You're going up there?"

He nodded, waiting for her reply.

"You must think it's the thing to do?"

"It is. I figure I'll be back by Christmas. Ain't much we can do about your drive before late winter. Oh, I agreed to take fifty head of Tina's uncle's steers north. Jim Bob wants to rob him."

"He knows how—" She stared across the room as if in deep thought. "Going by yourself?"

"Yes. This marshal said he'd go along for a fee."

"These men are killers."

"Yes, they killed my best friend, Dave Ivy."

Rosa brought them a tray of food. "You two better eat. You both look like your best friend died."

"Thanks," Unita said absently.

He added his.

She frowned at him hard. "Don't fall in the damn bottle up there."

He never answered her. Instead he reached over the table and clutched her hands. "I'll be back by Christmas."

Her blue eyes showed the concern in her. "If you're still breathing."

"I'm a hard-shelled old buzzard."

"Eat, you two," Rosa said, delivering two plates of food and going back in the kitchen.

Unita laughed. "Mother has spoken."

He couldn't swear to it, but it looked like there were some tiny diamonds of moisture on Unita's eyelashes. She ducked her head when he released her hands, then blew her nose in a kerchief from her dress pocket.

"You better eat." She managed to smile, bringing her chin up.

He agreed. "I know how bad that stagecoach food is."

"You will send us letters about your progress?"

"I guess I could. I never planned to, but I will if that would suit you."

She nodded real quickly. "It would."

After lunch, he lingered as long as he dared, then rose and nodded. "I'll be going now."

She trailed him to the front door and caught his sleeve. To check that Rosa wasn't spying on them, she rose on her toes to look back. Satisfied they were alone, she put her arms around his neck and kissed him. He woke up from his absent thoughts about the trip north with her in his arms, then realized where he was and what was happening. *Damn, this couldn't be happening to him.*

"Here," Rosa said, coming from the kitchen with a poke. "I fixed some things for you to eat on the way."

They broke apart with a longing look of regret in her eyes. He wet his lips and nodded to her. "Christmas."

"Christmas."

He took his hat off the hook, then hugged Rosa's shoulder and kissed her on the forehead. "Thanks for putting up with me."

She gave him a friendly push and blushed under her olive skin. Then she unstrung the small silver cross from around her neck and made him bend over.

The crucifix in place, he nodded to her. "That was very kind of you."

"May God ride with you."

He replaced his hat and went out the door to join

Unita. With her arm wrapped around his waist, they went to his horse.

"The roan and I'll be in San Antone tomorrow. I hope in time to catch a northbound coach."

"What'll you do with the roan?"

"Board him with Joe Nichols. He's an ex-ranger. He'll take good care of him."

She buried her face in his shoulder. "I should go along."

"You have the ranch to run. I'll be fine."

"I'll worry about you."

"Besides my bad habits, why didn't our trails ever cross before?"

"They did. You never noticed me."

He chuckled. "I noticed you. Who don't?"

"Oh—"

He kissed her quickly, knowing he'd never get away at the rate they were going. Her fingers slipped off him as he backed to the roan and mounted. With a big knot in his throat, he mounted and eased the horse around. A salute off his hat brim to her, and he set out for San Antone. Damn, this parting with her was harder than he ever imagined.

The uneventful thirty-six-hour stagecoach ride to Fort Worth left him sore and stiff. The wire he'd sent to Marshal Conway before he left San Antone should have reached him by then. Ed dismounted and went to find a decent meal. Then, two hours later, he climbed on the Fort Smith–bound coach. He shared his back-facing seat with a woman of ample proportions in her twenties, whose cheap perfume and strong musk irritated his nostrils. Wrapped against the cool air in a blanket, he tried to sleep. His seat companion ate.

She used a sharp paring knife to cut thin slices off a thick stick of dry sausage that reeked of strong garlic, and she ate it on soda crackers. He swore she must have eaten a couple of sticks of it before they reached the Red River ferry that night.

"I hate ferries," she confided to Ed.

Just awake, Ed sat up and nodded. The coach was halted and he could hear men outside talking. The two drummers opposite them were sound asleep, snoring on the back bench. The cold north wind came in around the loose-fitting canvas curtains.

"It won't sink on us will it?" she asked, wringing her short, pudgy fingers and her entire huge body shuddering.

"No, it's safe enough. Just lots of folks crossing right now from the looks of things."

She took a slice of the sausage off the blade of her knife and, chewing on it, appraised him in the dim light. "You married?"

"No."

"Shame. You ain't bad-looking."

"You married?"

"Widow."

"Sorry."

"No need to be. He wasn't too valuable."

"Oh," he said, anxious to get out from under the confinement of her huge butt, which wedged him in, to stretch his stiff muscles.

The driver opened the door and nodded to them. "We'll be a few minutes, folks. You can get down, but be ready to get back on."

"How long a delay?" she asked, leaning forward to try to look outside.

"Oh, fifteen minutes I imagine, ma'am."

"It never mentioned this on the schedule." She began to rise.

"Sorry, ma'am. Guy that makes them out never got here when the ferry had this much business."

She rose, with her large posterior stuck in Ed's face and, with her head out the door, peered at the line of vehicles ahead of them. "We should have priority."

"Yes, ma'am, but we don't," the driver said.

Settling back, she pointed her paring knife at Ed in the starlight. "There should be a law."

"Excuse me," Ed said, and climbed out, anxious to escape her. He smiled at the driver, who was going off in the night shaking his head. Mrs. Fatso was the demanding sort.

He took his blanket with him, resting on his shoulders, and it helped ward off some of the cold air, but he'd need more layers. The wind went through his britches. A pair of wool long handles would be the thing. In Fort Smith he'd buy a set, if he didn't freeze to death before then.

Over an hour later the stage and team rattled onto the ferry. Ed decided that the woman held her breath the whole time, including the entire time while the barge was winched across the river.

When the coach rocked around while going up the bank, she finally exhaled and her chubby hand clamped on Ed's leg. "Oh, thank God."

He was grateful it wasn't the one holding the knife.

In Fort Smith, he parted with Trudy Stanton, whose entire life story he had heard without any emotions except relief to have gotten rid of her dead husband. She'd come to Arkansas to claim some farm her late husband had inherited.

It was early evening and, after stowing his saddle and gear at the stage company office, he found a store open on Garrison Avenue. Aided by a clerk, he bought some red woolen underwear, a new wool shirt, and a waist-length lined duck coat to replace his unlined jumper.

The blanket rolled up under his arm, he headed for a Chinese bathhouse that the clerk pointed out for him and soon was clean, clothes washed, dried, and pressed, as well as dressed for the bitter cold and on his way to find a meal and a good night's sleep in a bed that he savored despite the thin walls and a very loud, talkative couple in the adjoining room who, when they weren't talking loudly, were busy making noisy love.

He woke the next morning, dressed in the new underwear he'd slept in because the room was unheated. Frost had painted the smudged windowpanes. Moping with his fresh-shaven face in his callused palms, he considered having a drink to warm his blood up. Damn! He might freeze to death before he ever found the Bradys. Instead he had a fried-pork-and-eggs breakfast, then walked the few blocks to the federal courthouse on the river. Smoke from the stacks of paddle wheelers on the close-by Arkansas River streaked the sky, mixed with all the wood smoke from heaters and fireplaces.

The marshal's office clerk said that Conway was in town, and for him to check the Lucky Owl Saloon, because he sometimes played poker there, but that he'd give Conway the message that Ed Wright was staying at the Grand Hotel. Ed thanked him and left, amused at the notion of the three-story building being called the Grand Hotel. From his past night's experience, and the ice in the washbasin pitcher, it could better have been better called the Arctic Circle.

The Lucky Owl looked empty when he managed to get inside and closed a door with a loose doorknob behind himself. Not overly warm, but it was out of the wind.

"Can I help you, sir?" the bartender asked from behind the luxurious, polished wooden bar.

"Marshal Bruce Conway here?"

The bartender nodded and pointed to the rear with a white rag in his hand. "Back room. Not necessary to knock."

Headed for the door, Ed considered ordering himself a drink, but the notion soon passed. He found the room filled with cigar smoke and heated by a coal-burning stove. Grateful for the first real heat he'd found since the Chinese bathhouse the night before, he nodded to the four players who looked up at his entry.

A short man behind a large mustache nodded back. "You must be Ed Wright."

"Yes. Are you Conway?"

"Yes, I am. But I'm right into this hand now, and about to clean these scallywags out of their life savings," he explained, drawing some gruff laughter.

A taller, thin man with a white beard scoffed at the words. "Like hell you are."

"I've got a hand that'll make you shiver like a wet calf out in this cold."

"Ah, bid and get on with it," a bald man said.

"That's Ed Wright, boys, from south Texas. That's H. T." He pointed to the bald man. "John Shanks." He nodded to the white-bearded player. "And Rumples, he's the captain of the *Lady Belle*." He indicated a man with a wide grin and a bowler on the back of his head. "Raise you boys fifty cents."

"Aw, hell, I thought you had four aces," H.T. said, and the others grumbled too.

"Go ahead," Ed said. "I ain't in no hurry to leave this stove."

"That's so for the four of us," Conway said, looking confidently at his hand.

"Damn cold enough," Rumples said. "May freeze my vessel in."

Conway won the hand and raked in the money. "Me and Ed here's got business, boys. Give you a chance to win this back later."

He put the money in the pocket of his brown business suit and then smiled at them. "See you all."

"Less we see you coming," H. T. said, and Conway led Ed out in the hall.

"I guess we'll ride horses up there," Conway said. "Better go find you one."

Ed agreed, and they made small talk about his stage trip while walking up Garrison in the bitter wind. He had no great desire to set out in the cold, but he wanted this business over. At the livery he bought a solid bald-faced chestnut horse with the ranch brand 86 on his right shoulder for twenty dollars. The six-year-old had probably come up from Texas on a drive to fill some of the Indian beef contracts.

Conway then took Ed to a diner in a basement off Garrison and they had lunch.

"I can't guarantee they are still up there, but last I got word they were operating near Sand Springs," Conway explained.

"I chased them plumb across Arkansas once," Ed said, seated and waiting the order some boy had taken. "I guess the nation isn't bigger than that."

"Them two are the scourge of the earth," Conway said, smoothing his mustache. "My boss sure wants them rounded up, too. They've been stealing cattle, hogs, and horses. Selling moonshine. And no doubt they're in on some murders and robberies out west on the drover trail."

The boy brought them coffee, and Ed cupped the mug in his hands. He dreaded the weather outside, but wanted this matter over regardless of the temperature. For the first time since he could recall, drinking had taken a backseat to getting back to Unita. Funny how it had been years since any woman had really struck him.

Conway talked like he knew the law business. Acting tough enough, but dressed a little fancy for a man who tracked down criminals: white shirt, tie, suit but for himself Ed never dressed up except for funerals. He looked up when Conway asked, "When you want to leave?"

"As soon as we can."

"Meet you at the stables at six in the morning?"

"We need some supplies?"

"Naw. I think we can find enough places to stay and

eat up there. Besides the roadhouses, most farmers welcome a little income." Conway sat back for the waiter to put down his plate of food before him.

"I'll be there and saddled, ready to go."

"Good. You married?"

"No." He might as well be, but that was beside the point. "Are you?"

Conway shook his head. "My wife left me for a much better deal."

"Oh?" The food on his plate looked good and smelled better. Roast beef, thin-sliced, piled high, mashed potatoes, gravy, and fresh-baked bread.

"She divorced me and married a lawyer here in town who makes real money, so she can go to fancy balls."

"I guess you can't please them all."

Conway bobbed his head, busy forking in food. "A marshal is never home, makes little money, and has no prestige."

"Sounds like me. I've been driving cattle up the trail ever since the war, and been gone from home so much I had no time for one."

Conway looked up. "I kinda regret it now. I'd like to have a son to go fishing and squirrel hunting with. But I don't know—" He shook his head. "Guess it ain't to be."

"Aw. Maybe you'll find someone."

With a head shake, Conway dismissed it. "You have a ranch, huh?"

"Yes. A good man runs it for me."

"Boy, what kind a pie you got today?" Conway asked the waiter.

"Apples and peach."

"Peach. You want some?" he asked Ed.

"Sounds good. I'll have peach too." He might as well, since he figured he was paying for it all.

"Driving cattle herds to Kansas sounds exciting."

"I bet it's a lot like being a marshal. Folks think it's exciting too." Ed smiled at him.

Conway's shoulder shook as he laughed softly. "Ain't that the damn truth. *The Elevator*, the local paper, carries all these exciting stories about U.S. deputy marshals going off in the Indian Territory and arresting murderers, pig thieves, and counterfeiters."

Ed nodded. He'd read Texas papers with accounts of cattle drives. Being a damn "hero" wasn't all it was cracked up to be in his book, either.

Conway stopped eating and drummed his fork on the plate as if in deep thought. "Been three marshals shot in the past three months."

"Goes with the job, huh?"

"I guess. Do folks get killed on cattle drives?"

"Way too many." Ed wiped his mouth on his cloth napkin. His appetite was gone. "I've lost more than my share of good men."

"I need to tend to some business before we leave. Tell the boss where I'm going. We talked about it before I sent you the letter. He approves, but I'm still going to make this official business. That way I can collect the small fee they pay for arrests that the grand jury's put out warrants for."

"Fine. Six a.m. at the livery."

"Wear your warmest clothes. This cold's unusual. We usually get a break after a day or so." Conway shook his head as if he couldn't understand Mother Nature's turn to the frigid.

Ed wrote Unita a short note and mailed it. *I made the long trip fine. Hate stages. Met Marshal Conway. He's short, thirty-five, big mustache, and dresses like a banker. Bought a bald-faced horse. We leave out for the country north of here in the morning. Very cold. Write more later. Ed*

Dawn came with light snow, like tiny chicken feathers, dancing in the sharp wind. Their collars turned up, huddled over their saddle horns, they had crossed the Arkansas River on the steam ferry and trotted past a junk town of derelicts, breeds, and Indians that squatted among the bare white sycamores and walnut trees that lined the sandy west riverbank opposite Fort Smith on the Nation side. Cur dogs barked at them. Cooking-fire smoke swirled around the womens' blanket-wrapped waists and several dark-eyed children followed their passing with suspicion. In the light snowfall, they looked like a blurry painting to him.

By late afternoon the short day's sun was an orange ball in the west. Conway had mentioned a place he wanted to reach and they rode up a narrow lane through the stubby remains of a large cotton field. Bits of the white fiber still clung to the open bolls and flagged in the wind.

"This will be the best stop on the trip." Conway motioned to a large, two-story house.

They dismounted at a rack and Ed found his sea legs. Then he followed Conway up the walk to double white doors. The two-story house was painted red with white trim, and columns rose to the top of the second floor to support a porch. It was a massive home like he'd seen in Mississippi during the war. Great pecan trees surrounded the well-kept yard.

A black man answered the door, obviously a servant.

"Ah, Marshal Conway, come in. And good day to you, sir." The man was old, but still sturdy-looking, despite the frosty fringe of hair around his bald head.

"Ed Wright." He stuck out his hand and saw a small smile in the corner of the man's wide mouth. "From Banty, Texas."

"Very good to meet you, sah. I be Adam."

"She home?" Conway asked as they stood in the entry room, holding their hats and unbuttoning their coats.

"Miss Ellie be right down. She done send word for the boys to put dem horses of youse up, rub them down, and grain them."

They thanked him and waited at the bottom of the staircase for her appearance after Adam took their hats and coats. Ed considered the house warm with his wind-burned face heated from the exposure.

Ellie Schaffer appeared at the head of the stairs and smiled at her guests. In a bright red gown with a low neck that exposed her cleavage, she appeared ready for the governor's ball. Her light brown hair pinned up and her face powdered, the thirtyish lady looked elegant. Her nose was a little pointed, and her blue eyes danced with excitement.

"My, my, two marshals have come by to see me," she drawled.

"One, and my friend from Texas," Conway said, and held out his arms to hug her. "Meet Ed Wright."

She nodded and then bent over slightly and hugged Conway's back, with a few pats on the shoulder. She turned her attention to Ed. "Welcome, Mister Wright, to the Indian Territory and my humble farm."

"Little more than that. Very lovely place," he said, indicating the house under the great crystal chandelier.

"Thank you, sir. And what do you do in Texas, if I may ask?"

He decided she must be in her midthirties, taller by several inches than Conway and, under all that southern drawling, expensive silk dress, and cleavage, she was no dumb sister. This woman had some steel in her—not unlike Unita Nance.

"I'm a small cattle rancher."

"Somehow I doubt the small part, but come. You two must need a drink. This cold weather has frozen us past sociability down here." She turned on her heel and led the way to an adjoining room where the fire crackled in a large fireplace and the reflection of heat really scorched his tender cheeks.

She poured drinks into glasses from a cut-glass decanter and handed them each one in the flickering candlelight of the room. "My late husband Carl liked good whiskey. Called this sipping whiskey. Of course, whiskey is illegal in the territory." She winked at Conway, who nodded in return. "But of course, how could civilized men and women live without it?"

"It would be very hard," Ed said, enjoying the fine liquor's taste on his tongue.

She showed them to leather hobnailed chairs with curled wooden arms in a semicircle facing the crackling fire. More like men's seats than horsehair-stuffed couches like he had expected. She took the central chair between them, crossed her legs, adjusted her dress skirt, and offered a toast.

"To warmer days." The half-filled glass was raised high in her hand.

They clinked glasses and she turned at the approach of someone. "Yes, Adam?"

"Dinner is in one hour?"

"Exactly," she said and then looked at them, receiving the nods she sought from both men. "That will be wonderful, Adam."

"Sell your cotton?" Conway asked.

"Most of it. I retained some bales at the Fort Smith warehouse, hoping the price might rise, but who knows. Cotton is not very exciting. Tell me about you gentlemen's business."

Conway told her about the Ivy murder and how Ed had trailed the Brady brothers to Fort Smith, then returned to go after them. She kept looking at Ed. Either to approve of him or something deeper. Slow like he savored her whiskey and nodded to Conway's details, making eye contact with her. But he hoped not to encourage her. She was a woman on the search. While he was not certain for what, it was not Ed Wright. He couldn't wait to get back to Texas, where it was a lot warmer.

Dinner was served on gold-rimmed, hand-painted china plates that he imagined were so expensive that he actually worried about eating off of them. He had learned in conversation that her late husband, Carl Schaffer, several years older than she, had come to the Indian Territory from Georgia, married a Cherokee woman, and laid claim to this bottomland, then began buying out his neighbors and owned several slaves at the start of the war. His first wife and four children died in an epidemic, leaving him a widower. Actually Ellie was his second cousin and their marriage had been arranged.

Not long after the wedding, bushwhackers shot Carl in a robbery attempt inside the mansion at the end of the war. Since then she oversaw the holdings and had a warm affection for the U.S. deputy marshals who'd run his killers down. The murderers not killed in the shootout were sentenced to hang in Judge Story's court in Van Buren, Arkansas, the predecessor to Parker's court in Fort Smith.

The meal consisted of rich-tasting, smoked, salt-cured ham, canned green beans, brown rice and gravy, with canned apples. Yeast rolls steamed when opened and the butter, freshly churned, made the saliva rush in Ed's mouth. No doubt this was no exaggeration of Conway's earlier forecast that this would be the best stopover on their trip.

"Do I understand you two must leave early in the morning and be on your way?" she asked from her position at the head of the long table, flanked by her company. The ring of disappointment sounded in her voice.

"Yes," Conway said. "No reflection upon your hospitality, of course."

"Of course," Ed chimed in.

"Your company, as always, is welcome. But I understand urgency in such matters."

"Thank you," Conway said with a seductive smile.

She clapped him on top of his hand. "You know the doors here are always open to you men of the law."

Then she turned and looked at Ed. "Brave Texas cattlemen as well."

He felt like squirming at her words, but thanked her.

After supper, Conway excused himself and they

were alone in the den at the fireplace, having an after-supper drink. She stood by the hearth and turned to Ed. "You have a woman at home."

"I made a pledge to one," he said, looking past her and wondering why her cleavage attracted him so. *Silly*, he finally decided, *it's on purpose*.

"Oh, so you will marry her?"

"No, I promised to take her cattle to Kansas."

She smiled as if relieved at the knowledge. "Then you have no wedding plans?"

"Ma'am, the way my life's been the last five years I don't need any wedding plans."

"She's a very lucky woman. I am a student of men." Then she turned away and looked at the north wall. "I have gauged you as a man who drives hard for what he wants done."

He nodded. "That's to get the Brady brothers, or send them to hell."

"Then take her cattle to Kansas."

"Try."

"No, you don't try things. You do things, Ed Wright. More whiskey?"

No, thanks." He handed her the glass. When had he done that before? For some reason he didn't want to get drunk. He shook his head and smiled at her. "You, too, are the type of person that runs on iron tracks, like a locomotive."

"Well, thank you. Many men find that unattractive in a woman."

"You're neither unattractive nor offensive to me. But I can understand how a weed-free cotton field in such large acreage is the product of your oversight."

She looked slightly embarrassed and wet her lips

before sipping her whiskey. Avoiding looking at him, she shook her head. "If I were the Bradys, I'd buy a cemetery lot and coffin, and go around in my stocking feet so I didn't die with my boots on."

Ed laughed and rubbed his palms on the tops of his legs. He hoped she was right.

"What's so funny?" Conway asked, coming back.

"I was ordering funeral arrangements for the brothers," she said.

"Good, I hope they need 'em."

So did Ed.

Later that night, he sprawled on his back on a feather mattress with the bedroom's fireplace casting a glow on a tin ceiling. He could have sworn he heard footsteps in the hallway, coming from Conway's room to hers. None of his business, but he did smile to himself at the discovery, roll over, and go to sleep.

Chapter 14

A cold sun shone the next day. The snow on the ground looked like powdered sugar on the brown leaves and around the bases of the tufts of yellow-brown sedge grass. They left the river country and rode over lots of waist-high blue stem and through some stunted post oak. Stirrup to stirrup, they passed several Indian homesteads with smoke coming from rusty stovepipes. Winter-thin horses and milk-cow stock stood about the places, guarded by leggy black dogs that barked at their passing.

At a trading post on the Grand River, they spoke with Jerky McClain, a white-haired Cherokee with small, thin braids, a high-crowned, unblocked brown cowboy hat, and two eagle feathers on beaded rawhide strings that bobbed on the back of the brim when Jerky spoke.

"Them Brady bastards may be denned up with that woman—what is her name?" Jerky turned to his wife, who, in her youth, must have been the prettiest woman in the Nation. Her beauty, though aged, still showed through her soft copper skin.

"You mean Ruby Heartkiller?"

Jerky narrowed his brown eyes at Conway. "You know her?"

"I think so. She lives up on the Arkansas near the Bear place?"

"Bear Springs."

"Bear Springs, yes," Conway said, as if recalling the location.

"You better have plenty of damn ammunition. There may be twenty of them no-accounts up there with them."

"Twenty?"

"Sure they're all about to starve out this time of year. Horses are too thin to steal, and no one would buy one anyway. They can't ride west over there on the cattle trail and rob any drovers cause there ain't none. You may find a shit-pot load of them hanging out over there."

His wife frowned at his choice of words.

"That's what they'd be. Twenty of those no-accounts would sure make a shit-pot load."

"You don't have to say that. What if there were little kids in the store?"

He raised up as if to look for them. "I don't see no little kids. Only two old marshals from Fort Smith. You see any kids?"

"No." She shook her head in disapproval. "Don't you two encourage him either."

They all laughed.

That night the two of them slept in the living room off the back of the store on cots and in their own bedrolls. By dawn, they'd eaten Mary's breakfast of bacon, biscuits, and flour gravy—she explained her hens had quit laying in the short days and cold. Full of her rich food, Ed paid her for it, as well as the horses' grain, and they left.

Day three threatened to thaw them out some.

"I know a man up near there that might help us. He's been a good posse man in the past."

Ed unbuttoned his coat and nodded as the temperature began to rise. "Guess we could use some help."

"Cost you a dollar a day and keep."

"I can afford that, especially if we can catch the Bradys."

"I can't guarantee that."

"I understand. Let's hire him. Where is he at?"

"On the way. Besides, he knows where Ruby Heartkiller lives."

"What's his name?"

"Gale Brown."

Ed nodded and they trotted their horses. It was past noon when they reached Brown's place. Brown's plump Indian wife told Conway that he'd gone to see about a neighbor and would be back later. She didn't act pleased to see either of them and went back inside and closed the door without a word.

"Guess you must have made her mad," Ed said, chuckling as he led his bald-faced horse to the edge of the yard and loosened the girth to wait on Brown's return.

"Aw, she don't like for him to ride posse. Afraid he'll get hurt I guess."

"That's real enough. From the looks of things he can use some money." Ed dug out some jerky to share. "Here. Guess she ain't killing no chicken for us to eat."

"By damn, I believe she'd let us starve."

Ed sat down on a large log and began to chew some hard, peppery jerky, moistening it with his saliva first. It was a long ways from eating on gold-rimmed plates at Ellie Schaffer's.

At midafternoon Brown rode in and pushed his winter-shaggy bay horse over to where they lounged in the sun. The thin rider looked to be in his forties. He walked toward them bent over like so many beat-up bronc busters.

"How you been?" he asked Conway with a grin.

"Fine. Meet Ed Wright." Both men shook hands and nodded.

"What brings you out of your card game?" Brown said with a wink at Ed.

"Bradys. They killed and robbed Ed's cattle partner near Memphis on a paddle wheeler."

"Plenty tough bunch."

"Ed's paying posse wages to get them. We're headed for Bear Springs country."

Brown nodded and then looked at Ed. "I could use some pocket money. I'll get a bedroll and my gun. Be ready to ride in a few minutes."

"Fine, take your time." Ed watched him head for the house.

The next thing he heard was the shouting and cussing of the woman coming from inside the low-walled shack. Brown soon appeared and looked unscathed, but the dark-faced woman on his heels was not to be ignored. She waved her fists at them and let fly a jargon of cuss words. Some must have been Indian, Ed was unsure but they sounded like large hail on a tin roof.

Brown, undeterred by her foot-stomping tirade at

his back, stuck his rifle in the boot and tied his bedroll on behind his saddle. Then he turned like he'd heard none of it. "Guess I'll be back in a couple days."

She stood straight, arms folded, frowning at him with her dark lips narrowed to a seam. "You should have dressed better."

He reined up the bay and looked hard at her. "Why?"

"They are going to bury you in those old clothes."

He grinned at her. "Hell, no one would know me wearing anything else."

She charged the horse, kicking at his legs. "Go! Go, you stupid bastard!"

Brown nodded to Ed and the three rode off under a barrage of cuss words and some small rocks. Ed looked back once and about laughed at the sight of her: hands on her hips, glaring after them.

"Ruby Heartkiller," Conway said. "You know her?"

"Yeah, she's up in them hills above the Arkansas River," Brown said, sounding not the least disturbed by his woman's anger.

"We need to scout the place. Several folks think she's got lots of boarders up there, setting out the winter."

"I heard that Bo Tinker was up there too."

"Who's he?" Ed asked the pair riding on his left and right as they trotted their horses northward.

"He shot a deputy marshal down on the Canadian last summer," Conway said, looking serious. "Tough guy. I've got a warrant for him. We need him too."

"We can stay at Sam Belham's place and scout

Heartkiller's before we rush in, if'n you don't look too hard for liquor," Brown said to Conway.

"I'd much rather have Tinker than a whiskey fine."

"Good. His wife's a good cook besides." Brown gave Ed a big smile of approval at the decision.

"We gonna make Heartkiller's by dark?" Conway asked, leaning over in the saddle to see Brown.

"No, after dark. I don't want them getting word we're coming. We get there in the daylight they might find out and hit the trail, or fortify themselves good in her place. Either way I don't want them ready."

"I told you he was good posse man," Conway said.

Ed nodded, his mind focused on the events ahead. Maybe he would get those two killers in his gun sights, and not far off either. Then he could go back to Texas. It had been clouding up since they left Brown's and he sensed moisture in the wind on his face. More snow or cold rain moving in; he felt it in his stiff bones and muscles. If they could get this over before it struck. . . . Maybe—but in his heart he doubted they could do it all—scout the outlaws' place and take them before the storm struck.

Hours later, dogs barked in the distant darkness, no doubt at their discovery of Brown's approach to their yard. He'd ridden ahead to talk to Belham while Ed and Conway waited on their horses in the timber. No moon or stars. Ed wondered how this plan might work. In this strange land he felt like a blind man, dependent on Conway. Ed considered the marshal level-headed enough, and he felt Brown had an uncanny way of handling things. Different from being a ranger. But whatever was necessary suited him. The temperature under the cloud cover was steady and not as cold, save for the wind that swept out of the south.

"Going to storm," Conway said, sitting his horse close by Ed. "Too warm."

"I've had the same notion all day."

"I hope Gale can get us in here."

"Someone's riding back."

Gale rode up and reined in his mount.

"He says come on in. Sam don't like that bunch. Says he'll even help us."

"Why's that?" Conway asked.

"I think some of that bunch helped themselves to Sam's wife." Brown sat his horse in front of them. "It happened when he was gone."

"Reason enough," Ed said.

"She's making more food, so we can go in, put our horses up, then wash up. Sam said he'd take us over there tonight, but hell, dark as it is we might just as well wait till morning, huh?"

"He know how it lays."

"Says he does."

"How many are over there?"

"Not over six or seven, according to him."

"The Bradys there?" Ed asked as they walked their horses toward the lantern hung up for them.

"They have been," Brown said.

"How about Tinker?" Conway asked.

"I ain't sure. We better ask Sam."

"I will."

Ed looked off at the shape of distant hills, barely visible in the inky night. Maybe this whole ride had not been in vain. He certainly hoped so when he dropped heavily out of the saddle and went to loosening his girths.

Sam Belham was a big man, framed by the light in the doorway. A dark beard and wearing overalls his voice sounded gravely and carried. "Howdy boys. Get them feed bags on them ponies, then come on down. She's got supper ready."

"What's this Sam like?" Ed asked, hauling his saddle and pads into a rough shed and tossing them on a wagon. Maybe they'd stay dry there.

"He's a little mouthy, but he's honest."

"Never met him," Conway said, putting his saddle up.

"Thanks," Ed said, wanting to add, "I hope all this works." He followed the others to the shack and washed up on the porch, then shook the big man's hand.

"Ed Wright."

"You a marshal too?"

"Ex-Texas Ranger."

"Damn, you guys brought both barrels, didn't you?"

"Yes, they killed my partner, them Bradys did," Ed said.

In the background, Ed saw a girl busy setting out plates of food on the table. She hardly looked out of her teens and was the only one in the room. Definitely Indian, she had a cute, full figure under a blouse and layered skirt. But her smile at them, and her eyes dancing over high cheekbones, would have melted a big drift of snow. She nodded to him and the others to sit down, then rushed off for more.

"That's Yellow Flower," Sam said, motioning to her, and they all sat down. "She's half Delaware, half

Cherokee, and mean as a badger." He ducked when she went past him with butter and a knife for the bread. Then he laughed and, over a smile, she made a put-out face at him.

"Coffee will be done soon," she announced.

Ed thanked her. They pitched into bowls of potatoes, gravy, and sliced, smoked ham. Ed savored her sourdough bread and the pale, winter butter. The sweet sourness filled his mouth and he savored each bit, then he filled his plate.

Conway had begun asking questions about Heartkiller's place between bites.

"It's a two-story house and a big barn. Used to belong to a chief. Was a fine place back then. He had slaves. There's a patch of timber behind it and we can come up through it."

"Can we in the dark?" Conway asked, pointing his fork at Sam. "What about dogs?"

"I got a bitch we can take with us that will take them damn dogs out of the country chasing her." Sam grinned at the notion of his plan.

"Just so they don't warn them," Conway said.

Sam dismissed his concern with a head shake. "They won't."

"That bunch might fight like wildcats," Brown said. "They don't have much to lose 'cept hanging."

Ed heard it all. His mind was in Texas, wondering how they were going along getting ready for the drive. As much as he dreaded it, he felt consumed to make this the safest drive he ever took. *Damn, it would have been lots easier staying drunk in San Antone. What did he say?* Sam had said something and he was so busy feeding his face that he'd missed it.

"I didn't hear that," Ed said to Sam.

Beside him, Brown wiped his mouth on a kerchief and then whispered, "He said that three of them outlaws came by, jumped his wife, and gang-raped her while he was gone to Kansas two weeks ago."

Ed nodded at Sam to show that he'd heard what he said, and shook his head. Jerky was right—they were a shit-pot load of worthless humanity. He could recall that first night Dave Ivy came by his place, when tin cans were all plinking with water from roof leaks, and him talking so big about cattle drives to Kansas. He had a score to settle, as much as the man behind the full beard with his coal-dark eyes staring off at the far wall. Eating at his guts—like it did his own.

"The plan is to get up after midnight, ride over there, and be in place at first light," Conway said, looking around the table at them.

Ed agreed with the others about the plan. Three tough men who no doubt had been under fire before with him. They'd take the Bradys if all went well.

Chapter 15

At midnight the rain started. A cold drizzle was falling when Sam hissed them awake like the outlaws might hear him. The three of them had been asleep in his shed on some hay. The horses in the pen were gathered with a candle lamp and saddled under the shed. Ed used his slicker to keep the saddle dry while he ate and looped the reins over the yard fence, then splashed through some puddles to wipe his feet off on the porch. Too dark for a bat to see, he decided except for the lamps inside.

"Morning," he said to Yellow Flower, hesitant to walk on her rugs, which he knew were laid over the dirt floor.

"Come in," she said, and held the door open for the others.

"I want to pay you for our food, too," he said.

She shook her head, but he insisted she take two dollars. At last she forced a smile, accepted it, and closed the door after Brown, who was the last one to come in. "I will buy some new hens with this money. A coon's been killing mine."

"Fine. Thanks for all you've done for us."

She nodded and hurried off to get the breakfast on the table.

They ate in silence as if the task ahead, along with the wet weather, had dampened their spirits. It was no time to wait—the outlaws might already have word that a marshal was in the area. Conway had explained that to him coming up—word of a lawman's presence was telegraphed around quickly once he arrived in a district.

After the big meal they thanked Yellow Flower and went outside for their horses. Sam, in a poncho and great felt hat, got the small gyp and carried her on the saddle across his lap. He rode in the lead. The light drum of the rain reminded Ed of the war and marching in Mississippi. Blacker days for him even than the cattle drives; his life had become a pattern of burying folks that he liked. Rangers, soldiers, drovers; he'd done those details, and now they were on another campaign in the darkest night he could ever recall. Rain ran off his hat brim.

Hours later, after crossing small, gurgling streams and winding through the wooded hills, they reached a place where Sam told them to dismount and hitch their animals. It was hard to tell where they were. Ed could see little of the outline of the post oaks close to him. The rain slacked some, but a wet mist on the growing wind swept his face and he shivered from the penetrating cold, even under the coat and slicker.

"Sam's going to bait their dogs off with his gyp," Conway said. "Then we can move in and be ready for first light. Cloudy as it is, that may be late too."

Ed and Brown agreed. From the scabbard, Ed slid out the .44/40 Winchester and listened. In a short while he heard dogs fighting in the distance, and then he listened as the gyp led the merry pack after her, over the hill for home.

"Sam had scent he put on her," Brown said.

"I figured so," Ed agreed and nodded, wishing the time for it to get light would come up. They went single file, picking their way after Conway. He stopped them at the edge of the woods and the close-cropped hay field.

"Ed, you take the barn and corrals and cut them off from their horses. Sam, Brown, and I can take the house."

"Keep your head down," Ed said after them. Rifle in his hands, he hurried downhill to the tall, once-white barn that showed up in the inky night. Must be getting closer to light. He eased the side walk-through door open with a creak and was inside the barn's dark interior that smelled of musty hay. That and the sharper whang of horse urine filled his nose as he stood in the darkness, listening to grunting horses sleeping at the tie racks. He felt grateful to be out of the wind and rain.

After hours of waiting, by his mental clock, dull light began to spread over the ridge and open pasture. He could see the second story of the house under the hill. Gunshots began to pop and the shooting sounded fierce. Did they need some backup? Conway wanted him to block anyone escaping—maybe he should turn the horses out; then they'd be harder to catch and ride off. More shots.

He decided to take a look and left the barn. On the brink of the slope, he saw a man running away from the house.

"Stop," he shouted, cocking the rifle and drawing it up.

"Hell with you—"

Ed threw the butt to his shoulder, squeezed the trigger, and the muzzle blast of black powder swept his eyes. The outlaw went down. More shots inside diverted his attention. Someone was moaning that they were shot. He could hear a turkey gobbling, but it wasn't a real one.

The bearded face of Sam came to the back door and waved for him to hurry to the house. The big man was jamming cartridges into a six-gun and spilling some on the floor in his haste.

"Ain't good. Conway's been shot and I don't know where Brown is at. Two of them's dead, but I don't think the Bradys are here. Bo's upstairs, barricaded in," Sam said in a coarse whisper, and spun the cylinder to check his work.

"How bad's Conway?" Ed asked.

Sam shook his head. "He's laying on the stairs. I can't tell, and Bo shot at me every time I tried."

"You keep him pinned down. I'll get Conway off the stairs and see if we can do anything for him. You figure they got Brown too?"

"Jesus, I can't tell. It all happened so fast."

"Easy," Ed said. "Cover me. I'll get Conway."

"I'll try."

Rifle in his arms, Ed stood against the wall and listened for a sound. Nothing. When he dared to stick his head around the doorway, a shot splintered the pine facing and fragments stung his face. Sam moved past him, took aim at the top of the stairs, and fired.

"Now!"

Ed broke past him through the eye-tearing, acrid gun smoke and saw Conway sprawled on his back halfway up the steps. He ignored the ear-shattering next shot Sam made to contain Bo. In a scramble, he reached the marshal and shouldered his limp body. Overbalancing, he caught the side of the wall and righted himself at the last second before falling with Conway. Then, quick as he could, he rumbled down the steps in his wet boots and ducked into the kitchen. There he sprawled the still lawman out on the table.

"Is he alive? Is he alive?" Sam asked, keeping guard at the door.

Ed felt for his pulse under his chin. Nothing. "No."

"Sumbitch—you sumbitch, Bo. I'll get you, you little stinking bastard!"

"Easy," Ed said, putting his hand on the big man's shoulder and listening to the turkey call again. "What the hell does that mean?"

"Cherokee death call. He's saying 'I am ready to die or kill you—come on, get me.' "

Ed removed his six-gun to check the loads. "Cover me. I'm going up there."

Sam caught him by the shoulder. "We can burn him out. Burn the whole goddamn place down—him too."

"No. Brown, or his body, is in here someplace. So is Conway's. They deserve a burial."

"That no-good devil upstairs—he ain't worth dying over."

"I'm going to try. Cover me till I'm near the top of the stairs."

"You're crazy—"

"Cover me."

"I will."

"Bo, it's your last chance to give up," Ed shouted. His answer was a wavering gobble.

Ed rushed across the room and slammed his shoulder to the wall at the base of the staircase. Gun ready, he watched the head of the stairs. Before proceeding, he shared a grim nod with Sam. Then he made his first step, the grit on his soles sounding loud. Step by step he advanced until he was at the head of the stairs and could peer down the hall. A familiar prone body lay on the pine flooring in the hallway—Brown's. A thin, bitter gun-smoke haze filled the narrow passageway. The first doorway was open. . . . Then the gobble came again and Ed knew his man was in the back bedroom on the right.

How to approach him? Bo'd be triggered on the open doorway. Somehow Ed needed to distract him for a moment. Nothing, nothing came to his imagination. *Cap'n, where are you?* In his grave under a granite stone, where he belonged. He had passed away in his sleep after a long career of law enforcement.

If he knew where in the room Bo was stationed— no help. He gritted his molars and switched hands with his gun to dry his palm on his pants. Then a notion came—toss the slicker in the room as a ruse and then come, guns ablazing. The only way he could throw it in was with his left hand. Then he must bring his right around to shoot at Bo. He'd only get one chance.

The Colt stuck in his waistband, he shucked the slicker as quietly as he could. His stare glued on the doorway, he balled the slicker up and held it in his left hand. Slow like he tiptoed closer—then Bo gobbled. He moved and threw the slicker into the room.

The blast he expected came. Instantly, he stepped into the doorway, standing sideways, making his first shot at anything. Bringing the muzzle up, he cocked and aimed at a snarling face in the veil of smoke. The vision disappeared and he shot again into the gray fog. His ears rang so loudly they pierced his thoughts.

Bo was down and what Ed had on was burning— his wool shirt was afire. He could smell it. He shoved the gun in his waistband and raised his left arm. The smoke was coming from that side as he beat it out with his palm, but the bullet had missed him.

"You all right?" Sam was in the doorway, gun ready.

Ed backed up against the door facing and nodded woodenly. "I'll be fine."

"You got Bo," Sam said, kneeling by the outlaw's body. "He won't rape no one else's wife." Rising, he gave the still body a swift kick. "Sumbitch, you—"

"I count four outlaws. One I shot running off is in the yard—"

"Naw, there's five. One more dead in this other bedroom," Sam said from across the hall. "Damn, I hate it about Brown. He was a good guy. Best horse breaker in the country."

"I hate worse telling his widow. She warned him about this happening."

"That's the trouble with being married to a damn squaw. They can tell your fortune." Sam had his hat off and was scratching his head. "Guess I better get an ax."

"What for?"

"There's a reward for all these guys. We need to put

their heads in gunnysacks and you can deliver them to
Judge Parker."

"Me?"

Sam nodded. "Yeah, they'd never believe me. But
I'd split it with you."

"How much reward?"

"I don't know what they got Bo's up to, but I'd bet
it's close to two hundred for him alone."

"I'll need their names." He holstered his six-gun
and caught Bo by a bare foot. He dragged him and
followed Sam, who tossed the other outlaw down the
stairs. Then the big man scooped up Bo with a roar
in his throat. Sam raised him over his head to toss
like something he detested off the top of the stairs,
and he crashed on the floor below.

"Now we better carry Brown down," Ed said, real-
izing that anger still raged in the big man.

Sam agreed, and they packed him down to the
kitchen to lay him on the kitchen floor. Straightening,
Sam shook his head. "Been a helluva day, and we
missed them damn Bradys."

Ed nodded. "They've lit a shuck by now. Was she
here?"

"Guess not. You and me can share the loot and
horses, huh?"

"What's legal?"

"Kinda unspoken. The marshals get their horses and
the money in their pockets that ain't loot."

Ed shook his head and grinned, amused at him.
"How do you tell that?"

"Well, like if it was in a strongbox or money bag,
then they turn it in. The rest is theirs."

"If I take their heads in, I want to split the reward between you and Brown's woman. She'll need it."

"What about you? You came a long ways and offered to pay all of this . . . Lordy, you gave her two dollars for food."

"I'm all right. You split with Brown's widow what you get for the horses, saddles, and guns, and bury the bodies."

"I'll do that. What about Brown and Conway?"

"I'm going to wrap them up. I'll take Brown by his widow, and Conway to Fort Smith. He deserves a hero's burial."

"They was sure brave."

Ed closed his eyes and nodded his head. "They were." Like all the rest he'd buried—too damn brave.

Chapter 16

Ed rode up and stretched his sore back. The dogs were raising enough hell that he knew she could hear them. He'd been in the saddle all night and his eyes felt full of sand when she cracked the door and looked past him.

Ed dropped heavily from the saddle and held the horn to get his sea legs working.

"He's dead, isn't he?" she asked, wrapping a blanket tight around her.

With a knot in his throat he turned to face her. "Yes, ma'am."

"Oh," she shrieked. "I told him not to go! Goddamn you!"

He caught her fist before she struck him and ducked a foot aimed for his shin. "Hold on. He made the choice, not me."

Her sinewy wrists in his grasp, he strained to contain her attack.

"You—you killed him." A mask of fiery madness faced him as she squirmed and twisted to free herself. Cuss words rolled off her dark lips as she strained and groaned.

"Stop! He's dead. This won't bring him back."

She collapsed to her knees in defeat. He did the same to hold her in case it was a ploy and she went back into the mad business.

Her large brown eyes began to flood. Her lower lip curled against her teeth and she began to sob. He reached around her and hugged her. "I'm sorry. He was a very brave man. The ones who killed him are dead."

She straightened, wiped the tears off one high cheek, and nodded. "His friend—the marshal?"

"Dead too."

"Where will you take him?"

"I'm taking Conway to Fort Smith."

In the weak sunshine, he dropped back on his heels. "You want me to help you bury him?"

"No. I will dress him and call my people in to help me. I don't want any bad spirits in his grave with him." She looked at her hands and wrung them.

"There are some rewards—some of their horses that Sam Belham will sell and bring you the proceeds, half of them. I will have the federal rewards split between you too."

She pushed the long, raven black hair back from her face and then nodded to indicate she'd heard his words. "I don't even know your name?"

"Ed Wright."

"I am Bird Woman, Ed Wright. I would fix you some food."

He shook his head. "No. If you're all right, I must ride on hard for Fort Smith."

She struck her breasts with a fist. "I have a big hole in my heart, but I will be fine."

Ed rose, dug out the money they'd taken from the pockets of the outlaws that he'd split with Sam.

"Here's twenty-three dollars and some change," he said, and kissed her on the cheek. "God be with you."

The money tied in a bandanna in one hand, she nodded in approval, holding her fingertips to the spot he had kissed. "May the Gods go with you, Ed Wright."

"I'll need help," he said, checking his cinch, then mounting Baldy. With a nod he reined the horse around, reached out and caught the lead to Conway's horse bearing his canvas-wrapped corpse, and started out.

When he looked back she still held the reins to her husband's bay and waved to him. He booted Baldy into a trot. It was a long ways to Ellie Schaffer's and he rode with dread in his heart over that meeting. Why him?

He'd slept some in the night, and bought some crackers and cheese at a small store about dawn. He also fed the horses some grain he bought there. The storekeeper had frowned at his load.

"Who's dead?"

"U.S. Marshal Conway and the heads of five outlaws."

"Oh!" The man's thin shoulders shuddered in revulsion.

"I thought the same thing, but the rewards go to his deputy's widow and the other posse man."

The horses were through eating and he needed to get on. He moved to the stirrup to check the cinch and mounted. "Guess I've done worse things. I simply can't recall when." A nod to the speechless man on the porch and he left.

A ferryman looked hard at him as he stood on the deck, recrossing the muddy-looking Arkansas, holding his horses to steady them, though he doubted, as tired as they were, they'd spook at much. It was long past dark before he reached Ellie's place. Lights were still on in the windows. He dropped out of the saddle like a dead man, caught himself, and got his numb legs under him while grasping the saddle horn. At last he bent over, hands on his knees, and tried to recover, ignoring the barking dogs.

Adam came out with a lamp. "Could I help you— oh, Mr. Wright."

"Evening, Adam."

He held the lamp up high. "You bring what I's think you brung?"

Mouth grim set, Ed nodded. "I figured she'd want to know."

"Oh, mercy—she be sure upset."

Ed agreed with a grim bob of his head. "She up—"

"Adam, what is wrong?" Ellie called out from the doorway. Then she saw Ed and gasped. "Ed, tell me nothing is wrong."

He hurried up to the porch and removed his hat. "There is, ma'am. Conway was killed by those men he was after."

"Conway—Bruce is dead?" Her hand went to her forehead and he could see her knees had buckled. He swept her up in his arms to save her a fall.

"You's got her?"

"Yes. I'll carry her inside. This has been a big shock."

"What can I do?"

"Have the boys feed and water the horses. They been rode hard to get here. They don't need to unload them."

"How's she?"

"She'll be fine. In time."

"I have the horses cared for."

"Good," he said, giving her limp body a boost in his arms.

She stirred and blinked at him as he entered the open doorway.

"Ed, I'm so sorry. You can put me down."

"I will when you can sit. You still look very pale to me."

"Oh, dear—" She put her arms around him and began to cry. "Why poor Bruce?"

"I reckon God needed him worse than we did." Easing her onto the couch, he started to straighten.

She patted the cushion beside her and looked up at him with teary eyes. "Oh, please sit beside me. I'm sorry I am such a baby, but I hardly know what to do."

"It is a helpless feeling," he agreed, and sat down. His arm curled around her and he put his cheek on the top of her head as she sobbed.

Words fell off her trembling lips as she spoke of things between Conway and her.

"He'd hoped we could be married."

"I guess you could have," Ed said, unsure what would have prevented it.

"I couldn't risk losing my land. My husband owned it because his first wife was Cherokee. I was his heir, but . . ."

"They might decide that if you had a white husband you didn't have a claim?"

She sniffed and nodded. "This land is very good. Lots of the other land is stony and won't grow crops. People get jealous and do bad things."

He agreed, and found her arms around him and her sobbing on his shirt inside the open jacket. Gentle as he could he rocked her, and thought about the fact that seven more men were dead and he still didn't have the Brady brothers.

His eyes closed at Adam's words. "You wish me to take your hat and coat, sir?" He started, agreed, and gently shrugged the canvas jacket off. Adam took it and his hat.

"I'll see about some food. I figures you ain't ate good on the road."

Ed smiled at his concern. "Thanks. I could eat some later."

"No," Ellie said, raising up and pushing her hair back. "Have them fix him some food. I'm so sorry; I never thought about you."

"Yes, ma'am, I'll see about it." Adam nodded and went off with Ed's coat and hat.

"Oh, Ed, what will I do?"

He hugged her again and shook his head. "Life ain't easy."

"But I lost my first husband to bandits and now I've—lost Bruce to others." She looked up at him for the answer.

"Maybe we need a drink?"

"Sure," she agreed and sat up, pushing locks of hair back. "I can see this has not been easy on you."

"I've got big shoulders."

"Did you get the men you went after?"

"Only part of them."

"What will you do next?" She rose and went after the decanter and two crystal glasses.

"I guess go back to Texas. I couldn't find out much about where the others went."

"Folks close ranks," she said, handing him a glass and pouring a drink.

He nodded. The entire ride down there, he'd thought about having a drink, but he knew too much depended on him. The smell tickled the inside of his nose when he lifted the glass. His first sip went down as smooth as a fire raced through dry grass. He closed his eyes to savor the whole thing. Damn, he'd sure become dependent on the stuff to deliver him from reality.

Two drinks more and, with her tucked under his arm, they went to the kitchen, toasting all the good things that had happened in their lives.

"I was so happy to be coming to the Indian Territory and marrying a man I'd heard about all my life."

"Things were better here than in Georgia?"

"You heard of General Sherman?"

"Who hasn't?"

"He burned my family's plantation to the ground."

He stopped in the dining room doorway and held her from going in. "We were talking about good things."

"I'm sorry." And she hugged him familiarly. "I promise only good things."

The whiskey on his long-empty stomach had taken a toll. He realized he was drunk. He was holding an attractive woman less than casually. Where would all this lead? He didn't give a damn—not then or ever. Poor Conway's body out there in the cold—stiff, and him long departed—and he was having an affair with his woman. He must not have any conscience, any code of ethics.

He released her and made a crude, gentlemanly attempt to seat her. That done he sat down and looked around. Things took time to settle down, and the smell of food about gagged him. He knew he needed some—maybe chicken soup and goat's milk. Lordy, he did feel drunk.

The food stayed down and he awoke hung over. Sunlight streaming into the room, he could see a ruffled white tent overhead. Under fine sheets and down comforters, he was buck naked. Where in the hell was he at, anyway? He realized he was under a bed canopy, and sat up to rub his gritty eyes. When he glanced to the side, he saw Ellie's curly, reddish-brown hair, spilling on her bare shoulders. She was lying in the bed beside him.

What had he done? He had no intention of becoming involved with her. Had she misunderstood his intentions? Looked like a damn mess to him. He turned to throw his legs off and a hand caught him.

"Don't leave me. It's cold out there. I want to snuggle while it's still warm in here."

He closed his eyes. Where were the words to deny her? They weren't on his list.

"I—I need to take them in."

Hugging the sheet to her, she sat up and tossed aside her hair. "You sound mad."

"I'm not mad. I'm embarrassed. Guess I got drunk as a skunk last night. I never intended to."

"It was my fault."

He swept his clothes off the floor, hugged them tight to his belly as cover, and headed for the screen with his face growing more heated by the minute. Behind the blind at last, he began to put on his longhandles.

"It wasn't your fault."

When he looked over the screen, she was wrapping herself in a robe. Something about the determination in how she looked made him wary.

"Are you mad?" she asked.

"No—" He pulled on his pants and stood straddle-legged while he put on his shirt. With it buttoned, he used the webs of his hands to hook both suspenders over his shoulders. His fly buttoned, he felt at ease. "I stopped off to inform you about Bruce's— Conway's death. I'm sorry if I took advantage of your sorrow."

Armed with a hairbrush, she'd attacked her thick hair. "No one took advantage of me."

He came out to sit on the bed and put on his socks and boots. "It sure seemed that way to me."

"Who did we hurt?" Busy rolling the hair out of the brush, she looked up at him. "I know I can't have you. Poor Bruce and I'd realized the same thing. There are five families here that rely on me. They were my husband's property. Now they are my responsibility. They have no urge to move away. Maybe we can hold this place together."

"I'll have that in my thoughts."

"Do. Because, like you I have . . . I pledged to them I would hold it, and make a home and work for them. So I stole something from you. Do you hate me?"

He shook his head in defeat. "No, disappointed in myself. You won't understand—"

"I might. Let's go find some breakfast." She pocketed the brush, put her arm in the crook of his, and they went downstairs. "You know they never had a ball in this house?"

"Really?"

"Shame isn't it?"

"Yes."

"Carl built it when the war started. Then he lost his family. We were married by a justice of the peace, and he died before we could even plan one."

"Maybe one day you can have one here."

She shook her head, taking him across the polished floor. "Who could I invite? Rich Cherokees? They dislike me. The former slaves? No, I will have this big hall, and keep it warm with the fireplaces, as long as my people will stay here and marshals stop over."

She showed him to a seat, then went to the kitchen and talked to her help. A young black girl carried in a tray with cups and coffee to serve him.

"Breakfast is coming," Ellie said, and took her chair. "Tell me about this woman in Texas?"

"I woke up in her shed. She had her mind made up that she needed a guide to get to Kansas."

"Her husband?"

"Killed in the war."

"She runs this ranch."

"Has since he left for the war."

"Then we have much in common."

He blew the steam off the coffee in his hands. "Yes, you do."

"Why are men so close-mouthed?"

He frowned. "I don't understand what you mean."

"I mean you give me little, short sentences and I want—" She spread her arms out. "A wagonload of answers."

"If I had 'em, guess I'd tell you."

"Oh, Ed Wright, you have answers for many things, but you'll ride off keeping them under that Texas hat."

"For you, for Unita, for my personal problems living with the ghosts from my past—those don't come easy."

She nodded as if she understood. "It's 'cause you care, darling. All those men you've buried trailing cattle, in the war, and as a ranger, are your personal ghosts."

The girl put a heaping plate of eggs, ham, and grits before him. He nodded to Ellie and waited until she put Ellie's dish in place and had departed before he spoke. "They're the ones that haunt me."

She nodded that she understood. "I will dress and we can take a wagon to Fort Smith. Your horses must still be very tired from the long trip."

"I didn't—"

"You didn't do lots of things, I am sure. But I want to see that Bruce is put away well."

"Yes, ma'am."

She wiped her mouth and rose, dropping the napkin on the table. "They will have it all loaded by then."

"Yes, ma'am."

"Damn it, Ed Wright—" She shook her head and rushed out to the kitchen, giving orders.

When she returned, he cradled another hot cup of coffee in his hands. "I'm giving you those two horses."

She turned and smiled. "You won't need them?"

He shook his head. "I'll take the stage back to San Antone."

"I like that bald-faced one."

"He's a good horse. Never bucked a time with me."

She nodded and left to dress.

He sat blowing on the coffee and readying himself for the authorities in Fort Smith. There'd be lots of questions to answer. All he could do was tell them how it happened so that they believed him.

The farm wagon was out in front. Adam came by to tell him all his things were loaded for when he was ready. He told him to keep Bruce Conway's saddle and bedroll, and the man thanked him.

"He was divorced. So his wife has no claim on it."

"Are you speaking about Bruce?"

He turned. Ellie stood in the foyer, dressed in black and putting on a long driving coat. "He was divorced?"

"The decree wasn't final."

"I thought he said she had married a lawyer?"

"More complicated than that. But her divorce was arranged and might not have been legal."

"Well, it won't matter now. You still keep his things." Damn, what kind of a mess was Conway in anyway?

"I'm ready."

"I'll be a long, cold ride," he said.

"I know. But someone needs to be at his funeral."

They arrived in Fort Smith via the ferry near midnight. He went by the federal court building, left her wrapped in a blanket on the spring seat and went inside. The shift captain of the guards, Emile Darby, was the person of authority on duty. After Ed explained the matter, Darby sent a swamper out to get the two gunnysacks of heads.

"They smell bad?" he asked Ed, looking wary about the deal after his man went for them. "Have a seat."

With a shake of his head, Ed refused the offer, knowing Ellie was out there on the seat in the cold night. "They ain't fresh apples, but the posse man said you'd need proof who they were."

"Goddamn, I hate dead heads."

"I don't like them myself. But I want those rewards for those two, the posse man's widow and the other man who helped get them."

Darby frowned at him. "What's your part in this?"

"I went looking for killers who murdered my partner. They weren't there."

"I hate worse that they killed Bruce Conway."

Ed agreed. "I'm taking his body to the funeral home."

"Chief Marshal Wade will want a full report. Man, Judge Parker sure hates any of them deputies getting killed. He'll be at the funeral."

"Fine, I'll be back in the morning. I'm tired."

"Sure. Wade'll want that report."

"I'll get him one." Ed left, passing the old man carrying the sacks over his shoulder and laboring down the hall.

They delivered Conway's body to Fall and Son's Funeral Home, and put the team and wagon up at the stables. Both of them walked the two blocks to the hotel under the stars in exhausted silence. At the Grand he took two rooms and carried her bag up to hers. Weary and looking to sleep, he stood outside her room's door. She appeared ready for her knees to buckle as she patted him on the chest. "You're a tough man, Ed Wright. I see why you can get cattle to Kansas."

"I know why I hate it so," he said, and smiled.

She looked up and down the hall to be certain they were alone, save for the loud snoring coming from the occupants of the various rooms. On her toes she pursed her lips and closed her eyes. He kissed her quick like and spun her around.

"Morning will come too soon."

"Oh, it will," she said cheerily, but he heard the disappointment in her tone.

When the funeral was over, he planned to head for Texas. Where he belonged. And perhaps with the woman he belonged to. He unlocked his own door, and waved at her as she disappeared into her room. For a man who'd been sleeping in his own bedroll and not had a woman around to even consider for several years, he'd suddenly gained two—if he wanted them. He was still upset by the entire turn of events, including Conway's and Brown's deaths, when he fell asleep under the covers.

The next morning he knocked on Ellie's door. To his surprise she was already dressed and ready to go when she opened the door. They had breakfast with the Chinaman; then he hailed a hansom cab for the drive over to the courthouse.

She went inside to wait while he spoke to Chief Marshal Wade about the incident. A short man with a mustache, he wore a nice tailored suit. He acted polite enough when Ed explained his purpose, and the man showed him a chair.

"Is the lady with you comfortable out there?" Wade asked.

"Mrs. Schaffer. She was a friend of Conway's. I think she'll be fine."

"All right." Wade leaned back in his screechy-sounding swivel chair and tented his hands before his nose. "What happened up there? Conway told me he was going with you after the Bradys."

"They weren't home, but the rest of the gang was."

"I'll get my secretary to take notes." Wade rose and went to the open door. "Clyde, come in here and take this down."

He returned and nodded. "She is very nice-looking. Conway spoke of her."

Ed nodded. "I think they were very serious."

"Shame, too. He was a good man. Now this is Clyde Butler. Mr. Wright was with Conway when he was murdered."

The fresh-faced young man wore the anxious look of someone eager. After he set down the paper, pen, and ink he had brought for the transcription, he and Ed shook hands.

Everything explained, Ed began his side of the story and the young man wrote it down.

Another deputy stuck his head in and told them Conway's funeral would be at two.

Wade nodded his head in approval. "Give Judge Parker's clerk the word too. He'll adjourn court to attend it."

"Yes, sir."

Ed had begun to realize that all the traffic and congestion going on in the outside hall was part of that man's court session, being held down the hallway.

Prisoners in chains and their lawyers paraded in and out of the courtroom. Marshals with fresh arrests lined them up at the clerk's desk. Visitors and more quickly packed the hallway, each in some way involved with the federal court system.

"Just a regular day here," Wade said to Ed at a break in the deposition session.

"What else will you need?" Ed asked when they were finished.

Wade shook his hand. "We should be fine."

The mourners at Conway's funeral were warmed by the afternoon heat. The red clay was piled high beside the grave, and the minister spoke quietly with Mrs. Schaffer on the side. Well dressed in black, she made an attractive widow. Several marshals came in their business suits. They shook Ed's hand and spoke of their gratitude for him taking the time and effort to bring Conway's body back for the services and recognition.

"Most would have buried him there," one man said, and shook his head.

Heads swiveled when a buggy and driver arrived.

"That's Quince, his lawyer, and Conway's ex-wife," one marshal leaned over and explained.

Ed thanked him, taking a place beside Mrs. Schaffer.

"She came for the life insurance?" she asked under her breath.

"Damned if I know."

"I'm ordering him a tombstone. She won't be on it."

Ed nodded and looked up. A cab was coming.

"That's Judge Parker," someone said and they

waited for a straight-backed man with a goatee to get out with Marshal Wade and join them.

The service was brief. Three women sang two hymns, and the minister closed it in prayer. Ed watched the judge go by and toss a handful of red clay in on top of the casket in the grave.

"That's Cherokee tradition," she said under her breath.

Then the judge talked to Wade, who pointed to Ed on the far side of the crowd. Parker came over to shake his hand and nod to Mrs. Schaffer. "Good to meet you, Mr. Wright. Marshal Wade told me of all you have done on this matter. We are all grateful. A very conscientious thing you did, bringing his remains back for interment here. Not many men would have done it."

"It was left to me."

"The federal court thanks you, and if we can reimburse you in any way . . . ?" He waited for a reply.

Ed shook his head. "Conway was a good man."

"Thanks again."

When they were at last alone, Ellie grew teary and dabbed her eyes on the way to the wagon. "Why refuse his money?"

"I didn't do this for money. I did this for Conway."

"Ed Wright, you have convictions that few men possess."

He shrugged and halfway lifted her lithe body onto the seat. "I don't know about that. I just wanted it right. He tried to lead me to those killers and I owed him."

She finished putting a blanket over her shoulders

and clapped him on the leg. "If I can ever help you, holler."

"I will." He clucked to the team, swung them around, and caught sight of two black men filling the grave. He couldn't forget Judge Parker throwing in the handful of dirt—a Cherokee tradition.

Later that evening as he and Mrs. Schaffer ate supper, Wade stopped at their table. "I wanted you to know that this afternoon Quince filed a petition for all the rewards and money coming to Bruce Conway for his wife to receive."

Ed raised up in the chair. "What did you do about it?"

"I told him if he didn't want to be slapped with a bigamy rap, he better withdraw it."

"What did he do?"

"Smiled like he does and took the papers with him."

Ed nodded at Ellie. "Mrs. Schaffer said she came today for his life insurance."

"She tried, anyway. I'm certainly pleased to meet you today, ma'am."

"Why, Marshal Wade," she said in her finest Southern drawl. "You're ever up my way, I always have a meal ready for a lawman."

"I shall. When do you leave, Ed?"

"In the morning. Fort Worth stage leaves at six a.m."

"Will you be going home too?" Wade asked Ellie.

"Yes, in the morning too. Ed arranged for Marshal Clark to show me home. Clark has business out west."

Wade smiled. "I bet he does. Both of you, thanks. You did Bruce Conway proud today."

Chapter 17

The coach seats were leather-covered and filled with horsehair, and gave little padding for his butt or back as he slumped under his blanket and tried to sleep. A picture of Mrs. Schaffer remained in his thoughts, of when he gave her a final hug in the cold gray light of the alley. She had waved to him as she mounted the seat beside the lanky marshal for the trip home.

He'd be in San Antone in four days, if he survived. No word around Fort Smith of the Bradys' whereabouts, though Wade had promised to send him any news he heard about them. Only able to doze until a pitch of the coach awoke him, he wondered what was happening in Texas. How many had signed on with a woman to take their cattle north?

He decided to stop over a night in Fort Worth when the stage reached there. Down in the livestock market district, where some local slaughter operations were carried out, horses, mules, and cattle were bunched for the trail north. Nearby, an element of tough thugs, gamblers and riffraff gathered in the saloons and brothels. There might be someone down there knew something about the Bradys. He watched the winter brown hills when the temperature warmed enough to put up the canvas covers and let some of the rank body odor out of the cramped coach. A stew of sweat, cigars, and bad whiskey mixed with infrequent farting made the air inside the coach resemble a raw outhouse and saloon combination. Then a drummer got sick and didn't get his head out the window soon enough, and the sourness of puke only stacked on top of the rest. He'd damn sure be ready for Fort Worth.

He was grateful there were none of the opposite sex on board this trip. His slovenly companions were mostly salesmen with small sample suitcases, and plenty of pints of whiskey in their boot vamps— original bootleggers, 'cause any whiskey in the Indian Territory was illegal. They also pissed close to the coach when the stop was made in the absence of any females. This saved them from a trip to hell into the violent-smelling, foul places called "facilities out in back" by the better-spoken drivers and crappers by the rest.

Food was never good at such stopovers, and every fifteen miles or so they changed horses at one of these outposts. One look at the scruffily dressed, unbathed help, fly-specked tables, and grease-smeared plates turned most away, but for the iron-stomached ones. Ed kept to his diet of jerky from his pocket, only drinking some of the bad coffee, so he didn't have to sip on the larva-infested water available. At least in the hot coffee they could no longer swim.

It rained the last day of the trip to Fort Worth. The muddy ruts were deep and made the coach swing hard on its leather hangers. The tossing around of the passengers added to their upset stomachs and the vomiting grew worse. So bad that Ed finally rode on top, wrapped in his slicker against the drizzle and endured rather than stay down there.

"You going on?" the gruff-talking driver asked him as he held the ribbons to the four horses in his gloved hands.

"After a bath, and a night's stay in a real bed." He turned his head from the cold drizzle and pulled down his wet hat brim.

"Can't blame you. This the damndest bunch of drunks I ever hauled. For ten cents I'd leave them all at some isolated station, 'cept the damn swampers there would get back at me for doing it." Then he gave a big belly laugh and leaned in to make the horses keep up the pace despite the mud wearing them down.

His canvas coat's collar turned up and bushy gray mustache twirled at the ends, he looked like the captain in charge, on the edge of the bench in the box, his goal getting there on time despite the uncooperative weather, horses, and mud occasionally flung at them.

"What the hell do you do for a living?"

"I used to be a trail drover."

The man turned and looked at him hard. "Well, what do you do now?"

"Run some cows in the hill country. Near Banty."

"I'd like that a damn sight better than driving this rig."

"It's not bad."

"Guess you been on a cattle-selling deal."

Ed shook his head and gripped the iron railing to hang on as the coach swayed from side to side in the ruts. Someone below threw his head out a side window and loudly retched.

"I had a partner who was murdered last fall by some outlaws. I was up in the Nation looking for them."

"Do any good?"

"No."

"You've got lots on your mind, I can see that. All you needed was a bunch of dumb drunks to share the damn coach with. Life's hell at times—get over, damn you!" he shouted and leaned to rein the horses hard aside for a fallen tree in the road. His run-down boots planted on the dashboard, he fought them to the left and the stage lurched as if it might tip, then righted itself and he swung them back.

"Good job," Ed said, impressed.

"Hell, that was easy." He laughed again and then shouted at the slacking horses to hurry. Slapping them with the lines, he drove on. "It's the real wrecks that are tough avoiding."

In Fort Worth, Ed found the too-hot, steamy bathhouse, and a small Oriental took his clothing to wash and iron while he smoked a cigar and lounged to his neck in hot water. At last, shriveled but clean, he climbed out, dried himself with the Turkish towel, and put on a robe to wait on his clothing. The place was devoid of any business and warm, so he soon dozed in the corner.

"Clothes all clean—" The boy awoke him, holding his folded clothing, and he nodded. How they did all that in that short a time he never knew. But at last, dressed and back in his slicker and hat, he hitched the six-gun on his hip and headed for a real meal and a bed.

A swish of moisture sprayed his face and every

porch roof of the businesses along the street made small waterfalls off of their eaves.

"Honey," a gal gasped, and hung herself on his arm. A short young doxy, with her hair all wet and plastered to her head. She looked slender and less than twenty years old. Beside him she raised herself up and met his stride. "Where you going, darling?"

"To eat."

She blinked her blue eyes at him and then turned back to dodging through the night full of barkers extolling the benefits of their various saloons to the cowboys, gamblers, fancy Dans, and more doves. "I know where you'll like the food. Want me to take you there?"

He felt her take charge of more of his elbow and ride familiarly on his arm. "Where's that?"

"On the corner. Amos's."

"All right, we'll eat there."

Her slender face lit up at his words. "You won't regret it, either."

"I don't regret much in this world."

"I mean it. Cross my heart." She put her forehead on his coat sleeve and never missed a step in keeping up.

"Good," he said.

They took a table on the side. He removed his slicker and hat to hang on the hook at the end of the booth. She indicated for him to go in first, then she slid up against him. With his left arm over her shoulder, she grinned like she had possession of him when the waiter came over.

"What do you drink?" Ed asked her.

"Beer all right?"

He ordered two, and two steak dinners with the trimmings.

"I can't eat all that," she said quietly after the waiter had left.

"What's your name?"

"Nell, short for Nelly."

"Nell, you eat what you want of it."

She drove a small breast into his side and rubbed the top of his pants leg with her palm. "I sure like you, mister."

"Ed, Ed Wright."

"Ed, you live around here?"

"No, I live at Banty, west of San Antone."

"That sounds like a neat place."

Rather than explain the dried-up, dusty place tucked away in the hill country to her, he merely nodded, which must have satisfied her. The waiter brought their beers, and some fresh, hot rye bread and a bowl of butter.

Ed buttered some and it melted in his mouth. He gave her a bite and she smiled like no one had ever done that before. Her wetness was seeping into his shirt and britches. It didn't matter—she was fresh, and her youthful eagerness was flattering. Besides, he'd been under lots of pressure for several days, bringing back the dead that he wanted to escape from. The damn Bradys were gone again, like smoke. By the time he got back up there, their trail would be cold.

"You got folks?" he asked.

She wrinkled her nose. "My maw lives up in Carrol County, Arkansas, with my stepfather."

"Oh?"

She nodded and looked at her small, chapped

hands. "I decided to come down here after Maw married him."

Ed nodded with his mouth full.

"Kinda dangerous business, isn't it?"

"Yeah, but I's got to eat."

He agreed. He couldn't save every waif. The notion knifed him. The food arrived and they ate it in silence. She consumed half her steak and fried German potatoes, then gave a sigh and sat back.

"Was I right about the food?" she asked.

"Good place," he agreed, forking in a bite of the browned meat.

She stretched her arms over her head. "I guess when we get done here, we can do business?"

"What's the price?"

"A dollar."

He nodded.

"Too much? I know you fed me."

"No."

"I'm ugly?"

"No, Nell. I knowed the time I'd of paid a lot more'n that for a toss in the hay with you. Just sit tight," he said as she started to scoot away. "I've got some problems and new things going on in my life. Things I can't answer, and all I see this doing is messing it up more. You set to keep doing this business?"

"Sure. They only pay two bits a day for dishwashers here and I tried it."

"I guess that's right."

She wrinkled her nose. "And then you can sleep with the cook if you want to keep your job."

He shook his head, and raised up to reach in his pants pocket. "Here's two dollars."

"Gosh, mister, what do I need to do for you?"

He smiled at her. "Just sit there and be yourself."

She hugged his arm. "If my daddy hadn't died I'd be up there at home. He was a lot like you."

He wanted to say he wasn't, but didn't want to hurt her feelings as she looked downcast.

She folded her hands in her lap. "I'll be damned. I never figured this would happen."

"There'll be stranger things than this. Someday you may run across two killers named Brady who I am looking for. They killed my partner on a riverboat. You drop me a line—Ed Wright, Banty, Texas, and I'd sure appreciate that."

"Brady?"

"Yes. Marsh and Corley Brady. They're killers so be careful. Just a line on where I might find them is all I need."

She scooted her butt up tight against his and clutched his arm. "I'll sure write you, Ed Wright, if'n I ever hear about 'em."

After the meal, on a street corner in the drizzling rain, Nell kissed him good-bye standing on her toes. Then he watched her run off and disappear into the inky wet night. Under his reset, sodden hat, he went to find a hotel bed to catch up on his sleep. San Antone and the roan horse were still a few days away. Unita'd have to wait a little longer for his return.

At dawn, he caught the stage for San Antone and rocked his way there over the next two cold days. Huddled in his coat, he half slept under a blanket and tried to ignore the drummers passing a pint of whiskey around the coach to warm their *inaards*. Damn, he sure didn't need any of that.

In San Antonio, with his head down to the north wind, he hired a hack and rode out to the roan's location at his ex-ranger buddy Nichols' place. A handshake plus a refusal to accept any money for keeping his horse and he was Banty bound. At least he hadn't gotten lost in some saloon, and he breathed a sigh of relief from the heights west of the Alamo. He'd missed that opportunity.

He stopped and got his mail in town, then headed for Unita's to return the roan. Sore and weary from a day and a half in the saddle with only a few hours' sleep, he sat the roan and looked at the Bar U ranch headquarters on the distant brown slope. Ready for the bath he'd evaded taking in San Antone, so he wouldn't be tempted to stay around, he reined up and grasped the saddle horn. He guessed she'd take him smelling like an old goat or turn him away.

Why was he going back there? Besides returning the horse, maybe he was drawn to her by the pleasure he expected, like whiskey. If it wasn't one thing in his life, it was another. But the thought of her had haunted him in Fort Worth the whole time that doxy Nell had clutched his arm. Strange for him to be admitting it, but he'd done dumber things.

Dogs barking at him like it was a celebration, Unita came out on the porch drying her hands and squinting against the midday sun. He shook his head in defeat. She sure made his stomach roll around to simply look at her.

"Ed, I guess you didn't find them from the long look on your face."

He hugged her when they met, halfway to the house, then threw his arm over her shoulder. "It's a long story. I'm filthy, more whiskers than a billy goat, and—"

She stopped him on the porch and, after checking around to be certain they were alone, kissed him. Her ripe body squeezed up to him and, the sweet musk of her body filling his cold nose, he felt good for the first time since leaving Fort Smith. Maybe even before then.

"Some hot food first, and we can heat water for your bath." She led him inside. "Rosa, heat some water. The errant guy is back."

"Oh, Senor. You are all right," she said from around the kitchen door, looking relieved.

"Yes, ma'am, and I'm glad to be here."

"The Bradys?" Unita asked.

"Run off before we got there, I guess. Got two men killed—" He dropped his head and shook it warily. "And several outlaws were also killed, but the Bradys got away or had left the day before we got there."

He nodded that that was it, and busied himself washing his hands and face on the porch. Then he followed her inside.

Unita closed the door, then looked him in the eye as if she shared his loss. "I'm sorry. The trip must have been hell." She took his coat and hat to put on a peg.

"One of those things." He finally shrugged and slid onto a bench at the sight of Rosa coming with a plate full of food.

"One thing I missed the most," he said to the Mexican woman. "You two and your cooking."

She clapped him on the shoulder. "We missed you too, Senor Ed."

"I don't know why." He grinned at them and the three of them laughed.

"I only have three bunches of cattle signed up so far for the drive," Unita confided to him as he slowly chewed the rich-tasting food. "Mine, yours, and Tina's uncle's."

"I'll make some rounds. There's more out there. I'm sure you can leave here with two thousand head, and cover most of our costs with their cattle."

"They don't think a woman can get them there."

His fork poised with slow-cooked roast beef on the tines, he looked at her. *Damn bunch of fools anyway.* "I'll talk to 'em."

"Good," she said.

After a hot bath and a shave, full of food, he felt better lounging in overalls while his own clothes dried. Heat from her fireplace radiated in his face as he stood in front of it and considered all that lay ahead. It was even cold in Texas.

"What will you do for Christmas?" she asked, joining him.

"Hadn't even thought about it. Sorry, I've been on my own so long without family—it's kind of another day."

"I'm getting the crew some little things like jack-knives."

"I'll get my bunch at the ranch some things."

"In town they're getting some ripe oranges in for Christmas. You want some for them?"

"Sure, order me some."

"Two sacks?"

"Be fine. I need to ride over there in the morning and be sure I still have the ranch."

"May I go along?"

He looked across the table at her. "Sure."

She smiled as if that pleased her. "You must be healed."

"That damn stage didn't shake me loose, so I should be all right. Guess I should move back over there. Don't look good, what with me—I mean—"

With her left hand she pushed the curls back from her face, and then shook her head. "I don't care who thinks what."

"That's plumb generous of you."

"Ed Wright—" She looked him square in the eye. "We have lots of business to do to get ready. I'm counting on you to show me the way. Stay here. Jorge has things under control. In fact, I wanted to know if Rusty and the boys that I leave here can help him at spring roundup while we're gone."

"He'd appreciate that. I know them big ranchers run over him some at those deals when I ain't there, and having a gringo partner might help him hold his own better."

She checked the kitchen door, then turned back to face him and, in a low voice, asked, "Are you tired of sleeping in the shed?"

He closed his eyes and shook his head, then reached across and clasped her hands. "I ain't through fighting demons. Shed's fine."

She bowed her head and accepted his words. "Stay here as long as you want. We have lots to do and I need your help."

"I agree. We'll ride over in the morning and check

on Jorge, then we can swing by town and I'll look up some of those guys who have cattle to ship."

"Sounds like a deal." Her face brightened.

"How far away is Christmas?"

"Two weeks. There's a ball at the schoolhouse—" Her shielded expectation didn't fool him.

"We'll go if you want your toes stepped on."

"Oh, I've seen you dance before."

"Not ever sober."

She laughed. "You might even be a better dancer sober."

He didn't know if he could dance without liquor, but he'd try.

Chapter 18

Tina rushed out and beamed at them when they rode up. The small, pert-looking Mexican woman acted as excited to see that Unita was with him. Tina told him the men were at the big tank north of the ranch house, and he told the two women to have a nice visit and rode out to see about the men. He doubted that they'd even miss him, they were so busy talking to each other.

Jorge smiled his handsome grin when he rode up. The large stone tank had been drained and the three—Jorge, Ramon, and Raphael—were inside it, looking at a large crack in the masonry.

"It was losing so much water," Jorge explained when he dismounted and stood outside the wall.

Ed agreed. "After you cement that crack, let it dry good before you refill it."

"*Sí.* There is water in the creeks for the cattle from the rains, so I thought to fix it now was a good thing."

"Sure is. No trouble?"

"No, everything she goes good."

"Good. Senora Nance's offered to have Rusty and her men help you some at roundup while we're gone."

"Oh, *sí*, that would be good. Some of those men think I work for them and not for you."

"I know. That's why I wanted Rusty to help you. We need to start bunching our older steers in one area after Christmas and the New Year. I figure we've got those few hundred head to go up there."

"*Sí*, there should be that many, and we can do that."

"You want to go to Mexico over the holidays?" Ed asked him.

Jorge's smile gave him away before he even spoke. "Oh, yes, to be with my people down there would be very nice."

"I'll stay over here with Ramon and Raphael, and you can take the little ones and Tina home."

"*Gracias.*"

"No, you are a good man for me. Be sure to come back."

Jorge laughed. "We will."

After the noon meal at Tina's, Ed and Unita rode their horses into Banty and stopped by at the store to reserve their oranges. Ed picked up a new shirt, gallowses, and britches to wear to the ball, and got a grin of approval from her. She threw a new black silk vest on the pile he'd started on the counter.

"You can use that too."

"Hmm," he said, appraising it. "I may look like some dandy in all that."

She chuckled and shook her head in amusement. "No, you'll still have that floppy-brimmed hat."

"Mr. Ed, would you like to look at a new hat?" James Lee, the tall youth behind the counter, asked.

"Guess if I'm going to the ball I better have one." A glance aside at her and he saw her nod of approval.

After trying on several, he settled for an ash gray Boss of the Plains with silk binding on the brim. It cost six bucks, and he shook his head while signing the ticket for all his things. About then she leaned over close and whispered, "You'll be the best-dressed one there."

He acknowledged her words. He'd also be the fanciest one, too—and that made him a little fretful. But with her on his arm going in that schoolhouse door, they could all gossip and be jealous as much as they wanted to be—he'd not give a damn.

They were headed out of the store when he saw Biff Tyler ride in on a big dun horse and dismount across the street at the Minnie Ha Ha Saloon. He turned and gave her his armload of things and said, "Hold this."

"Don't—" barely peeled off her lips, but his somber head shake forced her to nod that she understood.

"Hang that hogleg on the saddle horn," Ed ordered Tyler, and stepped off the porch, ready to undo his own.

"Well, if it ain't that damned old drunk, Ed Wright," Tyler sneered and undid his buckle like he'd been ready to do that. "I just love the fact I'm going to kick your ass in public this time."

His holster off and rebuckled, Ed looped his rig over the horn. "You ain't going to be doing much more than eating dirt today, Tyler."

Tyler snickered as he stripped off his fine, embroidered vest and then hung it and his flat-brim hat over the gun. "You're going to be riding a pony again when I get through with you."

"Like hell," Ed said, moving in a circle with his dukes up and ready.

"Here, have this!" Tyler charged in, but instead of hitting his opponent he missed, and Ed landed three quick jabs to Tyler's chin that forced him backward.

With Tyler retreating, Ed moved in and slammed him hard in the face. That force sprawled him into the hitch rack. His horse spooked, breaking the reins, and distracted him enough that Ed freight lined two hard fists to his gut, which drove the air out of him. With Tyler seated on his butt, Ed gave him a swift kick to the ribs and sent him sprawling with a sharp cry of pain.

With Tyler's shirt collar in his hand, he dragged him over to the water tank and stuck his head under the suface. He might just drown the sumbitch. Then he jerked him up. "You had enough?"

"Hell—"

Ed cut off his protests by slamming him back under the surface.

"Don't! Don't! You'll kill him!" Unita shouted, breaking his concentration.

With a shake of his head in disgust, Ed at last pulled the flailing Tyler up. Sputtering and coughing up water, Tyler indicated he'd had enough.

"Next time I hear you've rode over there and cussed her out, I'll kill you like the low-life dog you are."

"I—hear—you."

"Good, cause I'll gut shoot you and leave you to die." Ed started to go, then his anger gathered up again. He whirled and kicked Tyler so hard in the chest that he lifted him off the ground with a groan.

Unita had Ed by the arm and forcefully dragged him away from the coughing and gagging foreman. Her face was black with anger. Ed submitted to her moving him, but he still wanted more revenge, recalling his own beating at Tyler's hands.

James Lee held all of Ed's purchases in his arms for them. "Whew, you sure beat him up."

"About halfway—" Ed looked back and scowled at Tyler, still on his knees and coughing at the edge of the horse tank across the dusty street. None of the shocked-face onlookers that fell out on the boardwalk to see the excitement even ran to the man's aid. Showed Ed how much Tyler was disliked in the small town.

"You ready to go?" she asked in a cold voice.

"Yes, ma'am." His gun belt on, he took the packages from James Lee and thanked the clerk.

In the saddle, he rode out of there with her, ignoring the rest.

"You could have killed him," she said under her breath at the edge of town.

"He needed killing."

She shook her head in dismay and they rode several miles in silence. When she at last spoke, it was very direct. "I suppose you don't think Crabtree won't extract some kind of revenge on you for beating up his man."

"He'll have to hire it done."

"He can do that."

"He sics any dogs on me he better be certain they kill me. Cause I'll damn sure go look for him in the end, too."

Twisted in the saddle, she frowned at him. "You can't kill everyone."

"I don't aim to, but I will if they try me."

"What is this get-even business that makes men like you so rabid?"

"Must have been born inside us."

"I can't understand it."

"I'm sorry, but every day I had to catch my breath getting on and off a horse, and the fact that he kicked me so hard, it knifed me."

"Goaded you on."

"Right."

"Now he's busted up and going to come looking for you."

Ed shook his head. "He don't want to lose his fancy looks. Tyler picks his fights with those he can whip."

She obviously didn't agree but went on, "I didn't want war with Crabtree."

"It's my war and any man talks that nasty to a woman in Texas needs to be either horsewhipped or hung."

"Well, you did not find anyone to ship cattle with us—today."

"No, but I sure evened up one deal." He juggled the packages to rub his skinned knuckles. They'd be sore.

She booted Star in close to the roan and took the hatbox from him. "I'll put some alcohol on those cuts and wrap your hands when we get back to the ranch."

He shook his head and smiled at her. *Yes, mother— now I've sure got me one.*

After breakfast the next day he set out for Billie Miller's. The short ex-corporal from his outfit in Mississippi lived on Lovell Creek. He arrived at midmorning and scattered a dozen large shoats that were bedded down beside the creek. They grunted as if pissed off that he'd even come by and upset their mud bathing.

Billie came out on the porch of his ramshackle house, putting up his suspenders and squinting to see who he was.

"Corporal Miller?"

"Damn right, Sarge. Hey, man, what you doing back up here?" Billie spat tobacco off the edge of the porch and turned back. "It's Sarge, and he's sober, Ida Mae!"

"Well invite him in. Land's sakes, ain't you got no manners?" A small woman without any front teeth rushed out and grinned big. "Get down. Get down."

"I can't stay long. Ida Mae Nance's outfit's taking steers north to Kansas in March. I come by to see if you all want to put some in."

Billie looked at Ida Mae as if uncomfortable, then back at Ed. "I don't put much truck in her taking my cattle and losing them."

"I understand, but who else you got?"

"Terrance Crabtree's talking like he'll take 'em."

"Crabtree? He ain't never been north of Fort Worth."

"Oh, he's got some guy going to head it up. Name's Luther."

Ed nodded. "What's he want to drive them up there?"

"Half," Billie said.

"Kinda high ain't it? He wants half the cattle he starts with, or half those he gets there with?"

Billie scratched his rumpled hair. "I guess half he leaves with."

"You signed that deal yet?"

"Why?"

" 'Cause if you have you can bet he won't get there with very many of 'your cattle.' "

"I never liked the deal in the first place," Ida Mae said, and folded her arms over her small bustline.

"Well, Frank Hogan said it was the only way for us to get anything out of them."

"Frank knows better than that."

"He's made a deal with Crabtree when we came back from San Antone after you said you wasn't going back again. We all kinda went along with him."

"We's got to have some cash." Ida Mae shifted from one foot to the other. "Or we'll lose this place, and all the fixtures we worked so damn hard on here."

Ed couldn't see much of value in the rusty tin and gray weathered-board shack and outbuildings, with the rundown corrals of rails, but it wasn't his place, either. He squatted on his boot heels and listened to her go on about their hard times, agreeing with them through nods.

"I understand, but Mrs. Nance is offering to split the cost with the outfits per head that get there."

"What if she loses them all?" Billie asked.

"Ain't no worse off than Crabtree's deal. You're taking all the loss with him. It won't cost half the cattle to get there, anyway."

"I heard you was going to be her guide?"

"I am."

Billie was rubbing his palms up and down the sides of his pants. "Damn it, Sarge, what about my neighbors? Will they think I walked out on them?"

"That's your business. I can find other cattle to go

north. I just wanted you boys in on the ground floor, before I go looking for others."

"Guess she needs to know." He looked over at Ida Mae. "Well, what do you think?"

"We better go up and see her in the morning. Thanks for coming by. I'll make us some dinner." She looked at Ed for his answer to her offer.

"No, thanks, I better ride on. I've got lots of folks to see about. But thanks, Ida Mae." He stuck out his hand to Billie. No way was he eating Ida Mae's cooking. "Thanks, she'll be looking for you."

Wamp Kaiser was next on the list. Ed made his place in midafternoon. His wife, Olga, came out in a checkered dress with a shape like a beer barrel and spoke in a heavy, accented, deep voice.

"Vot jew vant?"

"Wamp here?"

She continued in her "v" version of English. "I don't know where he is, but I can ring the bell and he will come." That done, she asked if he drank his coffee with cream.

"Black's fine," he said.

The loud peals brought Wamp on the run, and she delivered them steaming dark coffee and some delicate pastry on a tray. Wamp talked about the Crabtree deal. After Ed explained Unita's deal, the dark-headed man in his thirties smiled in relief.

"We be up there in next two days, save us lots of money, huh?" the German rancher said.

"It'll help," Ed said, and left them after the midafternoon treat.

He returned to the Bar U satisfied they'd have plenty of cattle committed in the next few days. The word was out. He dropped off the roan at the saddle shed and began to pull the latigos loose to unsaddle him.

"Well?" Unita asked, joining him.

"I talked to some today. Your old buddy Crabtree is heading up a bunch he has consigned. It's about as good a deal as McGregor, or maybe worse."

"So? So?" She stepped back to let him go by to put his saddle and pads inside on the rack.

"We'll see how I did in the next couple of days." He put the roan in the corral.

"What do you think?"

"I'm not certain."

"Oh, I'd hoped you had some real good news." Her hand in the crook of his arm, he headed for the house and listened to her promise of the food she'd saved for him.

After washing up and drying his hands on the porch, he leaned over and kissed her in the dying sunset that reflected off the clapboard siding. His affection brought a smile to her face and she opened the door. "Thanks anyway, for trying."

"It ain't over yet."

"Sure. Sure. Come and eat before it's all cold."

The next morning, breakfast came and went. He left the house and chopped stove wood. He had a large stack completed when she came out.

"You aren't going out to see any more of your old buddies today?" she asked, looking around.

"Well, no."

"You don't think any of the others will join us?"

He set the next block up and busted off a small sliver. "We'll have to see."

"Maybe I should go see them?"

"Aw, give it time."

"Time? In less than two weeks we'll only have three months before we head out."

He split off another small slab. "Yes, I understand that."

The reality of leaving on another drive kicked him hard in the guts. All this time he'd avoided facing the reality of actually going back to Kansas again, by chasing after the Bradys and doing anything to distract himself and ignore the truth. Why did he ever agree to go again? That he'd go back one more time and cross those blame rivers—stampedes and the rest. *Sweet Jesus, why did he ever promise her he'd do it?*

"There's someone coming in a buckboard. You expecting anyone?" she asked, moving aside to try to see who it was. "I don't know them. They must be coming to see you."

With the hatchet, he cleaved off another stick of stove wood from the block and shook his head. "Naw, they must be here to see you."

She frowned at him and then gathered her skirts and went to greet them. He had to hide a grin. She'd be liable to hit him with a stick of wood up beside the head when she learned the truth. The hatchet driven into the chopping block, he brushed himself off and started around the house to join the conversation.

"Miller's my name, Billie. I was in the army with Ed. This here's my wife, Ida Mae, Mrs. Nance." With a look of relief on his red, clean-shaven face, Billie said, "There's my old sarge now."

"Come in and we'll have some coffee," Unita said, cutting a suspicious glance at Ed.

"Sure good to see you two," Ed said, acting like he hadn't expected to see them there.

"Mrs. Nance—"

"Unita, Billie."

"Yes, ma'am. What we came over about was seeing if'n we could put our cattle in with yours and send them to Kansas."

"I think we still have room. How many?" She motioned to the table and Ida Mae nodded, sliding into the bench quickly.

"Two-fifty I figure I can gather up that's big enough. Ed—he's hard on grading them. I guess you will be too?" Billie swallowed hard, taking his place by his wife and handing Unita his beat-up hat.

"Three and four years old is what the market wants."

"Oh, I know about that. Now, we always done business before with Ed. Never had no papers to sign—"

Rosa brought coffee and a tray with cups, sugar, and cream. She privately smiled at Ed, who remained on his feet behind Unita.

"Here, let's have coffee," Unita said, and became the hostess while Rosa went back for the pot. "I don't think we need any papers, Mr. Miller."

He stuck his hand across toward her. Ed noticed his short, stubby fingers and how Unita never hesitated as most women did over a handshake, but grasped it and looked him in the eye. "We'll do our level best to get them there."

"Ida Mae and I are counting on it. But we know all you can do is all you can do."

"Mrs. Nance, I mean Unita," Ida Mae said. "I sure

do like your house. Don't look like I thought it would none. But it's sure nice."

"You thinking it might be full of stuffed chairs and doilies?"

Ida Mae grinned with her toothless mouth and nodded.

"Aw, I'm not high on that stuff. Besides my hands eat and lounge in here. This isn't some fancy tea parlor."

"Yeah, that's what I like about it."

The Millers left after lunch, and Lou Carter arrived to consign his two hundred steers. When he rode out it was suppertime, and Ed had avoided Unita enough that they'd never had a chance to talk privately. But he could see it coming. It was written all over her face—she planned to get back at him over this surprise business. He'd sure better hide his amusement, too.

Chapter 19

"We're going to have to turn down any more cattle," she said in his ear. They were sitting in the dark in the front room on a bench, alone at last. The fireplace crackled with live oak wood, and a glow of orange lit the room. Her arms draped around his neck and her cheek was on his shoulder. It felt relaxing and reassuring to him to have her so close. He couldn't recall ever having the cozy feeling he felt all over when he was close to her and they were by themselves.

He put his arm around her waist and drew her closer. He never got her close enough to him, but it helped to squeeze her. "Yes, we'll have to turn 'em down after all the sign-ons we've had the past week. However, at the moment, I'm not really thinking about steers."

"Oh?"

"I'm thinking it would be nice if there wasn't any. Wasn't another soul but you and me."

"I don't think there is anyone but you and me in here."

"Oh, there is always reality. I'd just like for it to be you and me."

"Coming from you I'm flattered."

He took his arm from around her and rubbed his palms on his pants legs. "I guess I aimed it to be. If I was real good at words I'd think of something flowery to say right now."

"Why, Ed Wright, whatever for? You're about as nice-talking a feller as I know when you get down to it."

"Aw, shoot, Unita. I've got words I'd like to say to you that are so far back in my head I can't grasp 'em."

She laughed and caused him to grin. Then she hugged him tight. "You suit me fine without them."

He looked off at the fireplace and watched the blue flames consuming the logs. He was a lucky man to have her. No one else would have dragged him out of the Shamrock Saloon and put up with him. No one else as good-looking or intelligent would have done that for him. He wanted her—Lord he wanted her— but something held him back.

"It's going to be four o'clock before you know it," she said.

"I know." He lifted her chin and kissed her. It was getting harder and harder to let go of her, but at last he stood up and helped her to her feet. "In the morning."

"Yes. You know you sleep by yourself because you want it that way?"

He nodded. Her words sobered him, but he wasn't that sure of himself—not enough to make that large a commitment, even to her.

The morning bell rolled him out, and he dressed and joined the ranch hands on the way to the house in the predawn chill, causing them to breathe clouds of vapor. He'd sure be glad when spring got there— or would he? Washing his hands in the cold water on the porch, he wasn't convinced that spring would be all that great. Among the chiding and teasing cow-hands, the usual bantering went on as Ed dried his hands and face. Then he ducked inside the warm front room, joining Rusty, who was holding his outstretched hands toward the fireplace.

"Trail branding comes next?" Rusty asked.

"Yes. We better contact Rip Meadors, the brand inspector."

"He needs to be here?"

"I usually invite him to watch it. Saves any hard feeling in case someone thinks we took their cattle in the deal. Some folks do that—gather as they go."

Rusty gave him a serious nod. He understood about "gatherers."

"Food's here," someone announced.

Rusty agreed. "I'll get hold of Meadors when the time comes."

Ed nodded and they joined the crew at the table.

After breakfast, he saddled the roan and Unita kept him company in the process. The boys had left earlier with a wagonload of posts and were taking the stuff down on Scully Creek, in the bottoms, to set up a squeeze chute operation for the branding.

"I'm going over and check on Jorge," Ed told Unita. "He's going home for Christmas in Mexico. But I'll be back Friday evening and go to the ball with you Saturday night."

"I'm counting on it."

He hugged and kissed her, then mounted up. It was

getting harder and harder to leave her. He winked and set out for his own ranch.

He heard her "Be careful" over his shoulder as he set the roan in a running walk and nodded that he would.

Jorge had a wagon, loaded and tarped down, parked by the main house. His two small children were busy rushing around, obviously excited about the prospects of going somewhere. Tina came to the door, smiled, and waved. It was warmer than it had been for several days, but harbingers of precipitation streaked the sky in a frothy high cloud layer. Also, on the way over, some rain crows in the brush had called to him. It would rain in three days.

"Where are they working?" he asked Tina after tousling some of the children's hair in passing them.

"They are building a bridge over the wash this week. Jorge said you'd thought that would be a good project for some time."

"Yes, it would be better to have a crossing. I'll ride up there and see them. When do you plan to leave?"

She shrugged. "He said he must talk to you about that."

"Why not plan to leave in the morning?"

She smiled as if pleased. "I will get ready."

He mounted up and headed for the bridge project.

The deep wash made it difficult to move stock. The over-twelve-foot cut ran most of the length of the canyon, and a span would help get riders on the far side or cross stock over short of driving them the half mile to the base.

When he found the crew, they were setting support

posts in the bottom and notching in cross supports to hold against a flash flood. Jorge climbed up the ladder and shook his hand.

"Good idea," Ed said. "We've needed this for years. But I want you to go to Mexico. We can finish it."

"Too late today to leave. I will go mañana, and that will be all right?"

"Yes, fine. We might get some rain in the next few days. I just wanted you to have a dry trip."

"I'll leave early then."

"Good. What can I do?"

"We will soon have the supports built, and then we can lay on the beams and nail the floor down."

The beams looked straight and the decking boards were over two inches thick. He loosened the girth and hobbled the roan to let him graze. Then he took a homemade ladder down into the gulch and observed their workmanship. Jorge never did anything that wasn't hell for stout, and the bridge support looked the role. Raphael was driving spikes into the boards that made the cross bracing.

"We didn't miss the wedding?" he asked, smiling hugely.

"No wedding," Ed said, and shook his head to dismiss the notion.

The rap of Raphael's hammer driving the spike echoed down the gorge. "Oh. Ramon said you were sweet on her."

"Hush," his cousin said, bringing over another board and looking embarrassed at his words.

"Hell, boys, if I ever get married you all will have new suits to wear to it. How's that?"

"Mucho bueno!" Raphael shouted.

That's what it would be too. Very good—he just wasn't ready . . . yet.

He and the boys floored the bridge the next day, and it began to rain late in the afternoon. They headed back huddled in their slickers. Ramon drove the wagon and they rode ahead. Rivulets ran off the brim of Ed's old hat as the cold sought inside the long-tailed canvas coat. Both of the hands had Boston rubber slickers, which Ed was convinced were colder than an icehouse in this case.

The wagon pulled into the barn alleyway, and the tools put up, he held a meeting as they squatted on the hay-strewn floor. Rain pecked at the cedar shingle roof, and in a place or two dripped.

"You boys can check on the cattle and the horses when the rain lets up. Then get some firewood cut when you get that done."

They nodded, looking intently at him.

"Guess you boys'd like to go down to Juan's and do a little Christmas celebrating?"

They both grinned and bobbed their heads in approval.

"I'll give you each a ten-dollar bonus. That ought to make for a good celebration."

"Ah, *si*."

"Don't get in no trouble."

"Ah, no, Senor. But we will have a grand time." Ramon beamed at his cousin, who shared his look of pleasure.

"I'll be at the Bar U if you need me."

"Give the senora our best wishes for a *grande* Christmas," Ramon said.

"I will."

He climbed on the roan, reset the gun in the holster on his hip, buttoned up his duster, gave them a wave, and ducked his head riding out in the drizzle. Besides being tired of his own cooking, he was anxious to get back to her company. Those two boys would have them a time in the small Mexican settlement. There was a cantina down there, several fiestas would be hosted, and there would be enough *putas* to solve their needs, as well as a church to attend mass. They'd come back hung over and worn out, but they'd have a good time.

He set the roan to a long trot. It would be dark before he reached the Bar U.

They came out of the cedars on horseback. Both riders wore masks. They were armed with pistols, but he didn't wait for them to shoot. He put heels to the roan and bent low. As he fumbled with his coat buttons to get to his .44 and urged the roan to go faster, a cold chill of fear swept over him. Expecting one of their wild shots to strike him at any moment, he reined the roan off into the tall cedars. At last, with the gun butt in his right hand, he reined to a halt, looking back for sight of any pursuit. Nothing.

Damn. Where in the hell had they gone? He turned the roan back. All he could hear was the rain on his hat and wind in the cedar tops. His heart still thumped hard under his breastbone and he breathed hard to get enough air. Who were they and why were they on this road? Worse, why did they want him? Were they headed for his place to get him?

He'd not recognized them or their wet horses in his haste to get away. Daylight was fading fast. Already over halfway to her place, he holstered the pistol and swung eastward. Who wanted him dead?

Grateful they'd been bad shots in the downpour, he put the Colt in the duster's side pocket and rode on. The notion of the attack still on his mind, he rode up to the house. She opened the front door and spoke to the barking dogs.

"Get in out of the rain, stranger."

"I'll put the roan up. Just wanted to be sure I was welcome."

She laughed and waved him on.

He hardly had the latigos undone before she joined him in the rain. Wrapped in a yellow slicker, she hugged and kissed him.

"Lordy, girl, you're going to get all wet."

"I'm fine. You're here."

"May catch pneumonia—" He swung the saddle and pads off and she opened the shed door for him. Once inside the room that reeked of harness oil he put his pack on the first open rack.

When he turned she tackled him, and their hungry mouths met in fury. At last they parted, out of breath, and he swept the wet curls back from her forehead in the dim light. "Damn, I sure missed you."

"Me too. You had supper?"

"No, but—"

"No buts. We'll go fix you some."

He nodded and fished the six-gun out of his side coat pocket to holster it.

"Why have it there?"

"Strange thing happened. Over on Scully Mountain,

two masked men rode out of the brush like they were going to rob me. I gouged the roan and we broke and run under their fire. Course, by the time I got my gun out they were gone and it was almost dark."

"Who were they?"

"Damned if I know, but they couldn't hit a bull in the ass."

"Well, thank God."

"I've been thanking him all the way over here."

"What can we do?"

"I guess when it lets up raining I can go back and look around." He didn't expect to find much, with the rain and all. Gun in his holster, he buttoned up his coat to go out to put the roan up and then, like two kids, hand in hand, they ran for the house.

On the porch he stopped to wash up, and she took his hat and coat inside. Drying his hand, he ducked inside. The crew sharing a huge bowl of popcorn in front of the fireplace nodded and chided him about being out in the annual drenching rain. He agreed, and decided a real rain made everyone happier.

Who were those two masked men? Robbers? Vigilantes? Troublemakers? He needed to get to the bottom of it, and soon.

Unita brought him a cup of steaming coffee and he nodded in approval. One sip and he knew it beat any he'd made at his place since Tina and Jorge left.

Rusty came over and motioned him aside. Making sure Unita was not in the room, he spoke softly. "Word's out, Crabtree ain't happy about us taking them cattle he planned to drive up there."

"When was Crabtree ever happy?"

"I wasn't worried none. Just wanted you to know—"

Rusty cut his words off when Unita returned with a huge plate of food for Ed and set it on the far end of the table.

"We'll talk more later."

Rusty agreed with a nod. "You better eat."

"I better."

He better find out all he could about Crabtree, and if there was any relationship to those masked men. "Looks like too much food for one man."

With a smile for her, he slid onto the bench.

"You look hungry."

He was hungry looking at her, but it wasn't for food.

Chapter 20

Water ran out of the ground everywhere in the bright morning sun. Dry washes belched with creeklike flows on their ride up there. He dismounted near the cedars where he first saw them and handed her the reins. Any tracks or sign were melted away. The moisture squished out of the sod at every step. It had been a great rain but it had also erased the signs of his attackers.

"Nothing?" Unita asked.

"Nothing here."

"What next?"

"Check on the boys, go by Banty to see if we can learn anything, and then back to your place."

"I'm ready." She grinned big.

He felt better when he found the boys crosscutting firewood. They'd seen nothing, but after sweeping their hats off to Unita, they promised to be on the lookout.

Ed shook his head at their gallantry and reined the roan around. They headed for Banty. After eating a cold-cut sandwich in Lorain's store, he brought Ed a letter postmarked Fort Worth. He opened and read it.

Dear Ed,

Yesterday, three men rode thru here asking about yu by name. One was a breed, I never catch his name, one was an Injun and the other a messikin called his self Roho. They sure looked like killers to me. Not the Bradys, but they was sure asking for Ed Wright. I thought yu should know.

Nell

"What is it?" Unita asked.

"It's from a waitress I met in Fort Worth when I was coming back and looking for the Bradys. I told her to send me word if they showed up." Waitress sounded respectable enough for Nell.

After she read it, she handed it back. "Who are they?"

"First that I heard about them."

"You may have a bounty on your head."

He agreed. But how would they know him? The only way was if someone over in San Antone way told them he rode a roan horse with lots of mane. Maybe he should change mounts, just to be careful. Did they work for the Bradys? Maybe time would tell.

Back at the Bar U ranch they started to get ready in earnest. They caulked the wagon box to keep out as much water as they could fording rivers. It wasn't perfect, but anything helped. Unita and Rosa helped them sew up a new canvas cover for the rig. All the bows looked good, and the hardware solid. They painted the undercarriage yellow after going over it for any cracks or separations, then gave the wagon box two coats of red paint. It looked spiffy, and then

Rusty, who was the best sign painter in the outfit, made a neat Bar U on each canvas side.

He also scripted Bar U Ranch, Banty, Texas, on both sides of the wagon. The boys found a Texas flag and a U.S. flag, one for each side of the driver's seat. And then they started asking about the cook's job. Who would Unita hire? His food had to be as good as hers and Rosa's, even if they didn't go—good food was important on a task like this one.

Shaved, bathed, and dressed up, Ed pulled the buggy around in front for the drive to the Banty Christmas Ball. He stepped down, adjusted his new hat against a gale of late-afternoon wind, and escorted Unita from the house to the buggy under the cheers of the crew.

The crew had their horses saddled to ride into town for some Saturday-night libations at the Minnie Ha Ha Saloon. No doubt some dove, or two maybe, if the boys were lucky; these females would have the busy windfall of being there for the populous and profitable preholiday trade.

Ed drove the single-footed bay horse, recalling how his earlier buggy rides had about killed him. This afternoon, with the elegant Mrs. Nance on his arm, he felt like they were riding a gliding bird. Dressed in a new blue gown the millinery in Banty had turned out for her, she looked like a bride. He had to admit the new blue silk bandanna she gave him early for Christmas looked mighty nice around his chicken neck.

Nothing could spoil this evening. Everyone, except the single ranch hands who found the saloon's attributes more tempting than the ball, would be there.

When they entered the spacious schoolhouse, the fiddle players were tuning up, along with guitars and accordions. Unita rushed her cake over to add to the long table built along the back side of the building. The raw boards were covered with white linen tablecloths, and heaped with food and sweets.

Billie came over and shook his hand. "My, my, they've done got a real crowd, huh, Sarge?"

"I don't think we've seen half of them yet."

"I guess not." Billie grinned.

"Ida Mae here?"

"Oh yes, and you're supposed to polka once with her. I get my feet all tangled up doing that dance."

"Tell her to be ready."

"Good. She said that would be the best gift I could give her."

"I won't forget." Ida Mae might not be the prettiest gal in the country but she could sure polka.

"See you," Billie said, and went on.

Unita joined him and casually held on to the crook of his arm as they spoke to various men and women from around the community. Ed had not spoken to Frank Hogan since that day in San Antone, and understood the man was mad at him for signing up some of the others. Hogan's association with Crabtree didn't endear him none in Ed's book, so he'd ignored the man. Obviously that was coming to a chilly climax as Hogan stepped over and removed his hat.

"Howdy, Mrs. Nance. Ed."

"How are you, Frank?" she asked.

"Fine, busy getting ready. I guess like you all are."

"Yes, we're very busy. Grass will be here before we know it."

Hogan nodded to her. "If Ed don't mind, I'd ask you for a dance later."

"Fine with me," Ed said, feeling the distant air of the man.

"I'll be honored," she said, and smiled.

"Good," he said, sounding relieved, and nodded, then made an awkward exit.

"Frank and you?" Ed asked softly.

"Nothing serious. He's come to call on me before. Frank's a good man. He's not my man."

Ed nodded and she gave him a threatening look in return. Then, in a low hiss, she said, "He's not your competition."

With his palms turned up, he surrendered, and she only fumed more until he laughed softly, then leaned over and lightly bumped his forehead to hers. His move broke her mood and she looked at the tin-square ceiling for help, then smiled. "Ed Wright, I swear at times you're ornery."

"I won't deny it."

Later he whirled Ida Mae around the dance floor and she beamed as the accordion player squeezed out a Bavarian polka. Round and round they went, dancing through the other couples until the song ended and they both gasped for their breath.

"My lands, Ed, you get better at it each time."

Ed thanked her, knowing that she wouldn't lack partners the rest of the night after the stand backs saw how well the woman could dance. She might not be the prettiest woman in Banty, Texas, but she was the dancingest one. A bow-legged cowboy cut her off going back to the bench, asking her to shuffle the next one with him.

"She really can dance," Unita said, impressed.

"Next one's yours."

"Polka?"

"No, waltz, I'd say. Eck's got his fiddle out."

"Good," she said and took his hand, ready to slide. The soap chips on the floor had helped and he whirled her away.

"You never married?" she asked.

"Only girl I ever asked told me I didn't belong to her church and she couldn't leave her town."

"Foolish, wasn't she?" She threw her head back as he swung her around to the music.

"Might have done me a favor."

"You must have been disappointed."

"I was—at the time."

"You ever see her again?"

He shook his head and drew her close. "She's like a dust devil that went through my life, away now and gone."

As if satisfied, she nodded, and they danced on.

Between dancing and snacking the night whirled away too. Hogan came over and took his dance with her. A little rigid in his movements, he swung her around the floor. Ed only occasionally glanced at them, busy talking cattle prices to Wamp Kaiser.

He was consuming some of Unita's layered chocolate cake when Frank brought her back and thanked him.

"You're welcome," Ed said, and looked at her as Hogan disappeared. "Well, he say anything?"

"Said he was sorry. He would have taken my cattle north and that I didn't need to get you."

"What he meant was you didn't have to put up with a drunk to get your cattle sent to market."

A frown crossed her brows. "Maybe. I wasn't impressed. I can make my own decisions."

"Maybe you should have this time?"

"Ed Wright, we better dance. I hate to argue in public."

He chuckled and took her hand with his other in the center of her back, and they went spinning away. Lots of woman inside that blue dress. Lordy, she could take his breath away just standing there. It was even more heady to him to have her in his arms and swing her around the dance floor to the music.

Long after midnight, wrapped in blankets, he drove the buggy horse toward home, with her sitting close to him in the cocoon and him occasionally stopping—so the horse could catch his breath, and he could kiss her. They were intoxicated by the time he stopped at the front yard gate.

"I'm going to put you in the house and then put him up."

"Oh," she said, and snuggled against him. "I may stay right here all night."

He looked out at the corrals and sheds in the starlight. No, his own life wasn't settled enough to take a wife. It wasn't what his brain wanted to do, it was what he felt obligated to complete; find Dave Ivy's killers. Besides, dread gnawed at his innards over rolling out for Kansas. He closed his eyes tight at the notion.

"I can wait for you," she said, sounding serious.

"Wait? You ain't waiting for much."

She clutched his vest in both hands and shook him with amazing strength. "Yes, you are—to me."

"Yes, ma'am." He grinned. "I won't argue."

"Good," she said, and climbed down. "Go sleep in your cold shed." Under the cloak of blankets, she went through the gate and he laughed.

"Darling, you really look beautiful mad."

She turned and glared at him in the pearly light. Then she smiled and melted away the cold air seeking him out. A kiss on her lips and she told him good night.

He waited till she was inside the front door, then he drove the horse to the corral. A short while later he climbed under his pile of blankets and cussed his own stubbornness, drawn in a ball, waiting for his body heat to warm the shell.

Chapter 21

Christmas came and he gave her a woolen cape the millinery had made for her. She could wear it on the early part of the drive. It would be cold many of those first days going north. She swirled around in the cape and smiled at him.

Rusty had shot a couple of wild turkeys, and the women stuffed them with sage and corn bread dressing that Ed recalled was like his mother's when he was a youth. Yams, green beans, gravy, and biscuits topped out the noon menu, and they all ate till they were about to burst. Then she gave the crew their pocketknives and Rusty a silver watch.

They all had small trinkets for her, to go on a shelf with the others. A small bear, a hand-carved mule with packs that Don Don had made for her, an elephant, some chickens, and longhorns made up the individual presents. She acted impressed by each one and they joined her "herd."

The boys chided Rusty about his timepiece, and the joke was to keep asking him what time it was. He took all that in stride, and they drifted off to town or the bunkhouse as the afternoon waned.

Ed sat in a straight-back chair with his elbows on his legs and stared at the flames licking at the logs in the fireplace.

"Penny for your thoughts," Unita said.

He straightened and stretched, making a place for her on his lap. "You'd not get much."

"I like to hear what you're thinking," she said, seated on his legs and blowing on her coffee.

"I wonder if those bushwhackers are still in the country. I'll wander over to the ranch and be sure the boys are all right. It'll take Jorge and Tina a week to make the trip back from Mexico. I better check on them boys."

"Can I go along?"

"Reckon you can behave?"

She shook her head at him in dismay.

"My paw asked me that every time I wanted to go to town with him."

"And I bet you promised to behave every time."

"I did, and every time I got into something after we got there. If nothing else I got into a fistfight and came home skinned up or with a black eye. One time I was riding a wild billygoat on a dare and got thrown into a corral and split my head open. That time I was sore on both ends when Paw got through with me."

She laughed aloud and shook her head. "Ornery doesn't even cover the subject."

He tried to dismiss it but didn't win. "We can go up there after breakfast."

"You don't sound so sure."

"I don't want them back shooters harming you is all."

"Think they're still in the country?"

"No telling." He hugged her tight and put his head to the side of hers. "I just don't want to lose you."

She looked hard at the cup, ready to sip it. "You won't."

No sign of any ambushers on the ride over to his place. He carried a Winchester on his knee and she'd stuck a double-barreled shotgun in her boot. No dogs were about when they rode in. He stuck a hand out for her to stay and slipped off the bay horse, the rifle cocked and ready. No sign of anyone. He undid the latch, then used the rifle's muzzle to open the bunk-house door. The boys' blanket rolls were gone, and maybe they hadn't come back. Unita was waving to him from the house and he looked around warily as he ran over there.

"Your boys smoke cigars?" Then she pointed to the short butts that littered the porch around the hammock.

"No. But whoever sat there must have been here for a day."

"Waiting, weren't they?"

"They might well have been."

He opened the door and frowned at the upset condition of the house. It had been ransacked, with flour all over the floor. Cabinets had been torn down. What were they looking for? Tina and Jorge lived there, and they had little money.

"What were they after?" she asked.

"Any damn thing they could find, which in this case wasn't much. I better ride to Juan's and see that the two boys are all right."

"You think they might have hurt them?"

"I don't know." He let out a great sigh. "But I never imagined they'd bother the place."

"Poor Tina," she said as they went out to the horses, "she'll have a real mess to clean up when she gets home."

He agreed with a sharp nod. Those outlaws better find a hole to hide in, 'cause he was on the prowl for them. On the way out he pulled the door shut behind himself, storming mad as he went to the bay horse.

They left at a short lope. A weak winter sun warmed the land as they rode for the small community south of his ranch. Past noon they looked down at the small bell tower crowned with a cross and the surrounding adobe jacals of San Juan. He checked his .44 and reholstered it, still seething mad about the mischief at his place. He turned and nodded to Unita as they rested their sweaty horses. The hard-breathing bay stomped around, impatient to be on his way again.

"Do you know where they will be?" she asked.

"No telling." He tightened his grasp on the horn and stiffened his arm to rock in the saddle. Hard for him to believe that those Bradys had sent assassins all the way down there to kill him. But he'd gone damn near to Kansas to look for them. Maybe they were simply outlaws out to rob him—too many things unanswered.

"Maybe—" He looked off at the brown hills in the west. Then he shook his head in surrender. There was no way he'd talk her into staying up there. "Keep an eye out and ride a few feet behind me in case I need to shoot to the side."

"Think they're here?"

"I'm too dumb to know, but they might be. I'll check the cantina."

Despite the cold, half-naked, brown-skinned children stopped playing in the dusty street and looked in silent awe at the two riding past them. Several sharp-eyed Latino women pushed aside their blanket doors to observe them. Even the cur dogs sought shelter under a *carreta* or back in a space between the adobe building to bark at them. No horses or burros at the cantina rack. He dismounted and the north wind swept up enough dust to cause him to turn his back to it.

"I'll be right out," he shouted at her and, bent over in the saddle, she nodded.

He fought the latch and the flimsy door to pull it open. The flickering candlelight was dim inside and, though he didn't expect an ambusher in there, he was ready for anything. Behind the bar a short, mustached man in an apron nodded to him.

"I am looking for my men—Ramon and Raphael."

The man shook his head. "I have not seen them, Senor."

"They didn't come here for Christmas?"

The man's slow head shake made his stomach roil. Something bad had happened to them. Nothing would keep them away—nothing but death. He stepped up to the bar and ordered a drink.

The man poured him one. "I wondered where they were when they did not come to the baile on Christmas Eve. But no one has seen them."

He put two bits on the bar and downed the liquor in one breathtaking swallow. Hell, it would take gallons to drown his losses. Then he remembered Unita outside in the rising wind. "You have any food?"

"*Sí,* some enchiladas?"

"My lady is outside. We have not eaten."

"I will have her fix you both some food. Bring her in. No one in here will offend her."

He nodded and set the glass on the bar. Pulling his hat brim down, he went outside and forced his way to where she huddled on Star. "Get down and come inside. He's got food and we can get out of this wind."

Off the horse, with one hand to keep on her cowboy hat, she turned to him. "Have they seen the boys?"

Ed shook his head and herded her to the door.

"Where are they?" A shocked look on her face, she backed into the cantina, waiting for his answer.

"I'm not certain. I think something bad has happened to them."

"Oh, no. But who?"

"I have to think those bushwhackers rode to my place after trying to get me and—" He shook his head. The knot in his throat was too large to swallow.

"But we never saw any sign . . ."

"It was up there, but we weren't looking, I'm certain. Of course, it's as old as those butts." He showed her to a table and an older woman brought them two plates.

"I have only some red wine," the little woman apologized to Unita.

"That would be fine," she said to the woman.

He agreed, and told her to bring a jug and two glasses. One thing for certain, he didn't need any more hard stuff. Not that he wouldn't like to stick his head in a trough of it and drink enough to forget it all, especially what lay ahead for him. Only hell itself could have kept those two boys from coming down there for the celebration.

"Maybe they went to Mexico?" she said under her breath, with her fork idle in her right hand.

He shook his head, chewing on a spicy mouthful. "They'd never do that. Something's happened to them."

"When will Jorge be back?"

"In a few days. He's using a team and wagon, but even if he started today, it would be three days getting back up here."

"Will we go back this afternoon?" she asked.

"Yes, so we can get a good start in the morning—" He shook his head and considered her. "You may need to get back?"

"They'll be fine at the ranch. I can help you."

He accepted her concession and looked at his food, the red sauce running on the plate from the white cheese-coated tortillas. If only he hadn't left them, but there was nothing he could do about that this late. He used the side of his fork to cut off a bite.

What had those unholy bastards done to those two? He'd damn sure get them.

"Maybe something—"

"Not something. Someone!" he said, sharper than he intended to her. Then he put down his fork and reached over to grasp her wrist. "I am so sorry you have to be mixed in my trouble. That's all I am anymore, is trouble to all and everyone I touch."

"I have a stake in you. It's lot bigger than a cattle drive, bigger than some ruthless killers, Ed Wright. You aren't any more trouble than any other man caught between some vicious men who want to kill you."

"I don't want you hurt."

"I don't want you hurt, but stop taking the blame on yourself."

"Excuse me, Senor?"

Ed looked up into the face of an older Mexican man. He had a snowy mustache and his great sombrero was held in front of him as he nodded politely to her.

"I am Ignacious Vargas. I am the uncle of Ramon and Raphael."

"Yes, I have met you before, up at the ranch."

"The bartender, Carlos, says that you ask about them."

"Yes. They weren't at the ranch this morning and I rode down here to check on them."

"We have been worried. They were supposed to come to my casa for Christmas, as well."

"I am sorry. Have there been any strangers here this past week?"

Vargas turned and asked Carlos.

"Only the three men who were here for two days," Carlos said. "I will get Maria and she can tell you. They were pistoleros."

Ed exchanged a questioning look with Unita and he nodded. Was it the three men that Nell wrote him about?

They finished their food and he thanked the older woman. He was savoring his red wine when the bartender returned leading a short girl in her teens with stringy hair and obviously hung over. Wrapped in a green blanket he had little doubt she didn't wear anything underneath it.

"Carlos said you asked about those pistoleros that were here." Her voice was a husky, smoky rasp as she retightened the cover around her and made a sign to recognize Unita's presence.

"Yes, what do you know about them?"

"The one called Roho was the boss. He was big man and not nice—" She glanced at Unita as if to see if it was all right to continue, then went on. "The kind who likes to hurt *putas*."

"Big man with a mustache?"

"*Sí*, Senor. The other one was a breed named Hatchet. He was, how you say, shifty-eyed?"

"Yes, and the third one?"

"They called him Warlock. He never came inside. They said he was an Apache, but he was no Apache. I knew some in Mexico. He was, maybe, Comanche." She risked one hand holding the cover closed and swept the greasy hair back from her face.

"He never came inside?" Ed asked.

She wrinkled her nose. "Some Indios are like that. They don't like to be in a white man's casa as if it would have some power over them."

"You didn't do any business with him?"

Her head back she laughed aloud, as if amused at his words. "Not inside."

He put a dollar on the table and thanked her. "When did they leave?"

She picked up the coin, stepped back, and clutched it in her small fingers. "A few days before Christmas, and they asked about you, Senor."

"Oh, what did they ask?"

"If you were good with a gun."

"What did you tell them?"

She smiled. "I told them you used to be a ranger and would shoot them dead if they crossed your path."

"That scare them?"

"Roho said he cut his teeth killing rangers, but I could tell it made him uneasy."

"They said they wanted him?" Unita asked, indicating Ed.

Maria shrugged. "They never say. Just ask about him."

"Like what?" Unita asked.

"Would he ride down there and see me."

"Oh?"

"I said I wish he would and kill them, because half the time they wouldn't pay me. They made me mad."

"Thank you, Maria. I'd of been mad too."

The two shared a nod and Maria left the room, sweeping the tail of her blanket on the floor in her exit.

"They were the men in Fort Worth, that the waitress saw," Unita said.

Ed nodded and rubbed his palms on his pants. Time to move on—Unita would sure get an education traipsing after him. At least he was not guilty of any past indiscretions with Maria.

Vargas asked to go with them out of his concern over the boys. Ed agreed and the man joined them on a red saddle mule. Headed into the wind twenty minutes later, the animals hated heading into the billowing dust and sharp sand striking them head-on He and Unita wore bandannas for masks, and the old man tucked his head, using his big sombrero for a shield.

The ride took much longer than Ed planned, and it was dark when they reached the ranch. With sundown, the wind abated some, but he was not willing to simply ride in. The three killers might have come back. He told Unita and the old man to wait in the cedars, and when they saw a light in the main house to come on.

They agreed and he circled, coming in checking the corral for horses first, or any sign. After hitching the bay, six-gun in hand, he made his way to the bunk-house. Inside the dark interior he found nothing. Then he made his way to the main house where Jorge lived, the headquarters for the place when he bought it several years before. But again he found nothing but a ransacked house. Lighting a lamp he put it in the window and went back to put up the bay. On the way he found Jorge's stock dog's body, his throat cut and dead for some time. He'd missed it the first time they were there—he'd never checked the area behind the corral. He'd been so upset about the condition of Tina's house.

He led the bay around and unsaddled him as they rode in.

"Find anything?" she asked.

"Jorge's dog. They killed it."

She slipped off the horse and shook her head in the starlight. "I'm sorry."

"I am too, but I'm more concerned by the hour about the boys."

"I'll go see what I can find for supper," she said. "There's no sign of them?"

"Nothing I found. You all right?" Ed asked the old man, still sitting on his mule.

"*Sí*, but I have a feeling of death here. I must apologize, Senora, but it is very strong."

"I agree," Ed said, and began to unsaddle Star for her. There was something different there. Maybe the old man sensed it better than he did.

"I'll fix some food," Unita said, and hurried off toward the lighted door.

At the house, Ed built a fire in the hearth and it soon drove the chill of night away. Vargas held out his gnarled hands to warm them.

"This is a fine ranch. It has water and plenty of grass."

"I thought so too. When Mr. Fairway offered to sell it, I bought it quick like." Ed turned to Unita, busy in the other end. "Can we help you?"

"I have some biscuits in the oven and think I have enough fire in the stove to bake them. I'll make some flour gravy, and that's about all I can find."

"We can eat that," Ed said, looking at the old man.

"Ah, *sí*, that would be good."

"I'll find us some eggs in the morning. If those hens are still laying."

"Doubtful this late in the year," she said. "I'll cook down some cornmeal and make fried mush for breakfast."

After supper, they made pallets on the floor in front of the fireplace. Ed didn't sleep well and the wind had returned during the night, howling at the building corners. He slipped out of his blankets, built up the fire, and then pulled on his boots, coat, and hat.

Outside, in the gray light, he struck out on foot for

the canyon. Something told him to check the bridge. No notion why—but all night it was in his thoughts. Sheltered some from the blasts, he followed the old wagon tracks made hauling in the lumber. The predawn was shaded by clouds, but the illumination grew brighter as he strode through the cedars, and at last he moved around them to where he could see the span.

The sight of the two bodies hanging under it stabbed him in the heart. No doubt, even at this distance—they were the corpses of the boys. He began to run. Words slipped from his lips. Words of protest. Words of hate. Even God, who he felt had forsaken him.

On his slick leather soles he ran harder, then he dropped to his knees on the pitchy-smelling flooring, jammed his fist in his eyes, and began crying. Those two innocent boys didn't need to die. It was all his fault.

It was Unita's hand on his shoulder that brought him to awareness. "Vargas has ridden for the sheriff."

He clutched her and buried his face against her breasts. Her arms encircled him and brought the first solace he'd found in an hour or more.

"These men have no value for human life."

"I know," she said. "I know."

As on the two days before, he was drunk in preparation for their funeral. Unita came over to his place early that morning, made him bathe, and shaved him. Also laid out were his best clothes, all pressed and clean for him to wear. Jorge and Tina were back, and they loaded the children up in the wagon. Jorge came to the bunkhouse and offered him a ride, but Unita said she'd take him.

"You able to walk out to the buggy?" she asked him.

"Hell, yes."

"Good, then fall down and get your nice clothes all dirty."

"All right, steady me then." He took another swig from the neck of the bottle and set it back down beside the chair he sat in.

Busy brushing out her hair, she finished and nodded to him. "Ready?"

"Damn right."

With a wary head shake, she came over to help him up. With her for a guide, and after two tries, he and the bottle made it up into the buggy.

"You could have left me here," he said to her.

"I could have done lots of things in my life. But I didn't." She clucked to the horse.

The bodies, already decomposed, were in the ground, but the priest in San Juan was holding a funeral mass so that all their relatives from as far away as Mexico who could come to the little church had a chance to be there. Outside the chapel an array of wagons, *carreta*, burros, and horses were hitched in the warming sun.

From his seat in the buggy, Ed looked hard at the tall, ornate, carved doors, nodded to Unita, and lowered himself to the ground. The bells tolled loudly and many people were going inside. Women with their heads wrapped and carrying babies slipped in. Men in their Sunday best suits nodded to him.

In the sanctuary, a young boy showed them to the front row. He sat on the bench as the priest's monotone in Latin began, the audience answering in Span-

ish. It was like his body was there and his mind in the
log rafters high overhead. He looked down on the
dedicated. The mother silencing a baby as the priest
prepared the way for the two boys to walk into
heaven. It was all miles away from him.

The straight-backed woman in the black dress beside him—why did she continue to mother him? She
ought to have had her fill by now. Why didn't she marry
Frank Hogan, even if he was a little stiff on the dance
floor. Just so she left him alone. Those boys were dead
as sure as if he'd pushed them off the bridge to strangle on the end of the hemp rope.

And the note pinned on Ramon. *If U follow us, we
will do this to U.*

Goddamn them!

He felt her hand squeeze his. Had he sworn out
loud? No, but he felt like it.

Chapter 22

Late February came, and the brave yellow jonquils bloomed in the last gasps of winter winds. Cheat and wild oat blades waved inches tall. Ed was sleeping off another drunk when he heard a wagon pull up. He could hear the mules outside in the yard breathing hard and snorting, and the familiar jingle of harness. Sitting up, he mopped his face in his hands. What the hell was it doing at his place?

Rusty soon blocked the door, and the blinding spears of sunlight that came around him forced Ed to shut his gritty eyes.

"The boss said for us to load your things and you in the chuck wagon."

"What if I don't want to go?"

"Then our orders are to hog-tie you."

"She think—"

"Ed, I don't really know what the lady thinks. But I do know orders, and they were to get you and all your gear on that wagon out there."

"I ain't ready—my steers . . ."

"They're already road branded and in the herd. Jorge and his new crew already did all that."

Ed blinked his eyes. Had he been that drunk? Probably.

"I'll need my saddle—"

"The boys are getting it. You want anything else?"

"Blankets—hell—I don't know."

He managed to tell Jorge, Tina, and the two children good-bye. And he left on the seat with a grizzly old man who called himself . . . Cuddle, but Ed discovered later that his name was Caudle. After a few miles of the old man's squeaky, toothless voice, Ed decided he must be Unita's cook.

Things were happening too fast for his numb mind. Hell with it. He had two bottles of good whiskey left. The next thing he knew, after just about being pitched off the seat a dozen times by Caudle's erratic driving, they were at the herd.

It was the Comanche captive boy he saw first. He'd forgotten all about Blondie. Unita had put him to work cleaning up around her place, cutting stove wood, etc. Blondie was working hard at slowly turning a beef quarter on a spit where the big iron kettle hung over the fire. He looked up and nodded to Ed.

"Goddamn Injun," Caudle said, and spit tobacco off the side. "He ain't white. Sumbitch is still Injun. Don't talk no English. Hell, he even stinks like one when you get downwind of him."

Ed wasn't sure that the old man wasn't smelling himself, and lowered himself off the wagon feeling stiff as a board.

"You ain't burned it, has you?" Caudle demanded in Spanish.

Blondie shook his head.

"Good to see you," Billie said, riding up on a small

Spanish pony with a dish face. "Heard you'd been under the weather. Lots of folks saying you'd never make this trip. Me and Ida Mae, we knowed you'd get off your deathbed to go."

"Good to see you too," Ed said, and went to where several hands were gathered, repairing girths and saddles around another fire. There was still a chill in the air and, while he dreaded any conversations, he wanted to warm up.

The big string bean of a swing rider Ich Strang came over and squatted down beside him. "Thanks. When Mrs. Nance's foreman came for me he brought the money. Hiedie'll be fine till I get home."

"Unita Nance is straight." The winey smoke from the fire was burning Ed's eyes until the wind switched enough to move it aside.

"I've seen that. Good looker, too." He cut a sly, knowing grin at Ed.

He ignored it. "How's Shorty?"

"He's here. I went down there with Rusty and they let us have him. He's so damn glad to be out of jail, he'll be fine for a while."

"For a while?"

"Shorty's got bad about appropriating stuff ain't his. I'll watch him close so he don't piss any of the boys off."

"Maybe we should have left him?" Ed absently tossed some grass he'd pulled up on the red coals and watched it melt in the flames. Maybe they really should have?

"Naw. Hell, I'd get my worst enemy out of there. That jail business ain't no joke."

"Who else she got? We ain't talked much lately."

"Pretty good bunch. Several green kids, but they can ride. She's got lots of sound horses and that wagon is a dandy, all painted up." Ich smiled and then rubbed his mouth with his palm. "I'm ready to ride."

Ed nodded. He wished he was half that anxious to be under way.

He heard the rowels of Unita's spurs, and both of them stood and removed their hats.

"There won't be time for hat removal on this drive. So we'll start skipping all that." She was using her teeth to pull off a kidskin glove. "I need to talk to Ed for few minutes. If you'll excuse us, Ich?"

"Ma'am," Ich said, putting back on his weather-beaten felt hat. "I'm dang sure he'd rather talk to you than palaver with me."

Ed wasn't that certain.

She smiled and agreed, waiting for Ich to get beyond earshot. "You met Caudle."

He nodded.

"You have an idea for a boss?"

"This is your show."

Despite her iron will, she looked a little uneasy with the notion of that role. "We'll need a scout, right?"

"It's best."

"Who did you use?"

"Several. Jim O'Donald."

"Where's he at?"

"Last I heard, up around Mason."

"Too far and too late. Caudle says he's been up there several times, and knows all the crossings and where to bed down."

"It would help if you had a scout. Someone to ride out ahead and see about things."

"Can you do it?" She looked hard at him.

He dropped his gaze to his scuffed boot toes. "I ain't worth much these days."

"I didn't ask for your self-centered, pity-crowded opinion. I asked if you could scout."

He rubbed his hands on the front of his pants and nodded. "I can. Let that Comanche Blondie wrangle your horses and find that old cook another hand."

"Why?"

" 'Cause he knows horses better than any white man."

"He is white."

Ed looked off at the trees on the hills in their fresh green coat of leaves. "No, he ain't, but we won't argue."

"All right, he's going to be the horse wrangler. Rusty's going to help Jorge if he needs him while we're gone."

"Thanks. He's got two new boys but he'll need some help."

"They have your bell steer here, too."

Ed smiled at the notion of the brockle-faced long-horn. "Sam Houston's a dandy. He's more help than ten hands."

"I know. I heard all about him. What else do I need to do?"

"Get up early and move them north ten miles. The boys will need to swap horses at noontime the first few days. These cattle will be hell getting to the Trinity River before they're broke to drive."

"That's Fort Worth?" She looked shocked.

He nodded. "That's a month away. Keep several

horses saddled on picket line at night. They'll stampede easy."

"I see they fight all the time."

"Settling who's boss in this new herd. That's another reason they'll stampede. They've got to get a pecking order from top to bottom, and until it's straight they'll fight and butt heads."

"And there isn't a cow in the herd and they ride each other like crazy."

"Nothing to do with breeding. That's how they subjugate the competitor in the pecking order."

She closed her eyes. "Guess I'm getting an education after all these years. No one ever had an explanation for those things that they wanted to share with a woman. It was just, drive them."

"I don't know it all, but I've been gathering things since I went north the first year."

"Obviously. You all right?" She looked at him hard.

"Nothing—nothing some of Rosa's goat milk might not clear up."

She winked. "I'll have some by night. Oh, all the consigners will be here for the evening meal as a send-off."

"I'll be there."

"The roan's here for you."

"Good. I've got where I really like him."

"Consider him yours."

He laughed. "No, I'd rather have the excuse of borrowing him."

"Suit yourself. I need to go find a cook's helper. You're sure Blondie needs to be the horse wrangler?" She narrowed her left eye at him.

"Yes, he talks their language, and besides, he might scalp your cook."

She smiled and left, shaking her head.

He watched her striding away in her leather chaps and gallowses crossing her back. The cowboy hat crowned her head—even in man's getup she made a helluva woman. Might even be a first. A woman heading up a cattle drive—if any female could do it, Unita Nance might just be the one.

He needed a damn drink.

Morning came too soon when someone came and shook him. His head hurt and his belly felt on fire as he crawled out of his roll. Sitting on his bedroll to pull on his boots, he shivered as the body heat from the blankets fled his upper torso in the predawn chill.

About to get up, he blinked at the squatted hatless man in front of him. His words, even in Spanish, were garbled about thanks and the horses. His face gleamed with pride, even in the starlight.

"Don't let me regret it," Ed said in a gruff voice.

Blondie smiled and was gone.

She rode by and handed him a mason jar when he started for the horse pen. "More from Rosa." Then she went on before he could thank her.

No telling how long she'd been up. He could hear the hands calling out horses' names to Ich and Shorty, obviously handling the horse-catching job in the rope pen. Some they had to give the two men the color or point a gelding out, since both men were new to the remuda. In a few mornings it would be old hat.

"Roan," he said to Ich when he reached the corral.

"It's the one with all the mane," Ich said to Shorty

as both men worked in the dark, save for the light of a lantern or two the boys held up.

The roan caught he led him down to the wagon, keeping him on the far side so he didn't rile the cook on the first day. He drank his jar of goat milk, put the jar up, and found his saddle, blankets, and bridle. With the roan ready to go and hitched on the picket line, Ed went to breakfast, especially for the coffee. The milk settled his stomach some and he felt ready to ride.

"We camping at Eastman's tonight?" Caudle, in his apron, asked, going by him on his way to get something.

"Fine with me," Ed said.

No need in him riding all over hell. Caudle knew so much, he'd kick back and help the boys hold them in on the first day.

It was noon, when the boys swapped for fresh horses, that Unita stopped him. "Don't you need to scout?"

"Caudle's doing it today."

"Caudle's kinda bossy. But he ain't the scout yet." She flipped the curls back from her face.

"Boys need all the help they can get today. I'll be fine. The old man has him a spot picked out up there and the water is easy. Tell Ich and Shorty to feed them in from the east and they'll be fine."

She nodded that she'd heard him. "I also watched your Comanche taking the horses out. He is good with them."

"Too good to wrangle wood and water."

"Strange acting." She looked at him for help.

"No, he's a Comanche and just looks like a white man."

"I see it now. You were right about this first day. Half these cattle want to go home."

"Be glad your boys are fresh. When the cattle get worn down they'll be close to dead."

"I can see that now. What else should I be doing?"

He shook his head. "Have Ich tie up the clapper on Sam when they get to the bed grounds each night, and turn the bell loose to head them out before a storm gets here. They're better on the road in one bunch than trying to hold them."

"What if there's a river ahead?"

"Best to get them across it beforehand or, if you can't, you have them swing boys take them in big circles. They know how."

"When will these boys buck up on me?"

He sighed. "I only had one bunch do that to me and it was up in Kansas. We'd been in lots of storms, no sleep, and I was pushing them hard to get across rivers before they flooded and we couldn't. Two boys drowned in a mill."

"A mill? What's that?"

"That's when cattle get in midstream of a river and go to circling instead of swimming for the shore. It'll lose bunches of cattle, and even hands trying to break them up."

She blinked hard at him. "How do you prevent it?"

"Pray."

"Pray?"

"Yes, and hope he hears you."

Blondie rode by them. "I go now."

"*Sí*, you can find Caudle?" she asked.

He grinned. "Oh, *sí*, Senora."

With a wave she sent him on. The hands were re-mounted on fresh ponies and the cattle moving again.

"When can I graze them more?" she asked.

"Beyond the Red River when they're trail broke."

"Good. Why aren't you doing this?" she asked, ready to mount up.

"I'm the pilot, remember?"

"I remember lots of things." She reined her horse around and sent him off in a short lope.

He mounted the roan and skirted the herd, waved to Ich, and headed north. He needed some whiskey to drink. There might be some at Alan's Spring, a small place north of the drive.

He reached the town in midafternoon. A couple of saloons, a store, a harness shop, and a blacksmith all clustered along a creek. A few ranchers were in town. Their rigs sat about and a couple of hipshot horses were at the rack. He dismounted at the Gray Bull Saloon, hitched the roan, stretched his stiff back, and then pushed his way in the batwing doors.

"Howdy, mister. What can I do for you?"

"Pour me some whiskey."

"You can pour your own." The bartender, a tall, thin man looked at the bottle to mentally mark the amount in it. He slapped down a glass and the quart. Then he reset the red garters on his white shirtsleeves. "What else?"

"Need some pints to get me to Fort Worth."

"Four enough?"

"No, but that's all I can put in my saddlebags."

The man nodded like he understood him. "Gets tougher to get north of here, don't it?"

Ed sampled his whiskey and let it run down his throat. Sure cut the trail dust—good stuff. "There's a sign 'cross that Red River says 'This here is Injun Territory anyone in possession of alcoholic products beyond this point will be fined and/or imprisoned for violating the federal laws. Judge Isaac Parker, Federal Judge for the territories, Fort Smith, Arkansas.' "

"Must be a long, dry drive across that country."

Ed shook his head. "There's more folks make and sell it up there than down here. You can find someone selling it everywhere up there."

The man laughed. "Why in the hell is there a sign like that?"

" 'Cause his deputies arrest folks every day up there for making it."

"You headed up there?"

Ed nodded and downed his whiskey, then looked at the four pints the man had set on the counter. "How much do I owe you?"

"Five bucks will cover it."

Ed paid him and gathered his purchase.

"Have a good trip, mister."

"I will, if I can find some more on the way." They both laughed.

He short loped the roan back west. Pausing before crossing a creek, he reached down and undid his saddlebag flap. A pint out, he broke the seal and pulled the cork to take a good jolt, then recorked, slipped the bottle in his boot top, pulled his pants back down, and grinned—he'd start boot legging right there.

He saw the horse herd first, spread out grazing, and Blondie's paint, hobbled near a blanket on the ground that no doubt covered his rider's form as he was catching some shut-eye. Ed rode wide of them into camp, where Caudle and his helper, a boy of about sixteen named Jocko, were busy building a fire and setting the chuck wagon up. Caudle looked in his direction and then he spit to the side. "Suit you?"

"Fine. Where you parking tomorrow?" Ed asked.

"Across Red Water Creek at the old pueblo."

"Should work," Ed said in approval. "I'll tell the boss lady. She's after me to earn my pay as a scout."

"Well, Lordy, I been up this way so many damn times, I can read it like the back of my hand."

"Fine," Ed said. As long as it suited him they'd use cookie's places.

He unsaddled the roan and turned him out to roll and then join the rest. He went over and tried cookie's small pot of coffee. It was done enough, and he stayed back from the two of them. The whole time Caudle was ordering the boy around and chewing on him about something. Blondie owed him a big premium for getting to be out there with the remuda.

The herd moved in and the riders watered them west of camp. After that they pushed them across the shallow creek to eat their fill. The riders returned to camp, and most got out their bedrolls and flung them open on the ground to nap. There was plenty of groaning and moaning about "those damn steers." Typical first-day whining he'd heard at the end of the day on every drive.

"You boys should have been with me the first time."

"When was that?" a young one asked.

"All the cattle we drove north that time were mav-
ericks and had never seen a man before we caught
them and went north."

"Was they steers?" one kid asked.

"Yeah, after surgery."

"Whew, they must have been wild."

"They stampeded every night and we spent days
looking for them."

"How did it go? I mean, when you got up there?"

"They were real fat 'cause we took twice as long as
the rest to get there, and they sold for a high price."

The hands all laughed.

"How many head?"

"Eight hundred, but counting the cook there were
only six of us."

"Five hands?"

"Right, so there wasn't any sleep. I'd better go talk
to the boss," he said to them and they all grinned.

"How did you get your job?" one named Jersey
asked.

Ed stopped and turned back. "I made one too many
trips up there."

They laughed, and he went over to talk to Unita at
the chuck wagon.

She gave a head toss and they walked to the edge
of Caudle's ring for privacy. "How did you think it
went?"

"Fine for me."

"No." She frowned to make her point.

He shrugged with his hands slid in his back pockets.
"One down and probably ninety more to go."

"Oh, heavens."

"They get to be a habit finally."

"Good. Red Water Creek, huh?"

He nodded. Obviously cookie had told her about it. "I talked to Caudle about it."

"He said so. But I hired him to cook—"

"When I think it's wrong I'll tell you and him. He's a good cook so far, and sent the boys out with extra grub in their pockets this morning. He's got cinnamon rolls coming up for a treat here in the afternoon. I'm fine with him."

"I'm counting on you to tell me what I'm doing wrong."

"Go help him dish out those rolls and talk to them boys. It will make their day."

Her cheeks reddened and she looked undecided. "All right, boss. Where're you going?"

"Talk to Blondie a little about them horses. He may know which ones would be best for night herding now he's been around 'em."

"You sure place lots of faith in him."

He shook his head. "He knows horses, trust me. Go serve buns."

"Want one?"

"Naw, it might ruin my supper."

She shook her head and went to help. He walked through the new grass for the ridge and the pinto raised up and stared at him. A small bell he wore barely tinkled over the growing wind. Smart deal; Blondie had that horse there as a sentry, and when he raised up the bell rang and woke him. Horses were better sentries than a dog and they didn't bark.

The former captive sat up on his blanket and hugged his knees when Ed reached him.

"You sleep?" Ed asked, and squatted down nearby

so he wouldn't stare at him and make him feel self-conscious.

"Some," Blondie said in Spanish.

"Well, how do you like the white man's world?"

"Different. Comanches only hunt. Women do the rest."

"You remember being with your own people."

"I can see the place."

"Know where it is?"

"No, but I will know it when I see it again."

"Your parents dead?"

When Blondie didn't answer, Ed twisted to look at him and Blondie turned up his palms as if he had no words.

"You can pick the night horses. Ones that see better at night. Won't step on a steer in the dark."

"*Sí.*"

"Help them night herders. They ain't Comanche."

"I will. I like it better with the ponies. That old man talks too much. He is like an old woman."

"I savvy that." Ed seated himself and drew out the pint. He never offered Blondie any, but took small pulls on it and replaced the cork.

Nothing bothered Ed by the time Caudle rang the triangle for supper. He put the empty pint back in his boot. Broken glass could cripple a horse. He'd find a place to stash it later. The sun was getting low and four of the boys were bedding the steers down on the big flat. They were full of water and grass. That fill would put them to chewing their cuds and then to sleep. He hoped so anyway. Maybe there would be no stampedes.

When Ed reached the camp, he spoke to Ich. "Tell these boys the rules about spooking cattle at night."

"Listen up, no shooting, no loud screaming, no clanging iron, and don't ride into a sleeping critter. It'll be dark out there, but keep your mind on it. Every man draws a two-hour shift. I'll show you the Big Dipper. If it gets cloudy, we can use Caudle's alarm clock.

"Someone hollers stampede, you get out of bed and catch a horse. We'll have some on the picket line. Try to turn them in a circle when you get to the head of the herd. You may have to ram your horse's shoulder into the leader's." Ich looked around at the crew. They all nodded.

"Everyone savvy that? Good, lets eat."

Caudle had cooked a large haunch of beef and sliced it thin. Plus brown beans, green beans, sour-dough biscuits, and he still had some butter left from the night before. Ed took his plateful and went to sit aside.

Unita soon joined him and sat cross-legged on the ground beside him. "Will they stampede tonight?"

He shook his head.

They crossed the Colorado and headed for the Brazos. Rain caught them, and some wind for two days, but no bad storms. Ed held his molars close, thinking they'd get pyrotechnics out of the rain that blew in, but aside from everything they owned being wet through and through, the weather finally moved on.

He replenished his pints from an old man and even found a Mexican woman with goats who sold him a quart for two bits. From the smile on her face, she was looking for more cowboys to drop by and buy her milk. He rode off thinking that Rosa's product didn't have such a hot, animal flavor, but he drank it down anyway. It helped his belly and he caught up with Caudle at midafternoon in camp.

"Where next?" he asked the cook, hitching the roan to a front wheel where the Texas flag would flutter in his face while the gelding ate corn from a nose bag. The remuda didn't get feed. The cowboys only used them one day a week, so they were well rested. He rode the roan every day.

"I don't think this weather will hold," Ed said, looking at the azure-blue sky. "I'd like to be on the far side of the Brazos tomorrow night."

"No way. Why, we can't cross the Brazos tomorrow," Caudle said, and spit sideways. "Must be better'n twenty miles."

"Close to that I figure. But if it rains again we'd be better off on the north bank."

"What're you looking at?"

"Hot as it is today, I figure there's a dandy brewing out there, not too far away."

Caudle spat aside and wiped his whiskered mouth on the back of his hand. "They could boil up any time. We know that this time of year."

"It's that time of year. If I was in charge I'd push them and have it behind me."

Caudle nodded. "You'll end up crossing in the dark and lose a bunch."

"No, before I'd do that I'd bed 'em on the south side and let the cowboys cross over to eat."

"Going to storm someday, but I think you're nuts, pushing 'em that hard."

"Well, Caudle, that's my take," Ed said, took off the nose bag, and remounted his horse.

When Ed caught up with Unita and the noisy, bawling herd, he realized he had never missed that drone of cattle voices, hooves pounding the ground, and horns knocking. She rode aside and looked tired when she reined up.

"What's it look like up ahead?" she asked.

"Same old, but I want to talk to Shorty and Ich tonight. I think we need to push them across the Brazos tomorrow."

"Why?" She looked up at him after mopping her face with her kerchief.

"Weather's been good so far. But it'll break one of these days, and if we get across another river, it's one less to swim in a flood."

"Can we do it?"

"We'd have to push them, but I think we can and if I was the boss that's the way I'd do it."

"Fine, what does the other guide think?" She smiled at him.

"I'm crazy."

"So?"

"There's a couple of creeks east of here. Why don't we slip off and you take a bath in one. I'll be the lookout."

She blinked at him, twisted, and looked around at the dust and cattle. "Guess they will be all right for that long."

"Trust me, they will."

She waved to one of the riders, making a sign that they were going over the hill, and he nodded. They set out in a short lope through the grass, pear, and mesquite. The creek was clear and looked inviting. When she dismounted, he tossed her a bar of soap and a towel from his bags. Then he bent over to catch her horse's rein and lead him off.

"We'll be up on the hill. When you get done, call me."

"Thanks," she said, and he rode off.

Seated on his butt while the ponies grazed through their bits, he wondered if his idea to push hard the next day was smart or only his desire to take charge from cookie. Still, his gut feelings said, *"Get across the Brazos."* He seldom went against his gut and when he did, he ended up regretting not listening. A good slug of whiskey might help settle him at the moment, but he decided to let his molars float in anticipation for one still later.

Unita called and he pinched off some blades of grass to toss into the wind before he got up. "I'm coming."

He brought her horse down to her. She did look refreshed and that made him feel better. In a vault she was in the saddle and they headed back. Hat on the back of her head, she brushed her hair as she rode beside him

"That was wonderful. Thanks."

"A little getting away once in a while helps."

"Yes, I'd forgotten what a meadowlark sounded like with all those cattle sounds in my ears all day."

He looked off across the greening country. The wild plum thickets were through blooming and the blue bells were about to start. Lots of the country they crossed would soon be a sea of blue flowers, along with the Indian paintbrush colors of white, pink, and yellow being whipped on their fragile stems in a growing afternoon wind.

"So we push for the Brazos in the morning?"

"Yes, ma'am."

"I've not said anything so far, but I know how hard this is on you. I mean, going back over this same ground." She rode in close, stood in the stirrups, leaned over, and kissed him.

He chuckled, and she sat down in the saddle and frowned at him. "What's so funny?"

"Aw, Lordy, that must have been like kissing a cross between a boar hog and a prickly pear cactus."

"That's my choice, said the old lady after she kissed the cow."

"I can't beat that. I worry lots about you. This is a tough game. These are days I regret forcing you to be the trail boss."

"Why? I'm fine. Why, I'll be singing after that bath for two days, anyhow."

He glanced over and appraised her. "I believe you will."

Chapter 23

The push was on before the sun even thought about shining on them. Cattle on the move and the swing riders on each side compressed the line of march. This put them in a natural, fast-swinging gait that longhorns must have crossed the north African desert with when the Moors brought them over to Spain. During the war, Ed had read a book about the Moors and their Spanish conquest and occupation—along with their Barb horses and long-horned cattle, they brought their buildings to Spain, and it all fell into the new world when the king claimed Mexico and the southwest.

There was no need to scout—they needed all hands. A cowboy's girth broke and sent him sprawling. Ed saw it happen and rode down his horse, coming back to see an embarrassed youth named Hurley carrying his pack in both hands and cussing.

"Give me the saddle," Ed said. "I can run down the chuck wagon and get a new girth. You can ride bareback till I get back."

The freckle-faced boy of perhaps seventeen blinked his dust-coated eyelashes and grinned. "Damn, thanks."

"No problem."

A cowboy on the right side flagged Ed down and waved a girth that he'd pulled from his saddlebags. Ed shook his head in relief, grateful he wouldn't have to catch Caudle.

"I seen you carrying that and figured someone's girth had busted," J. T., another youth in the bunch, said.

"Thanks. I'll see you get paid for it." Ed turned the roan back and found Hurley.

"Damn, that was a fast trip," Hurley said over the herd's noise.

"J. T. had one."

"Well, bless his pea-picking heart."

"I thought the same. If you ain't got the money to pay him for it, I'll give it to you."

"Naw, I can pay him. I was fixing to buy a new one in Fort Worth anyway."

They dismounted and tossed the saddle on Hurley's dun horse. In minutes they had the latigos in place and the bellyband cinched up. Hurley stepped aboard, waved to him, and rode off to bring in a steer that had broken off from the bunch.

Pushing hard was that—hard work. The pokey cattle grew even more so, and Ed put up his bandanna and helped the drag riders prod them along. Noon came and went. Then the word came down the line that they were close to the river.

Ed set his spurs to the roan and could see that the swing riders had eased off making the cattle loop to the east for delivery to the water. Experienced hands in the right places made lots of difference and he knew those two were the best. He managed to cross in front of Sam Houston and rode the last mile at a hard run, pulling the horse down when he could see the river.

It wasn't flooding and looked fairly manageable to cross. Caudle had gone to the ferry downstream, but he should be making his way to the point on the far bank where the cattle crossed. A herd had crossed that day. Probably in the morning, from the looks of the cow pies.

Watering the cattle took over an hour. Then came swinging them out and heading them back. He told the two hands preparing to swim across to be on the other side not to let the cattle reaching the far side ever stall on the bank. "They stall, we'll have a backlog in the river. Do what you have to do but keep them moving."

"Yes, sir."

"Use your pistols to shoot in the air if you have to, but keep them moving."

Both grim-faced boys agreed that they understood, and set out to swim the river.

"I think Sam Houston will head right across," Ich said, and Shorty agreed.

Ed smiled, checking the sun time—close to five o'clock and the cattle looked weary. Many had laid down. "It'll be up to him to get us across."

"I'm glad you sent Unita with the wagon. Them boys can cross in their underwear that way," Ich said.

"She'd not complain about that."

"No, but it would sure make them uneasy," Shorty said.

They laughed and Ed nodded to them. "Let's cross over."

"We're ready." Ich stood in the stirrup and shouted, waving his large hat high over his head. "Head 'em up! Move 'em out!"

From a high place on the bank, Ed watched the lead steer take to the water and the swing pair press the string on his tail into the river. Then one black steer spooked and turned around. Tail over his back, he headed against the tide. But Shorty drove his pony at him while waving a lariat coil. The black steer tried to duck aside but the bay, head down, ears flat, teeth flashing, covered his move. The black one thought better of his plan, turned tail, and in three leaps dove into the water belly deep, with a great splash, and began to swim with the others for the north shore.

Ed used his brass telescope to view the slick-hided cattle reaching the far side. Shaking off water like wet cats when they emerged, the two hands were still keeping them rolling on and so far everything looked good.

He checked the sun time. They had another forty-five minutes of good daylight left. It would take all of that, but the moon should be up with enough light to bed them. The last head were midstream when he tied his boots around his neck and, with the two drag riders, prepared to seek the far shore.

"Sure went good, huh, Mr. Ed?" a short boy called Stubby said, bursting with pride.

"It sure did," Ed said, and smiled at them. "Helluva job."

The choppy water looked bloody in sundown's glare. The roan drove off into the stirred-up, muddy water being cleared by the current. The water felt cold penetrating his clothes and soon Ed was hanging onto the horn and letting the roan swim. Both boys were laughing and oohing over the river's chilly temperature until at last they rode out of the Brazos like triumphant knights and their horses shook hard enough to rattle their stirrups.

"We made it," Unita said as she rode down the mud-slick bank where the water shed from two thousand cattle and their hooves had made a slurry.

"Caudle make it?" Ed asked.

"Oh, he's acting like this was all his idea."

Ed shook his head. The boots around his neck weren't too badly wet, but they'd dry. He had clean socks in his bedroll. He'd change in camp, so he slung his linked footgear over the horn.

"You have a good day?"

"Fine, but I worried all day about the herd and the boys and not being with them."

"I savvy worry. Blondie make it?"

"He was waiting on us up here."

Ed frowned at the sight of the chuck wagon and in the lantern light he saw several hands gathered round. "We better get up there and see what's wrong."

"What is it?"

"Damned if I know," he said, and they hurried their horses.

When he stepped down at the wagon he realized he was stocking-footed. "What's wrong?"

"It's J. T. got hisself snake bit," Caudle said on his knees, tending to him. They had the boy's pants off and his longhandle split up to the knee.

The cook was using a tourniquet on his leg and one of the boys held a jackknife.

"Pass that blade through the fire," Ed said to him.

"And Hurley, get that bottle of whiskey out of my war bag." He nodded to J. T. The sweaty-faced boy seated on his butt, trying to mask his worst fears behind his ashen face, returned the head bob.

Then the boys parted and Blondie came through them with a small, limp bobwhite quail in his hand. He took the knife from the cowboy and split the bird open, then dropped down beside Caudle. He indicated for cookie to take off the wrap, and then he slapped the bloody, split bird on top of the bite marks and pressed tightly on it.

Ed saw the hard look in Blondie's cold blue eyes as he held the quail to J. T.'s leg. No one said anything. Hurley handed Ed the pint and he nodded to thank him. Somewhere in the night a hoarse-voiced steer was bawling for his partners, lost in the crossing.

"That going to work?" Caudle finally asked Blondie.

"Sí. Mucho bueno."

In the lantern light, Caudle rose with a scowl. "Beats the hell out of me how it would work." He pushed off Ed, who had uncorked the bottle the cowboy brought him and handed it to J. T.

"What beats the hell out of me is how that Comanche ever got the damn bird in the first place," one of the hands said.

"Ain't'cha heard of rocks, Nort?"

"There ain't none around here."

Ed took the bottle back from J. T., who quietly thanked him as if settled. The cork in place, Ed sat back on the ground and watched Blondie, who continued to press his feathery hands full on J. T.'s calf. Then he realized that Unita was squatted beside him.

"What's it doing?" she asked.

"I guess drawing the poison out," he said softly.

She nodded.

Ed had to join the cowhands' line of questioning how Blondie, without a gun, ever killed a bobwhite that fast?

It was late when they finished supper, with the cattle bedded down and the night guards out. Ed and Unita sat on his bedroll and watched lightning streak the western sky as storm after storm ran northward, parallel to them.

"J. T. going to be all right?" she asked.

"His leg ain't swelling like most snakebite victims I've seen. I think Blondie saved his life."

She leaned over and put her head on his shoulder. "It was a helluva day."

He agreed. "But we're across the Brazos. If we ever get past the Red, I'll kind of relax some, 'cause the rest, outside of the Arkansas, ain't too bad."

"It was a good move. Those storms out there could have been here."

"Yes, and it gave us a chance to rest up."

"I better get to my tent," she said. "Morning will sure come early."

Light rain fell before the sun crept up and everyone was crowded under the fly eating a breakfast of ham, biscuits, gravy, and fried mush off their tin plates, standing up to make room for everyone.

"Take you some biscuits and ham for your snack today," Caudle said to them. "We may have to eat jerky tonight."

"We're going to eat that cursed black steer next,"

Shorty announced. "If he cuts back on another river crossing he'll be dead meat."

"All your beef used up?" Unita asked.

"Used it all last night."

"There will be one turn up," Ed said. "If not, we'll sacrifice Shorty's pet black one."

Everyone laughed. Even J. T., who was on crutches, but recovering in shorter time than any snakebite victim Ed could recall. He was to ride with Caudle in the wagon for a couple of days, which Ed considered just punishment for letting a diamondback bite him.

They only went five miles in the cold drizzle and found some good graze. It was a day to get caught up. Under Caudle's fly, Ed even shaved and felt human again, though his boots were not drying out and had squished all day in the stirrups. He went over to Unita's tent after shaving and cleared his throat, waiting for her to answer. The cold mist on his slick face, he looked across the gray world and nodded to himself. They always needed the moisture.

"Come in," she said, parting the tent fold.

"How're you doing?" he asked, squatting down in his wet boots.

"Busy making a list." She sat on the folding cot, brushing her hair. "We'll need more supplies when we get up to Fort Worth."

"I know. Take us a month to cross the Indian Territory. Oh, about six weeks from the Red River to Newton."

"Take a week to get up there from Fort Worth. So that's an even two months."

"Close."

"I want you to go into Fort Worth. Get the supplies and have them hauled out to the herd. Figured you'd want to check on those killers while you were there."

He nodded, busy reflecting on what all the trip entailed. "I can do that."

"Good. I know this trip has pulled a curtain between us—" She was busy rolling the loose hair out of her brush. "Ever since the boys' death you've pulled yourself back into a burrow."

"Had lots on my mind. Sorry."

"No need. I appreciate all your hard work and guidance. Knowing men like Ich and Shorty, and what they could do. I'd never have made it without you, but I am worried you're falling back in the bottle and will waste a good life you could have."

He raised his gaze, looked at her, and nodded. It was the first time she'd addressed his drinking since the drive started, and it wasn't like he'd expected her to act. It was like she'd given up on them and only worried about him.

"When I get to Kansas and these cattle are sold, I'm running down both sets of those killers. Roho or whoever, if they're up here, and the Brady brothers."

"They might kill you."

"They might but I don't aim for them to. This old ranger is tough enough to find them and bring them in or end their misery."

"You better be sober when you try. You'll need every edge."

"Yes, ma'am."

She shook her head in disappointment. "I'm not your mother."

He closed his eyes and threw his head back. "I don't expect you to be."

"Come sit up here," she said and patted the cot.

He shrugged, rose, and joined her.

"Hold me tight," she said, burying her face in his shirt.

For a moment, he hesitated. Then, when he heard and felt her sobs, he shrugged off his coat and encircled her with his arms. Resting his cheek on the top of her head, he knew she wasn't crying for herself. The tension of their three weeks on the trail was all balled up inside of her and finally coming out.

Chapter 24

He hitched the roan outside Riley Brothers two-story brick building in Fort Worth and walked through the left-hand double door with all the glass. The large store carried odors of leathers, spices, and raw wool. Several customers were walking about the tables examining various goods.

"Mr. Wright, sir?" a young clerk asked from behind gold-framed glasses.

"Back again. What was your name?"

"Albert, Albert Goldberg, sir."

"Good to see you again. I need some things for a cattle drive."

"Will it be cash or carry, sir?"

"Carry, I guess."

"That's fine. You have good credit here."

"I'll need it hauled out later."

"No problem. What do you need?"

"A half dozen girths, a dozen shirts, a dozen waist overalls, two slickers to start."

"What sizes?"

"She wrote them down," he said.

"Oh, you have a wife?"

Struck by his words, Ed looked hard at the youth wearing the bow tie and shook his head. "No—it's—ah, Mrs. Nance, a widow who I'm guiding for."

"I'm sorry—I just thought."

"No problem. She's outfitting the crew with a new set of clothes."

"They probably need some by now."

"They do. I also need some dry-cured hams, two barrels of flour, two hundred pounds of brown beans, a hundred pounds of rice." He paused as the boy scribbled with a pencil on a pad. "Six tins of lard. Three cases of airtight peaches. Six cases of tomatoes, and a case of raisins—better make it two of them."

"How many hams?" Albert asked, looking over his list.

"A half dozen, and a couple crocks of lick."

"Molasses?"

"Yes."

When Ed had finished the entire list, the boy nodded. "When do you want this hauled out?"

"Early in the morning. They'll be bedded down on the South Fork. Get there early enough so the boys can transfer it to the chuck wagon, in case I'm not here to go with them."

"We can do that. Will your camp be far down the South Fork of the Trinity?"

"No. Ask for Caudle; he's the cook. You can't miss the Bar U wagon. It's all painted up red and yellow with flags."

"I guess you want to see about other business in town?" The boy gave him a coy smile.

"Yes."

"Then drop by later and sign the bill."

"Thanks," Ed said, and left the mercantile.

There were only swampers dumping slop buckets in the gutter in Hell's Kitchen at midmorning, when he rode into the district and dismounted at the Lion's Head Saloon. He pushed through the batwing doors and saw a familiar face standing at the bar. Johnny Bentson from Abilene, Kansas, was lifting a glass of whiskey when he recognized him.

"Ed Wright, you old dog. What're you doing in Fort Worth?"

"Trailing cattle," Ed said, and motioned to the bartender to bring him a glass.

"On your way to Newton?"

"On my way. What do you know?"

"Not much. Looking for a good card game." Johnny poured four fingers of whiskey in Ed's glass.

"You ever run across two brothers named Brady?"

"They're a pair of back-stabbing no-accounts. They were in on the Frank Green robbery and murder last fall."

"I didn't hear about that one."

"Frank had sold his herd. Two herds in fact, and was headed back for Texas in a buckboard with the proceeds. Didn't trust banks. He had two tough men along. Somewhere near the Indian Territory—Kansas border they all four vanished like smoke."

"Four of them?"

"Yeah, Frank's wife was with them."

Ed downed part of his glass and let the whiskey cut through the dust in his throat. "How do they know that the Bradys did it?"

"They don't. Green had a diamond horseshoe stick

pin. Must have cost a blue fortune. It was his trade-mark. If you ever saw it you'd not forget it." Johnny shook his head like he was bad hurt telling it, took a sip of his liquor, and then swallowed hard. He set the glass down hard and wet his lower lip. "Last winter Marsh Brady threw that diamond pin in a pot to cover his bet during a card game."

"What happened?"

"Some of us recognized it and demanded to know where he got it."

"He tell you?"

"Said he got it off an Injun down in the Cherokee Nation. We all knew better than that but what the hell could we do? No bodies. What law do you go to?"

"They fed my partner to the fish on the Mississippi. Same deal. I tracked them across Arkansas last fall and lost them at Fort Smith."

"Never found 'em?"

"I got close last winter. Hired a deputy marshal out of Parker's court." Ed gave a deep sigh and shook his head to dismiss the pain he felt from telling it. "We had a shootout up there with another gang where they were supposed to be staying. The deputy and his man got killed. The Bradys were already gone."

"They're somewhere over on the main cattle trail, like buzzards waiting for carrion."

"Ever hear of a Messican named Roho?"

"Name rings a bell. What did he do?"

"I figure the Bradys hired him and a couple more to get me, and instead they hung two of my cowboys." Ed downed the rest of his whiskey and set the glass on the bar. Close to shaking all over, he tried to turn around to hide the hurt he felt inside.

"Damn, man, you have had lots of troubles. Here, have some more whiskey."

Ed straightened and nodded. His composure restored, he straightened up and lifted the glass. "I won't need any law when I find them."

"How do I send you word if I hear about them?"

"Banty, Texas is good enough. Or Schroeder Commission Company. Les does most of my selling. He'll be in Newton by now."

"I know him."

Ed held the glass up and looked through the amber liquid. "I've worked my ass off the last five or six years, taking cattle north. Got a nice ranch paid for in the hill country. Stocked with cattle and lots of water—the things a man dreams about, and I can't stand it."

"Maybe if you track these bastards down you'll feel different."

Ed closed his eyes and threw his head back. "I damn sure hope so. I came through here last winter and there was gal named Nell working the streets. She sent me the word this Roho was coming to get me. I owe her."

Johnny closed his eyes and shook his head, not looking at Ed. Elbows on the bar, he drew up a little and then raised his glass. "Someone killed her in the alley last week. Arkansas Nell—cute little thing. Had a helluva funeral for her."

"Who killed her?"

"Hell, if anyone knew they'd have hung him. Damn, bartender, bring us another bottle. Ed's buying."

"If we can go sit at a damn table I will—" That

was her, all right. Arkansas Nell. For a long moment, Ed closed his eyes, recalling her spunk and ways.

". . . cut her up with a knife."

"Oh, damn, I don't need to know. I'm going to buy you this bottle and get the hell out of here." He dug the money out of his pocket. "You get drunk for me and—Nell. There's some things I need to do."

"Don't run off in the heat of the day. Hell, I can afford the whiskey." Johnny held out his hands to protest.

"No, I'm buying. How much?" he asked the bartender.

"Six dollars—"

"Here." Ed put the money down and nodded to Johnny; then he left. Not a minute too soon; he'd felt the walls and mirrors moving in on him. He unhitched the roan and rode him back by the store, signed the bill, and rode west to the mouth of the South Fork. He found a hill and watched the familiar horses flowing in from the south. Blondie was there with the remuda.

Ed sat cross-legged on the ground to observe everything. Nearby, the roan, with his long black mane and tail being swept around by the wind, grazed through the bits. He raised his head to observe the herd's arrival on the flats.

He had a pint in his lap, but he hadn't uncorked it. All he could do was turn over and over in his mind all the dead people connected with him. Why were they all his fault that they had died?

After a while, Blondie rode up to his position and took a seat beside him. He never said a word for a long time. Finally in his broken Spanish he began to talk. "The day they came for me—I saw it in a dream. Three of them took turns raping her on a bed. They held me and made me look until I puked."

"Bad, bad dream." Ed nodded, thinking of a small boy being forced to watch such savagery.

"Now I wish I never remembered."

"I know. But it is a curse we must face—somehow."

"Does whit-key help?" Blondie indicated the bottle in his lap.

Ed shook his head. "Makes it a damn site worse." Shaking his head, he translated that into Spanish for him. *Hell, no, nothing helped.*

Chapter 25

"You have any trouble getting the supplies?" Unita asked, joining him on the ground with her plate of food. The evening sun was sinking fast way out on the Illano Estacado and everyone was chucking down for the day.

"No, I signed for them. So you better pay him on the way back."

"Oh, I will. I could have taken a letter of credit—"

"They know we'll pay. I never mentioned it was your herd. Too much to explain."

She nodded. "You learn anything?"

"Not really." He considered the light brown crusted biscuit on his plate.

"Why do I feel you aren't telling me everything?"

"Seen Johnny Bentson up there. He's a gambler and a fairly honest one. He told me the Bradys killed a rancher named Green, his wife, and two men on the Kansas border."

"Did you see that woman who wrote you the letter?"

"No, I was too late. Someone killed her last week."

"Oh, Ed, I'm sorry."

A knife stabbed him in the guts. He shook his head to dismiss it. "She was just an acquaintance, but she did write and—"

"Ed, where are you going?"

"I'll be back—" No way he could eat. He tossed the contents of his plate out under the mesquite and then, in passing, drowned his plate and utensils in the tub of soapy water. He walked for a distance until he was by the shallow stream.

"Ed, I'm sorry. I never—"

He turned and saw her coming downhill in the twilight. With her spurs on, she was liable to topple on her face. The effort she made to hurry and still keep her balance was funny. He began to laugh at her antics, and ran over to catch her in his arms. To at last savor her closeness. He felt like all of his trials had fled on the wings of a flushed quail.

"Yesterday it was me," she said. "Today it's you."

"Forget it. I guess hearing the Green story, which was like Dave's death, and then learning she had been murdered too—it was more than I could stand."

"But you didn't get drunk."

He looked down at the top of her head; her hat rested on her shoulders on a string. "No, I didn't do that."

She squeezed him. "Six weeks and you can go find them."

"If we can sell the herd."

Her cheek nestled on his chest, she shrugged as if that was matter-of-fact. "We will."

Four days later, the snag-filled Red River faced him in the morning light. It was not any higher than usual, but the Red was one of the tougher rivers to cross.

Ed knew the warning sign from the federal judge, prohibiting the importation of spirits, was posted right beside the passage where the cattle went up the bank. Caudle had gone across with Unita on the ferry, and two cowboys on horseback as well.

Blondie was driving the horses down the bank. Ed frowned. The leader was a long-legged mare he'd never seen before, and she took to the water like she knew the way.

Ich reined up and chuckled. "That Comanche don't need no help getting them ponies over there. He could drive a thousand of them damn horses across here by hisself."

"Where did he get that mare?" Ed asked, shaking his head.

"Hell, how should I know? Probably stole her. He ain't ever going to be a white man. Lived too long with them redskins. But he damn sure can wrangle horses."

"He can, all right. We'll be ready to go in fifteen minutes."

"No problem." Ich turned his pony back toward the herd. "Oh, I got word back there at the store. Crabtree's bunch lost a lot of cattle in high water at the Brazos. Word is they're five days behind us now."

"I knew she could get up this time of year. Just so we don't lose any here," Ed said, and looked at the buttermilk sky for some help from his Maker.

Sam Houston struck the river and, like a veteran, struck out dog-paddling across the current and headed for the far bank. The cattle looked orderly enough going into the muddy water to Ed, seated on horseback with his boots tied around his neck.

J. T. was one of the first riders to come down the bank to help push them after Ich and Shorty went in. His horse acted the part of the fool, leaping out into the river and busting his belly in a great splash. His crash unseated J. T. and Ed saw that the young cowboy was off in the water, and that he was no swimmer.

He put heels to the roan, trying to keep his eye on the wet head bobbing in the dingy water. He and the pony slid off the steep bank into the Red's murky water. The cold was a shock to both. Ed aimed the roan for where he last saw the boy. He undid the boots and slung them over the horn.

Where was he? Then he spotted J. T.'s shirt under the surface and drove the roan beside him. He managed to catch the boy's collar and pulled the limp body across his saddle. Then he slipped off the roan's back into the river and urged him for the north bank with shouts, knowing they'd never climb back up the steep one he had come from. Swimming to help the horse, the fact that the boy had not moved upset him as he took in a mouthful of fishy-tasting water himself.

They were at last on the bank, the roan shaking off enough water to drown someone. Ed had J. T. in his arms and was searching for a place to lay him down. Finally he sprawled him out in the new grass and weeds, facedown, and went to pushing hard with both hands on his lower back to try to expel the water if he could.

"He alive?" Unita asked, arriving out of breath beside him.

Half rising, J. T. upchucked a mouthful of water and began to cough. Ed nodded. "I think so."

He looked back across the river. The stream of cattle was coming over in an orderly fashion for the most part. Maybe, just maybe, they'd make this crossing without any loss of life.

She had the boy, who was on all fours, by the shoulder, shaking and reassuring him. "Cough it up. You're going to be all right, J. T."

Yes, cough it up. The whole damn Red River.

Chapter 26

Two days later a band of blanket-ass Indians rode over the hill with feathers sticking up like half-molted roosters, looking for passage fees. Even at a distance, when Ed first saw them he instantly knew their purpose. They wanted to be paid for the "wa-hoos" grazing their land.

"What do they want?" Unita asked, indicating the party and sliding her horse up hard beside him.

"Money, marbles, and meat."

She frowned and shook her head. "How much?"

"All they can get."

"I have little money and no marbles. What do we do?"

"We negotiate a deal."

A tough look of skepticism swept over her face. "Can you handle it?"

"Yes, ma'am. Sure you don't want to talk to them?" Ed asked with a grin.

"No."

"I'll palaver with them awhile then."

"You need any backup?"

"All I need are them two quarts of whiskey I've got hid in the chuck wagon."

"Where at?"

"In your other carpetbag."

She laughed. "Why there?"

"No one would ever look in there for them. Trust me, they've all looked for those bottles."

"I'll send Jocko up to wherever you set up to talk to them."

"That hill looks good enough," he said, pointing to the rise where they sat their ponies.

"And be careful."

"These ain't bloodthirsty Comanches. They're just some starving bucks that the government forgot to feed this month."

"I certainly hope so."

"Send along the whiskey as soon as you can. I'll be out of my short supply in no time."

"What'll you do without any to drink?"

"I don't imagine I'll need it."

"I'm not so sure of that." She reined her horse aside and set out for the chuck wagon, no doubt several miles ahead of the herd.

Ed booted the roan for the hill. Holding his right hand up, he approached them. "Ho! Great chiefs and warriors."

A prune-faced man with the most feathers rode downhill to meet with him. "You got many wa-hoos."

"Let us go on the top of this hill, smoke the pipe, and speak of the cattle."

The chief agreed and said something guttural to the rest. The other stone faces agreed and turned their skinny ponies that way too. So far his negotiations with this bunch was going fine. That camp boy better burn daylight getting back with the firewater. He'd sure need it.

He dismounted and the roan went to chomping grass. He drew out two pints of whiskey and they went to sit over the north brink so the wind that rippled the short green carpet of grass wasn't so bad. He looked off anxiously to the north for the boy he knew could not possibly be there yet. *Hurry* was all he could think about.

At last the six Indians and Ed sat cross-legged in a semicircle, the chief using his flat hand to show from right to left all the land the great chief in Washington had given his people. The man's high cheekbones looked encased in old buffalo leather and his dark eyes were dulled by many years of squinting from the too-bright prairie sun. Ed decided they still missed few details—including the two pints of rotgut in his lap.

"You come to eat our grass," the chief said.

"There is plenty of grass now," Ed said, indicating the new crop of blades sweeping in the wind.

"When buffalo return we will need more."

"They won't come back this year," Ed said and put the rest of them to whispering.

The chief reared back and frowned. "How you know that?"

The others quickly backed his question and leaned forward to listen to his words.

"The Missouri is flooding." He indicated with his head to the north where he expected they used to come from. "They can't get across it, so they will stay up north this summer."

There was a moment of reflection for the men to talk in their own tongue about what he'd said, until at last the chief asked, "Where is this Miss—our—ie?"

"Four moons' hard ride." Ed pointed north. "Many large tribes live in the land between here and there."

"Need much money for you to cross our land."

"How much?"

"Maybe thousand gold dollars."

Ed shook his head. Impossible. Perhaps it was time to smoke a peace pipe or do something to stall. He needed time. Time for that boy to ride back with his prize trading items. If he let them start on his whiskey they might sober up before Jocko got there with the rest.

"We are friends." Ed pointed to his own chest and then to the chief's. "We should smoke to that."

"Smoke pipe?" The chief pushed his gray-black braid back and scratched his ear like he was unsure of what he wanted to do next.

"Yes. Smoke peace pipe."

Looking satisfied, the chief grinned and told the next guy what to do. He rose, wrapped his cheap blanket around himself, and went to the horses. Indian tobacco, or whatever they smoked, was always strong, so Ed steeled himself for the harshness ahead.

"We smoke pipe, then we drink whiskey like we big friends, huh?" the chief asked.

"Sure. We can work this out."

"What we have to work at? I can send for squaws." He smiled as if he had an idea. "You want squaw?"

Ed shook his head. No way did he need a squaw. Did he need lice or crabs? No.

"Squaw keep you warm at night." The chief looked

hard at Ed and elbowed the man on his right. His words to him must have been: *"Won't she?"* The other nodded in agreement.

"No, thanks."

An Indian returned with a pipe and pouch. He took his place and the chief held the pipe up to show Ed. "Great pipe."

"Great pipe," he agreed.

Chief opened the pouch and used his thumb to pack the bowl with the shredded tobacco.

"Secret tobacco?"

The chief nodded and finished. He put the beaded purse down and found a match. He struck it and tried to light the tobacco, puffing in and out. The match went out. Ed rose up and gave him more matches. Leather Face started again, and soon smoke came in little puffs from his wrinkled, dark lips. Using the sides of his hand to slice the universe, he said some prayer and then handed it to his right. Scar Face looked very seriously at the pipe in his hand with its leather strips strung with multicolored beads. He looked very harshly at the job ahead and puffed, blowing out some small bubbles of smoke, and then passing it on until it became Ed's turn.

The last buck's spittle was trailing off in a small wisp, but Ed never hesitated and took it to his mouth. The hot bitterness flooded his mouth and bit his tongue like hot peppers. He issued some smoke from around the stem under the close scrutiny of the others, then, as casually as he could manage, passed it on. Suppressing his cough was bad enough. Maybe they used dry horse shit for flavor—it tasted bad, anyway.

The pipe came back to the chief, who puffed on it

and passed it on again. The whole thing took some time, until at last the bowl was half full of white ash. The chief rose and used his thumb to press a spot of ash on each man's forehead. After that, he said a prayer and sent the rest of the pipe's ashes on the wind.

"Now we are at peace," he said, seated again on the blanket. "How will our new friend pay us the money for our grass?"

"We must talk more."

"You got whiskey?" The chief indicated the pints.

"Yes. How far does your land go north?" Ed stalled for more time. That boy better be hurrying—half-drunk Indians could be mean, tough, and demanding. Drunk ones were a pushover.

"Where the river flows to the sun."

"Flows to the sun, huh?"

"Yes."

"How many wives do you have?"

Leather Face laughed and stuck out his chest under the bone vest. "Four."

"Four?" Ed acted impressed. "What do you do with so many wives?"

"Make babies."

In a chain reaction, they all laughed at the chief's frank reply.

"You have squaw?"

Ed shook his head.

Leather Face frowned at him. "Who is woman with cattle?"

"My boss."

They all laughed at the translation. The chief made a face like he understood his problem. "All women are bossy. You must beat their ass sometimes to make them stop."

Ed leaned back and dug his jackknife out of his pants pocket. The buck next to him had to examine the knife, so he showed him both blades. A thin-faced one about his age looked it all over and smiled as he opened and closed it, as if he'd never seen the likes of one. At last he nodded in approval, gave it back, and Ed cut the seal on the first pint.

He closed his knife and held the bottle up so the sun shone through the glass and the brown liquor. "O great maker of whiskey, deliver me more and be quick about it."

From the corner of his eye he saw the roan lift his head and look north. The Indian ponies did too. Someone or something was coming. It better be his man. He pulled the cork, put the rim to his lips, turned the bottle up, and used his tongue to keep most of it in the pint. *Here goes the deal.*

Each one around the circle had a swallow apiece. They were well behaved and did not try to drink it all at their turn. The chief wiped his mouth with the back of his hand. "Good whis-key."

"Two bottles of whiskey and two wa-hoos." There were two limpers in the drag they'd have to eat before too much longer.

The chief shook his head and the last Indian on his left finished the rest of the pint. Hurry. Ed sighed and considered the last pint in his lap. Better stall a little longer and hope. "I am a poor man with little money. I can pay two wa-hoos and two bottles of whiskey for passage, and you can ask the next ones for money."

"They have much money?" The chief's look lightened at the notion.

"Yes. His name is Crabtree. He is very rich."

"Crat—bee?"

"No." Ed waved that away, delighted with his latest idea. "Crab—tree. Very rich man."

One stood up, looked north, and said, "You boss comes." The rest laughed.

Ed blinked, then he smiled. She was delivering it herself. He cut the seal and popped the cork on the last pint, handing it to the next buck, then he rose, brushed off the seat of his pants, and went to meet her.

"How're negotiations going with them?" she whispered, cutting worried looks at the seated Indians.

"Going fine. Couple bottles of whiskey and a few limpers and we'll be on our way." He went to her saddlebags and undid the one on his side. The bottles retrieved, he took the second one from her, chuckling.

"What's so funny?" She frowned at him.

"They think you're my squaw."

"So? Is that so funny?"

He stopped, taken aback, and then shook his head. "Only out of context."

"What does that mean?"

"Means 'lean over so I can kiss you for this whiskey.' "

She looked uncertainly at the ring of Indians passing around the pint and talking in their group. "Why not?"

Bent over the pommel of the saddle, she leaned over and pursed her lips. Ed, with his arms full of bottles, kissed her and winked as the Indians all hooted.

Red-faced at their hollering, she rose in the saddle and turned Star aside. "I hope that helped."

"Don't know if it did a damn thing for them. It sure gave me the strength to go back and deal with them."

She shook her head and he could see her shoulders quaking from chuckling at his words as she rode off down the hillside. With a final head shake and a hand wave she left him.

He went back to the ring, nodded, and sat down.

"Your boss, go back, fix food?" the chief asked with a smirk.

"Yes. How is the whiskey?"

"Goddamn good!"

The next round of the big bottle and two of the bucks got up and did a war dance. Making big steps, they danced around chanting and the rest began to join them, clapping and singing. "Hey-yo. Hey-yo, hey-yo . . ."

The chief and his war council were soused and they soon pulled Ed up to join them. He tossed his hat aside and went to pounding his boot heels in the ground, following his brothers around as they danced and screamed at the sun and at hawks. Damn, they acted crazy drunk. He stopped, closed his eyes, and stood with his chin up, sucking in air he needed to fill his aching lungs.

Two Indians were lying on the ground moaning. One was trying to get on his paint pony and it kept circling away from him. The chief had found the two full bottles and held them in Ed's face.

"Send squaws in the morning—get two wa-hoos—

you goddamn good man—call you *Bossy Woman's Man.*"

Ed nodded, looking the drunk Indian in the face. "Bossy Woman's Man." He couldn't wait to tell her.

"Trap—tree coming?" The chief waved the right-hand bottle to the south.

"Crab—tree's coming," Ed reminded him.

"Him rich sumbitch, huh?"

"Yes. See you."

"See you Bossy Woman's Man." The chief waved a bottle after him.

His hat on again, Ed checked the cinch and swung into the saddle. Then, using his hand over his mouth, he rode the roan off the hill yowling like a banshee to the cheers of his Injun friends.

Bossy Woman's Man. He couldn't wait to tell her.

Chapter 27

He heard first the hissing of the lodge poles in the grass. Armed with pans, axes, and butcher knives over a dozen women and many small children arrived at the cow camp before sunup. In the dancing fire's red light Ed could see they were dressed in an assortment of ragged clothes and castaway army uniforms, as well as tattered blankets.

A tall woman stepped forward, shoulders back, her hair in tight braids. She looked like the boss. "Where is the Bossy Woman's Man?"

The crew snickered when Ed stepped forward and nodded to her.

"Where are these cows?"

"At daylight they will rope them and drag them from the herd for you."

"Good. We wait."

"Caudle, you got a bunch of biscuits?" Ed asked over his shoulder.

"Sure, why?"

"Issue one to each of them."

"What'll them boys eat for snacks today?"

"Cook some more. We'll take time."

"Aw—" Caudle started to complain.

"Feed them," Unita said, and walked out to join him.

"You, Bossy Woman," the Indian leader said to her. "I am Red Water." The crew's low snicker at her words made the line of Indian women and children laugh too. That and Jocko with a big plate of biscuits, who started handing them out to eager brown hands. As he went down the line issuing them, his efforts brought impressed "oohs" from them, big and small.

"How nice to meet you, Red Water. We will have some bread for all of you," Unita said. "Come, we will have some coffee and talk about your business."

The woman hesitated and looked at two others near her.

"Them too," Unita said, and waved them toward her camp.

Ed would never forget a small, dark-haired girl in the lineup—half naked in the cool predawn, with her cheeks full of bread like a gopher and tears big as acorns flowing down her brown cheeks. He headed back for the rest of his breakfast.

Grumbling like a sore-toed bear, Caudle was greasing up both of his big Dutch ovens. On the sideboard was a pile of dough.

"Making snacks?" Ed asked, picking up his plate.

"You and your ideas—no, that ain't near enough for them starving kids. I'll make them hands some in the next batch."

It was late when they moved out. Ed stopped and watched how hard the women worked at butchering the two steers, saving it all to load on the travois and pack saddles. Steers on the move again, Caudle

packed up and headed north with the horse herd, and
Blondie swinging a blanket over his head and charging
around them on his paint pony.

"Those horses won't ever be the same, will they?"
Unita asked, riding beside Ed.

"Someday he'll tell me where he got that Thorough-
bred mare. The more I see her out in front, the more
I wonder about her source."

"Oh, you warned me he was more Comanche than
white since that day you decided to take him back
with us."

"I've never been sure why either."

"No, you knew him then. He's not a person with
much to share." She looked ahead.

"I ain't telling you this to shock you. All he recalls
about his mother is three bucks making him watch
them as a small boy, while they took turns raping her.
That was his only memory of a woman he thought
was his mother."

"Oh, Ed, that's sad as anything I've ever heard."

He nodded to that. Maybe the little crying girl he'd
seen earlier was another.

"What're you going to do for whiskey?" she asked.

"Try and forget it. I need to get going. Caudle says
we can make a camp on some creek ahead. I better
check out the water there."

"I may ride along."

"Fine, but we better get going."

They short loped their ponies a long ways, then trotted them, crossing lots of grassland and small streams.
Ed was pleased that they'd reached midway across
the Indian Territory. The hard-bottom crossings of the
streams signaled to him that they were halfway to the

Arkansas River, and it wasn't far to Newton from there. They passed Caudle and Jocko riding on the seat of the chuck wagon between the flags. They waved as they rode on. Ed's destination was a large flat where he hoped to find grass and water for the steers, enough to hold up a few days and fill out the steers some. They needed to make fewer miles from there on, and to put more meat on the product. The new grass mixed with the old would do that from there to their destination.

"What if another herd runs over us?" she asked after he explained his plans.

"Then you shoot the dumb headman of the outfit. That's too big a mistake to take as likely, but it happens."

"Ever happen to you?"

"Once. We were five days sorting them, and I got a check for thirty head we didn't get out of their bunch."

"Well, they paid you anyway."

He looked over at her and laughed. "Yeah, at fifteen bucks a head less than I sold my entire herd for."

"Oh."

Near midafternoon they found the open country he had hoped for, and the grass looked good. Dismounted, he was chewing on a stem when a rider appeared, and he frowned at Unita as a warning.

"This is a land of outlaws. Don't forget it."

"I understand," she said, standing beside him slapping her chaps with her reins.

"I know him," he said, recognizing the cowboy in the distance.

"Who is he?"

"A drover who once worked for me. He's all right."

"Why, Ed Wright, you've got a herd this far north already?" The cowboy drew in his reins, sat his Texas pony down, then took off his hat quick like for Unita. "Nice to see you too, ma'am."

She acknowledged him with smile and a nod.

"Unita Nance, meet Freddie Lynn Castro."

"Nice to meet you," she said.

"Aw, shucks, I thought she might be wearing your brand by now."

"No." Ed shook his head. "What're you doing up here?"

"Spend the whole da—dang winter up here for John Blocker, ah, looking after his herd that he never got sold last fall. And I won't do that again for the good Lord."

"He get 'em sold?"

"Sure, even before they finished the shipping pens at Newton."

"Good, they have the pens done."

Freddie Lynn shook his head "Almost, but the guy who bought the herd has his own help, so I'm headed back."

"I'm looking for two brothers named Brady."

"I've heard of them, but never saw or run onto them up there. Why?"

"They killed Dave Ivy last year."

"Aw, hell, Ed, he was one sure good feller."

Ed nodded. "And three hard ones led by one named Roho, he's a Messican, rides with a breed and a full-blood."

"That's easy. They're at a small place called Wichita up on the Arkansas."

"You sure?"

"Hell—excuse me, ma'am. My maw'd washed my mouth out with lye soap, talking like that in front of a lady, but I've been sleeping with the hoot owls too long." Freddie Lynn shook his head, took off his hat again, and with his fingers combed his too-long greasy brown hair back. "They was there three days ago. Tough bunch. Denned up in the La Paloma Saloon."

"They hung two of my cowboys, I guess for spite, when I was gone on business."

"Aw, damn. You better take lots of help with you. They've got a bad reputation. They say Judge Parker's men won't touch them."

"That tough, huh?" Ed wondered how he'd handle them. *One problem—one ranger.*

Freddie Lynn nodded with a serious look written on his face. "I ain't no gun hand, but I'd go with you. You gave me my first job coming up here, and I owe you."

"No, Freddie Lynn, you get back to Texas and bring another herd up the trail. Blocker's got one waiting for you?"

"He said he did."

"Rest up overnight in our camp. Ich and Shorty are riding swing for her. You'll want to talk to them. The chuck outfit's coming."

Freddie Lynn blinked at his words. "You said she?"

"That's the boss lady." Ed hooked a thumb at her.

"Ma'am, you got some of the best help I know of on the trail. I hope I can find that good a help down there for my drive back up here."

She smiled and laughed. "I wasn't easy."

They spent the next few hours exchanging stories about things that had happened to them. How Freddie Lynn near froze to death wintering two thousand longhorns in southern Kansas. His experiences in snow and ice made them laugh until they cried.

After Caudle arrived, they snaked him in all the wood they could locate. It was a big reunion after the herd was spread out and Shorty rode into camp with Ich and found their old compadre.

"What will you do about them?" she asked when they were aside by themselves, drinking fresh coffee.

He blew the steam off his cup and looked across the acres of the black-brown mass, with heads down, busy grazing. A few were lost and bawling for their own. He nodded at last, fully decided. "Ride up there and settle with 'em."

"I'm going too."

He looked sharply at her. "No way. Ich and the boys can get these cattle to Newton from here. You're within a month of reaching your goal. Don't be foolish."

"So I can go back to Texas and pay off the bankers and live like an old maid, rocking on the front porch."

"There's plenty of deserving—"

"I don't give a damn. You ride out, I go along."

At a loss for words, he shook his head vehemently. "There's no damn way."

"I'm sticking like a tick."

Her look melted away any arguing. Damn bossy woman, anyway.

"When do you plan to go up there?" she asked.

"In the morning." He had to figure a way to get her to stay with the herd. That was all there was to it.

"How long can the cattle graze here?"

"You can move them north like a carpet each day."

"I can put Ich in charge, can't I?"

He shrugged and looked away. "Your herd. Your call."

Her eyes narrowed and a stern look filled her face. She caught him by the gallowses and jerked him close to her face. "Ride off without me. I'll find you, damn it, Ed Wright. I'm going to Wichita with you, like it or not."

Ed nodded, set his cup on the fly and headed for the brush. If he ever had needed whiskey— Right then he needed a barrel of it. Why couldn't he drill any sense in her pretty head? Thoughts of carrying her limp, dead body in his arms up some dusty street made him shudder under his shirt.

He found a place to sit with his back to a walnut tree and looked off to the north in the warm sun. He hugged his knees and visions of whiskey passed through his thoughts. At a soft shuffle in the grass he about jumped, and Blondie squatted down by him.

"I will ride with you."

He frowned at the youth. "You do a good job wrangling horses. Stay here."

"No, I tell them I would go."

"Who did you tell?"

"Boss woman. She agreed and gave me a rifle."

"Good, then she's not going." He felt relieved. That was settled.

"No."

"No? What the hell do you mean, no?"

"She says she's going."

"Why are you going along?"

"I could be dead in Mexico. You and her treat me like I am your son."

Ed shook his head. "You could be killed. These men are killers."

Blondie rubbed his palms on his pants and nodded. "I am like her. I am going."

So he'd have a beautiful woman and a Comanche captive kid tagging along. He never should have said a word to anyone, just ridden up there and settled it. She'd known anyway. If only he hadn't given away all that damn whiskey acting like some kind of reformed preacher. *Oh. God help me.*

Chapter 28

Wichita's few false-front buildings sat scattered under the buttermilk sky across the shallow and wide Arkansas. A couple of saloons, a two-story cathouse, and three businesses marked the place on the trail. Many a cattle outfit lost a hand or two at the outpost in passing, either to the charms of some dove or the derringer of some gambler in a crooked card game. Others' bodies would be found downstream, facedown in the dingy Arkansas—killed for whatever was on them.

Ed knew from the buttermilk sky that it would be sure to rain before nightfall. He'd thought about going in after sundown, but decided that crossing the river that late might be dangerous. He put Blondie in the lead and sent Unita into the water after him. He and the roan brought up the rear.

A quick check behind and he sent the roan after them. The crossing proved easy and the horses shook hard on the far side. The spray caused him to smile at her and then shake his head in disbelief over what he was doing there; then he booted the roan up to Blondie.

"Remember, the Indian may be outside."

"You ever seen him?"

"No, but a dove told me their names. Roho is a loud Mexican with a mustache. Hatchet is a shifty-eyed breed, and she figured Warlock was a Comanche, though some said he was an Apache. But she claimed he wasn't one because she knew them."

Blondie used his fingers and repeated their names. Then he nodded. "I will be in back."

"These men are killers. If you must shoot, shoot to kill them."

Blondie nodded, resting the rifle butt on his right leg, and booted his paint up behind the buildings. Ed sat the roan and wondered what else he should have told him. Nothing. Then he realized Unita sat Star and was beside him.

"You hitch your horse at the store. Take the shotgun and start down the boardwalk. Don't shoot less you have to. Don't go past that second saloon."

She nodded. "I suppose you're going to wade in there."

"I suppose someone needs to."

Visually upset, she shook her head in disbelief. "Ed, damn it, be careful."

"I will," he quietly promised her and booted the roan up the empty street. Three horses stood hip shot in the bloody light of the setting sun at the rack. They were the only ones in sight. A swamper came out of the first saloon and tossed a pail of slop water in the dust. He gave Ed a hard look as he rode past and spat tobacco off the boardwalk, then went back inside.

He slipped off the roan and dropped the reins a yard or so from the hip-shot horses at the rack. The roan would be there later. The huge horn of the Mexican saddle on one of the winter-poor, long-haired broncs told him enough. The killers would be inside. Probably all three. Ed stiffened his spine and shifted the Colt on his waist.

He stepped through the batwing doors and let his eyes adjust to the dim candlelight and went to the bar. In the back of the smoky room he saw a sombrero's outline, and a man rose to his feet with the sound of chair legs scraping the floor.

"What's your brand of pizzen?" the bartender asked Ed.

"Whiskey—got any good kind?"

"Hell, no, but I got some."

Ed nodded that that would do. "Set the bottle up."

He could hear the ring of the sombrero wearer's spurs jingling as he came from the back. With the left side of his hip to the bar, his holster and gun hand were open. He could see the man's approach in the back mirror and poured himself some liquor in the glass.

"Ah," the mustached one said. "Senor, you must bring the cattle, no?"

Ed never answered him. He wished he had a better idea where the other two were back there. He'd seen one silhouette, but wasn't sure if there was another. Then Roho bellied up to the bar and ordered a cigar.

"The cat, she got your tongue?" Roho started to turn, but his eyes flew open at the sight of the pistol in Ed's fist.

"Roho?"

"*Si*—"

The Colt bucked in Ed's hand. The bullet struck the outlaw in the forehead, and the deafening explosion made Ed's ears ring. Percussion from his shot put out the candles. A cloud of acrid, eye-burning gun smoke filled the room, dark save for the light coming in the front doorway.

A chair scraped the floor and someone rushed across the room. On his knee at the bar, Ed aimed his Colt toward the back of the inky saloon, expecting the one on the move to crack open a back door when he did not shoot.

"Bartender," Ed ordered. "Run out the front door with your hands in the air, or get ready to meet your maker."

"Don't shoot."

"She won't if you keep your hands high."

The back door opened then and Ed fired at an outline. Two rifle reports from outside cut the figure down. Ed's eyes were seared by the gun smoke and watering. He could hear Unita outside, ordering the bartender to get facedown in the street.

"Blondie?" Ed called out in Spanish. "You see the Injun?"

"He's out here."

"Then we've got them?"

"*Sí.*"

He rose on sea legs, used his left hand on the bar to steady himself, and headed for the light from the open back door. The heavy weight of the cocked Colt in his right hand, he walked across the gritty floor and used his boot toe to nudge the breed sprawled on his back. His blank, open eyes staring at eternity told him enough. Like Roho, he'd hang no more innocent ranch hands.

Blondie squatted a few yards from the back door.

"Where is the—" Ed saw the facedown body of the third one with his braids exposed and the back of his skull bashed in until pink-tinged brains leaked on the dust-soiled black hair.

With a head toss for Blondie to join him, Ed headed back inside. He could hear Unita calling to him.

"I'm coming, Boss Lady," he said, and headed through the door.

"You all right?" she asked, out of breath and about to collide with him.

"Sure, and so is Blondie." He came back inside with a wave to his man.

"What should I do with him?" she asked.

The saucer-eyed bartender stood behind her, his hands reaching for the clouds. Ed about laughed. "Uncock the scattergun. We'll save him to set two more glasses up, have us a drink and try to scare up some food."

She put the shotgun on the bar, and drew her head up as if her entire back was stiff. "It's over?"

"Yes—all over. What's your name?" he asked the bartender.

"Gustoff."

"Gustoff, I'm going to give you ten dollars to dig a hole and toss all three of them in it." He slapped the gold coin on the bar.

"One grave?"

"One's enough for that worthless trash. Watch you don't step on him," Ed said to Blondie when he joined them and had to step over Roho.

Ed poured them each two fingers in the glasses and put the cork back. "We won't need that anymore. How much we owe you for the whiskey?"

"Nothing. Nothing."

Ed raised his glass. "Here's to lots better times— God, I hope so."

He watched Unita blink, swallowing hers, and then her arm encircled his waist and hugged him to her. Damn that felt good.

"Blondie, it's been a long day. Thanks."

Stiff lipped, Blondie nodded. "You need me, you call." Then he downed the last of the whiskey in his glass like it was water.

They rejoined the herd the next afternoon. Caudle looked up from his cooking and the campfire smoke swirling around his knees and the bottom of his apron. "Well, you find 'em?"

Ed nodded and dropped off the roan. He looked over at Unita as she swung down. She must be tired. They'd made a whirlwind ride up there and back. Blondie never stopped in camp. He went out and sent back the puncher who had been looking after his remuda.

Ed took Unita's horse and went to unsaddling. She quietly thanked him and headed for her tent to freshen up before the evening meal.

"Well, well, damn it are they dead?"

Ed looked at Caudle and nodded. "They won't kill no one else."

"Have a hard time?"

He stopped unlacing the wet latigos and looked at them. "Caudle, it ain't ever easy killing men, even worthless ones like them."

"Hell, I was just asking." He stalked off to rattle his Dutch oven lids and complain out loud about asking a simple question and expecting a simple answer.

Ed lifted the saddle and pads off the roan, and the nose-burning smell of hot ammonia escaping the horse's back stung his nose. *Nothing simple about killing either.*

Chapter 29

Maybe his life simply grew easier. They'd crossed the broad Arkansas wide of Wichita, and never lost a steer or rider. Ed had seen that Crabtree's outfit was about to catch them, so he pushed east some to let them pass. He wanted plenty of graze while they arranged a sale, and it spared their herd from getting mixed with any of the others, a thing he dreaded for all the hard work involved in separating them.

Cattle settled on some good graze, though the new grass was still short up there. He and Unita headed for Newton the next day. Ed considered the truth of a cattle drive was in the receipts. He rode with her into the tent city set up on the newly staked-out streets. Every pickpocket, tinhorn, con man, demi-monde, and other professional women from Abilene had descended on the small community beside Cotton-wood Falls and the fresh boards and posts smelling of pitch in the shipping pens Joe McCoy had built over the winter along the new spur siding of the Atchison-Topeka Railroad.

He rode the roan up the crowded street with her, looking for two men he'd never met or seen that he knew about. If they were in Newton he'd find them. Shots rang out and his hand struck his gun butt in reflex as he swiveled around in the saddle, searching for the source.

"It's only some drunk," she said to settle him.

He could see the shooter by then. In a red silk shirt, pants tucked in his knee-high boots, he stood outside a tent and whooped, waving his hat in one hand and shooting holes in the sky with the other. If Newton didn't hire Wild Bill Hickok or his equal at once to put the rowdies down, they'd take this tent city over. No sign of law anywhere around—Newton would be wide open without some tough men behind badges to keep them in line.

"What are you thinking?" she asked.

"I'm thinking this place will be pure hell by the time the herds arrive up here."

"I hope we are gone by then."

He agreed and they rode on. Schroeder Commission Company had hoisted up a freshly painted sign on two tall posts and he pointed to it. It was in a smaller tent than the nearby dance hall.

He found Les Schroeder inside unpacking his office.

"Well, Ed Wright. How's Texas?"

"Last I seen of it, fine. Meet Unita Nance. She's got about two thousand steers to sell. How's the market?"

"Ten cents a pound, if they have those new scales done. Joe McCoy said they'd be working this week."

"Can't get twelve cents for some good ones?"

Les looked at him and grinned. "Hard man to trade with. I'll check the telegraph in an hour. You staying at the Cattleman's Hotel?"

Ed shook his head. "We were going back to the

herd after we found someone needed our herd at twelve cents."

"Aw, give me a chance. You never brought a bunch of culls with cows mixed in with them up the trail. I'd like to buy them and see how stout those pens Joe built this winter are. I was down here in January getting this site and I never figured then he'd do it. But he has."

Ed nodded. "They sure need some law."

"Law?" Les laughed. "They can't keep a marshal. They quit after the first night."

"They need to hire a Wild Bill."

"There ain't many like him. You want the job?"

"Not for what they must pay."

"You were a Texas Ranger, right?"

"Mister," Unita interrupted, "we came to sell cattle, not pin a badge on Ed. Besides, he has a place down in Texas now that needs him."

Les blinked at her. "Yes, ma'am. I'm going to the telegraph office, and will be back here in a short while with an answer on the cattle from my boss in Chicago."

He produced a bottle of whiskey and some tumblers, and set them on his desk. "Here, help yourself while I run down there and check the telegraph. Have a seat."

"Thanks," she said, looking at the canvas camp folding chairs and nodding.

Ed flopped on one when Les left them alone. He watched her go to the open flap and stand in the sunlight. Then she turned back and looked at him.

"You weren't serious about wearing a badge here, were you?"

"No. I want those Bradys brought to justice and then I'd be satisfied." He dropped his gaze to his dusty boots and shook his head in deep concentration. "No. No, a marshal's job doesn't appeal to me."

"Good. If they're here, we'll find them."

"Aw, I don't expect you to have to—"

She swept across the floor and seated herself on his lap, pressing a finger to his mouth. "I intend to keep you in my sight from now on."

"In that case—" His mouth closed on hers, and he hugged her hard enough to break her in two. He fell into a deep abyss that consumed his every thought with tasting her.

When they parted, she pushed her curls back, straightened up, and shook her head at him. "You really think your bluff on twelve cents a pound will work?"

He winked. "We can always take less but I figure that's top dollar. Being the first shipment out of here and all. He might pay it."

"What will those steers weigh?"

"Eight to nine hundred pounds in the shape they're in."

She whistled. "That's neat. Almost a hundred dollars apiece."

"You could use eighty thousand dollars?"

She threw her arms around his neck and squeezed him. "Ed Wright, do you know how much money that is?"

He snuggled up to her and savored the musk that filled his nose. Then he let go of her and leaned back in the chair. "I think he's serious."

She used her fingers to comb the hair back from

her face and smiled. "Should we get a room at that hotel?"

"Better get two."

She nodded and looked away. "I meant that."

"They just nailed up this fresh floor setting on the ground and stuck the tent over it," Ed said, observing the construction from his seat with amusement.

"They call that the boomtown way, don't they?"

More shots punctuated the air, and Ed shook his head. "It'll really get wilder here in six weeks when the herds stack up outside of town."

"We should be loaded up and on our way home. Right?"

"I sure hope so." He looked warily around. These folks had lots to learn and not much time.

Les returned and Ed knew by the look on his face that they had made a helluva deal.

"Well, the old man wants them." Les motioned to her and smiled.

"When're Joe's scales going to work?" Ed asked, looking as bored as he could.

"Day after tomorrow. There's fifty cars on the side tracks now, and the rest should be here by then too. We can weigh and load a thousand head the first day, Joe says."

"We'll have them at the pens by sunup," Ed said, and rose out of the chair and shook Les's hand.

"Want a drink of the good stuff?" Les asked.

Ed shook his head. "No thanks, we've got work to do."

"I'll be damned, Ed Wright. You never turned down a drink before in your life."

"Guess I've got a new one."

"I never heard what happened to your partner, Dave Ivy."

"The Brady brothers murdered him on a riverboat."

"Brady brothers? Why I seen them this morning—"

Cold chills ran up Ed's spine and he blinked in disbelief at Les. "Where? Where did you see them?"

"They were in the diner where I ate breakfast. They're a real shady bunch, but they came down from Abilene with the rest of the garbage."

"You know where I can find them?"

"Try the Royal Flush Saloon. I'm sorry about Ivy. If I'd known they'd done it, I'd sure have sent you word."

"Come on." He turned around to see that Unita was ready. "Where's the Royal Flush at?"

"On the next block behind here. You can't miss the sign."

"We can find it."

"Thursday we weigh the first half," Les reminded him as they left.

"We won't miss it," Ed said, going out the flap.

"What now?" she asked as they went around Les's tent and edged their way through piles of empty boxes and crates. He could see the ace high card hand-painted on a sign. When he stopped she about collided into him. He laid the revolver on his left sleeve, checked the loads in the cylinder and, satisfied, snapped the cover shut.

"You stay here and keep an eye out to see if any rats run out from under the tent."

"Rats?"

"Two-legged ones."

"You expect them to run?"

"Yes, I do."

"Will you know them?"

"If they're in there—they'll either run out or come out feet-first."

"I'll watch," she said.

Ed crossed the rutted street, which had been prairie grass only months ago but was now cut up into a boggy mess by freight wagon deliveries and traffic. Some boards spanned the swamp and he did a balancing act to reach the far shore and save his boots.

On the other side of the mud, he nodded to her and headed for the flap. A tinny piano cut the afternoon's warmth and he stepped into filtered sunlight penetrating cloth, and saw a long, raw bar made of boards on barrels.

"What's your pleasure, laddy?" the big Irish bartender asked as if he was in the fanciest bar in the U.S.A.

Ed looked around at the empty tables and chairs. "The Brady brothers."

"Well bless me soul, you're late. They took the stage out of here an hour ago."

"How come?"

"Word came up that some acquaintances of theirs in a small burg south of here got themselves all shot up by a band of Texas Rangers."

"Band of Texas Rangers?" Ed blinked at the man in disbelief, about to laugh.

"I heard the tale secondhand." He turned up the ends of his mustache and leaned his elbows on the bar. "Twelve steel-eyed rangers rode into this small burg called Wichita under the cover of night. Found the three men in their beds, made them go downtown barefooted, and strung them up one at a time on a saloon porch to strangle to death. Then the captain shot each one in the face to be sure they were dead."

"Who were these ones they hung?"

"Some of the Bradys' bunch. A Mexican named Roho, a breed called hisself Hatchet and an Apache— he was some kin to Cochise—Warlock was his handle."

"They all work for the Bradys?"

"Who knows, but when Marsh heard that a dozen Texas Rangers was coming up here, they closed up shop and shagged out of here."

"Where they headed?"

"I heard Fort Laramie mentioned."

Ed found a couple of silver dollars and slapped them on the bar. "Anything else?"

The big mick shook his head and nodded thanks for the money before him. "You know them rangers, mister?"

"Yeah," he said, and left the Royal Flush.

He waved at her that it was all right, and then started for the crossing boards. "They took a powder."

She nodded, looking relieved.

When he reached her side, he hugged her shoulders. "You won't believe what I heard that sent them pedaling out of here."

"What's that?"

"Twelve Texas Rangers hung his gang on a saloon porch in Wichita."

"What?"

"They heard the rangers slipped in at night, woke them up, and took them to the saloon, barefooted, and hung them."

"Twelve, huh?" She laughed. "You tell them anything different in there?"

"No, ma'am, let them think that many rangers are after them. Now we need to find a steak and then get back to camp. Boys got lots of work to do to be ready to load that many head in a day."

"What about the Bradys?"

"I'll get them after we load and get paid for those steers."

She made him stop and looked him hard in the eye. "You know you can't go without me."

"I had that notion, back down the trail. Can I tell you how rough it might be?"

"Rough doesn't matter. I'm going along."

"About to become the richest woman in Banty, Texas, and ain't got any more sense than that?" He looked into the deep set of her eyes and shrugged in defeat. "All right. Let's go eat."

A shot rang out and he stepped in front of her, trying to locate the shooter.

"You forget I'm a Texas Ranger now, too," she said, looking slyly at him and stepping out from behind him. "That means I'm your equal."

"Yes, ma'am." Cattle sales and then Fort Laramie. *Those two dogs couldn't hide from a dozen Texas Rangers.*

Chapter 30

The clack of horns, cattle bawling, dust boiling, men cussing and prodding them on and off the scales ten at a time, then into pens, and finally up the chutes into slat-sided cattle cars. It took all the trail hands she could spare from the herd, and every one of Schroeder's men, working from dawn to dusk. But, the task finally done, they drank buckets of beer she'd ordered for them with all the barbecue they could eat. She even bought an armload of French bread loaves and a big tub of fresh-churned butter from a farmer's wife for a treat.

"Best damn day we've had so far, boys," Shorty said, sitting on the ground, floured in dirt and looking red-eyed as a mad cow, with an empty tin plate in his lap.

"Amen," one of them shouted, and raised a cup of beer. "Here's to the best boss lady in Texas!"

"Throw in Kansas too," another said.

"We've got one more tough day," Ed said. "Then you can go see paradise. It's all here."

They cheered and began moving stiffly toward their horses to drag back to the herd and camp.

"I'll pay them Saturday morning. I've arranged for Caudle and whoever wants to take the chuck wagon, your big steer Sam Houston, and the remuda back," she said.

Ed frowned at her. "Isn't Blondie going back with the ponies?"

She shook her head. "He said he wanted to tag along with us." Then she raised her chin and met his gaze. "He's tough help if we need him."

"The rest of a dozen rangers, I guess?"

"That's what I thought."

"Half or more of this bunch will be dead broke and hung over in two days. Tell Caudle not to be in any hurry to head for home right away, and to take the ones who need a way to go back. They can earn their grub by herding the horses and doing camp work."

She squinted her right eye at him in disbelief. "They'll spend it all that fast?"

"Oh, that's why all this riffraff came down here from Abilene. This is where the money will be. Those boys and some drovers will sure make the money change hands."

"You never did that?"

He shook his head. "I never mixed business with pleasure." Thank God.

A thousand more head to do the same with, and only a few hours' sleep what with night herding and guarding and all. The second day proved even tougher. But at last the sale was over and they set the boys free. Ed, Unita, and Les were in his tent under the glow of two lamps.

"They weighed better than you thought," Les said,

poring over the tickets. "Where do you want the money?"

Unita looked at Ed, and at his nod began. "I need to draw some money to pay my crew. Some expenses, and the rest we want in a safety deposit box or vault."

"Don't trust Kansas banks?"

Ed shook his head. "Besides, it's not all her money."

"I understand. I'll be a couple of days reaching the total, you understand. My latest accountant took one look at this place and quit. How much do you need?"

"Three thousand five hundred should do it." Unita shared a glance with Ed.

He agreed. "We'll be back in a few weeks for the balance."

Les looked across at both of them. "I'll get the money out of my safe for you. Be careful. Those back shooters are tough ones."

Ed agreed and they left with the crew's money.

"Any urge to get drunk?" she asked as they negotiated the muddy streets. The loud sounds of music, doves laughing, and screaming and general hell-raising filled the night.

"No, ma'am."

She hugged his arm. "Thanks. Thanks for getting me here, and thanks for being you."

He looked at the dark skies, threatening rain. "Thanks to you."

"We'll get all the crew's part settled, and then?"

"Take a stage for Fort Laramie."

"You ever been there?"

"No." Just another place, but if it contained the Bradys, he wanted to be there and confront them.

*   *   *

Four days later, at a stage stop in Beaver Creek, Nebraska, a horse hustler told Ed the Brady brothers had quit the stage there and gone up in the Platte River breaks.

"You sure it was them?" Ed asked, looking around in a cold north wind.

"Mister, I'd know them two skunks anywhere." The whiskered man spat aside and wiped his mouth on the back of his hand. "They killed my brother Job in Ellsworth two years ago."

"They recognize you?"

He shook his head.

"What's in the breaks?" Ed motioned to the south.

"There's a guy makes whiskey down there named Gilmer. He's got kind of a hideout for their kind down there."

"How many will be there?"

"No telling."

"Wait, throw down our gear and saddles," Ed said to the driver, who was getting ready to leave, the stopover. "We're getting off here."

"Suit yourself—" He looked around at the rolling prairie as if they'd lost their minds. Then he climbed up and threw down the gear for him and Blondie to catch.

"We'll need three horses," Ed said to the hustler.

"I can get them in a couple of hours."

"There's a bonus if you find them quicker."

"I'm on my way," the man said, and hurried off.

"You must have information," she said coming out of the soddy stage stop and seeing the luggage and saddles piled on the ground.

"They're up in the Platte River country at some whiskey maker—we think." Ed heaved up his saddle and her war bag. "We've sent for horses." He hauled his load of gear out of the mist that the wind blew in. Blondie brought more in with a nod.

"Horses be better than stage," he grumbled in Spanish.

Ed laughed. "You ain't seen the horses yet."

The mounts the hustler brought back were winter-shaggy brown ponies. Ed and Blondie saddled them. Then Blondie tried each one. One bucked some, but they acted broke. They saddled her the tamest one. Then, with a memory map the hustler drew in the dirt that satisfied Blondie, they set out southwest across the prairie in midafternoon. That evening they ended up at a homesteader's and slept on the hay in his shed. His wife, a German woman, fed them supper and breakfast while her husband puffed on his clay pipe and talked about the tall corn he planned to grow on the acres he'd plowed that winter with his oxen and the new John Deere steel plow.

After breakfast and more words from their hosts about how to find Gilmer's place, they rode on. Ed looked over the neat furrows the man'd made that looked like cornrows of hair. The job of plowing with oxen sounded like a prison sentence to him—he'd hardly enjoyed breaking out land for oats with mules in Texas, years earlier.

By midafternoon they had reached a ferryman on the Platte named Ned who looked them over. "Texans, huh? Got cattle coming?"

"Yeah, a couple of thousand. Plenty of good grass

around here." Ed indicated the short, new greenery waving in the wind.

"This country's going to be settled by farmers, mister. Law and order, not no border ruffians like you all bring up here. Railroad is recruiting them folks now. Settlers to grow crops and use my ferry."

"Good," Ed said, and indicated the barge. "Us ruffians want across the river."

"Cost two bits apiece." He held out a callused, unwashed hand.

"Man we stayed with last night said you charged ten cents." Ed pushed his bluff with a wink at Unita.

"That's for locals."

Ed narrowed his eyes and reined up the short-coupled mustang. "Anyone ever threaten to shoot you for overcharging folks?"

"No—but ten cents a piece is enough."

"That's better. Now, for a silver dollar, tell me how many men are at Gilmer's?"

"I don't make it my business—"

"How many?"

He scratched his shaggy beard and nodded. "Maybe four. Two rode in a few days ago, and far as I know ain't left."

"One have a mustache and a goatee?"

"Yeah. They both looked like tinhorns. Said they was land buyers."

"Land buyers?" she asked.

"Yeah, ain't no one buying land around here, lady. You can homestead it easier."

Ed paid him, and they dismounted and loaded their mounts on the hollow-sounding ferry. Ned began to crank them across the choppy brown Platte. On the high far bank, the hills were eroded and chocked in red cedars that towered above them. Gilmer's place was a few miles west according to the farmer.

"Good luck. Hope you find them," Ned said when they disembarked on the shore. "They give me a counterfeit ten for their crossing."

"You give them change?"

The ferryman nodded.

"What did you do with it?" Ed asked, ready to remount his anxious, head-tossing bay.

"Paid a freighter for my coal with it."

Ed nodded that he heard, and guessed that would work until someone got caught.

"He did what with it?" Unita asked, leaning over toward him as their horses climbed the road.

"Paid for the coal some freighter brought him."

"Oh, no."

Ed nodded matter-of-factly. "The further you get in the frontier, the more bad money there is." He twisted in the saddle. "We can make camp somewhere and let you go scout them?" he asked Blondie.

The blue-eyed scout nodded. "They not far."

Ed twisted in the saddle again, looking over the broken country. "If we can find any shelter we'll be lucky."

"Quit worrying about me," Unita protested and redid the blanket she was wrapped in against the wind.

"I'm more worried about the three of us. This threat of rain we've rode in all day might increase, and we need some dry shelter."

Even Blondie agreed from under the unblocked felt hat he wore. *Malo* was his word for the driving chill and there was a scowl on his face over the weather when Ed conversed with him in Spanish about finding a place to den up.

Rocking in his saddle, Ed considered it was one of those dreary late-spring days when even the small sprays of wildflowers regretted blooming. About then Blondie pointed to some fallen-down rail fence that indicated an old homestead, and they turned off the road. The soddy was fallen down but a small shed was dry save for a few leaks in the slab board roof.

Blondie left them to unsaddle and hobble the horses, and rode off into the dreary afternoon.

"Guess we're eating crackers and dry cheese," he said, rubbing his hands together to increase the circulation.

"What we've been eating on the stage—those stops are sure no fancy cafés," she said and laughed at him.

"If I can find some dry fuel, we can have a small fire at the doorway."

"Might be all right. But I'll be fine." She stopped and looked at him in the shadowy light. "You'd have gone with him if I hadn't been along, right?"

"Probably. But that Comanche can find out more than I can."

"You should have gone with him."

"Well, he'll be back and we may know something."

She came over and hugged him. "Ed Wright, this has been the bleakest day in my life. I've worried since morning that those killers are going to get you, and I'll be all alone up here in this winter land."

He hugged her tight. "Ain't none got me yet."

She raised her face and the tears ran down her cheeks. "These may be the worst ones yet, too."

He used the side of his finger to stop the tears. "It'll be fine."

Blondie returned at dark. He swung the blanket from his shoulders and sat down on the floor facing them. "There are four men at the whiskey man's place. I see the bearded one."

"Two in suits?"

"*Sí. Dos. Ono esta* breed. *Ono esta* big belly man with black beard."

"That must be Gilmer," Ed said to her. "Is the breed tough?"

"Maybe."

"They well armed?"

"Have *pistolas*."

"Can we take them?"

Blondie nodded.

"Sunup?"

"*Bueno.*"

"Have some crackers and cheese," Ed offered. "We'll find something better to eat in the morning."

They slept a few hours, then made their way on horseback across the ridge and down the ridgeline a ways in the darkness. Blondie signaled for them to go right and they started down a steep canyon till he held them up and they dismounted. Unita held the horses while they loaded their rifles and then picketed the mustangs. Darkness engulfed them and the cedars' big, looming shapes rose all around them. Ed could smell sour mash and hear pigs grunting in their sleep.

"Smells bad here," she said, and followed on his heels with her shotgun.

The wind was down but their breath made vapor

clouds in the cold air. They rounded the pigpen and Blondie indicated for them to squat and stay. He was soon gone soundlessly into the night. Above the pigs' nocturnal grunts, Ed heard several hard blows. Then nothing until Blondie returned.

"Breed gone."

Ed nodded. "How do we take the house?"

The dim light of dawn was coming over the ridge. The faint light was fast bringing things in focus for Ed.

"You cover the back door," he said to Unita. "Blondie, the window. I'll kick in the front door and we'll see how much fight they've got in them."

She shook her head in disapproval. "These men have killed—I know. I don't want it to be you."

"I'll remember that. Let's go."

They set out for the soddy. Satisfied that his man was in place and that Unita was out back, Ed used his boot to bust open the door. Rifle in his fist, he burst in the room.

"Hands in the air or die."

"What the hell—"

Blondie broke the window out on the side and stuck his rifle inside to back Ed's words.

A big man dove off the bed for the floor, and another in the next bed on the right reached for a weapon in a holster hung on the poster. It was one of those moves that proved fatal as Ed's and Blondie's rifles poured lead into him and the room billowed with acrid, sulphur gun smoke. When the ear-ringing shots were over, he flopped on the smoking bed in the arms of death like a fish out of water. The other brother— where was he?

"I give up! Goddamn it, don't shoot no more!" Gilmer screamed. "I give up! I give up!"

"Where's the other one?" Ed demanded. The rifle in his hands was cocked and ready.

"Must have gone to the outhouse. How should I know?"

"Unita?" Ed called. "You all right?"

"Sure."

The sound of her voice relieved him. His hands shaking from the tension he reloaded the side gate on the rifle. "Blondie, go look for any signs out there."

"I didn't see anyone go out," she said, coming around as Blondie ran off to check.

"He may have left the house before we even got down here, and slipped away. Keep your rifle on him." He indicated Gilmer in his underwear, sitting on the bed. "Shoot him if he moves."

She nodded woodenly with the right ear-hammer cocked back and the barrels pointed at the pale-faced whiskey maker. "Watch yourself."

"This way," Blondie shouted from above them on the hillside.

Outside the shack, Ed could see his man going through the cedars.

Ed was breathless when they reached the ridge. Obviously Brady was headed away from their animals, which Ed considered lucky. He must have been outside for some activity when they moved in.

"He's barefooted." Blondie pointed to his tracks as they both sucked in wind.

"Good, he won't go far."

The scout nodded and they set out along the edge between the prairie and the cedars.

Then a bearded man stepped out of the boughs a hundred feet ahead, dressed in his pants and underwear. He held a derringer pistol pointed at them in each hand. Ed held out his rifle and stopped Blondie

"Damn you, Ed Wright. I sent men to kill you, but I won't fail this time."

"They were like you're going to be. Get ready to meet your maker."

"Ivy was his name, wasn't it? Tough little sumbitch. I cut his throat—he was your partner, wasn't he—"

Ed's reply came from the muzzle of the .44/40 in his hand. The butt was pressed hard to his hip. He kept levering in cartridges and pulling the trigger as he advanced, the bullets thudding into Brady as he crumpled into a pile. The chamber clicked on empty and he raised the smoking barrel. "That's for Ivy." And he kicked him—hard.

Ed came off the hill and Unita rushed to meet him.

"What about Gilmer?" He looked hard toward the shack for any sight of the man.

"He saddled a horse and left for Canada." She fell in his arms. "I told him not to look back."

Ed agreed and hugged her. "Let's get married."

"You sure?" She gave a toss of her hair and looked up at him.

"I don't say much I'm not sure about."

"Took you long enough." She wet her lips and smiled at him.

"I think I've got this all finally settled. Let's head back to Newton, get your money, and head home." He pushed his hat back and scratched his head. "Where're we getting married?"

"There must be a JP around here or a preacher," she said, and leaned her face on him.

"No big church wedding?"

"I had one of those—make it simple this time."

He rubbed his palms on the sides of his pants legs. "I can do that."

"Good. Where we going to live?"

"Bar U, I guess. My old place ain't much."

"Good, I like it there."

She let go and looked around. "What about all these hogs?"

"I'm going to send word to that farmer who put us up for the night to bring all his friends and have a hog killing up here in two days—"

"And bring a preacher?"

"Bet he can find one. A free hog killing and a wedding." He grabbed her around the waist and swung her feet off the ground in a circle. "They'll sure have a time."

Ed sent Blondie with a note, and he began to dig a single grave for the breed and the Bradys. It was the only grave he ever remembered not dreading his purpose while he spaded out the dirt. The three planted, she brought him some fresh, hot coffee and they shared it, sitting on a lumber pile.

"You won't regret this?" she asked.

"What, planting them three?"

"No—I mean about us."

"Lord, no. There's over thirty fat hogs here. We're going to have a real hog killing."

"What about the sows?"

"Guess at one apiece they'll start the homesteaders' own bunch."

She leaned over and kissed him. "Gilmer sure won't need them in Canada." And they laughed.

The "hog killing" was a huge success. Thirty-five families came. A boy of maybe twenty with a bobbing Adam's apple read their vows and pronounced them man and wife. The fiddles played and, like Ed's daddy always said about such affairs, there wasn't one little kid didn't have a shiny mouth from eating fresh-cooked pork. Full of food and weary to the bone, they finally took a bedroll and slipped off from the maddening crowd into the night.

He unfurled their bed with gusto and laughed. "You ever figure it would end like this when you got me in that wheelbarrow that day?"

"Something like this." She nodded in the affirmative and gave him a sly smile.

Epilogue

Ed and Unita Wright's union produced four children. The oldest, Ellen, became a schoolteacher and married a cowboy named Roy English in New Mexico. They later ranched above Pie Town, New Mexico. The second girl, Edie, was killed at fifteen in a runaway buggy wreck coming home from town. Jason left home at sixteen and was never heard of again. The youngest son, Lyle, ran the ranches, both the Bar U and his father's place, after Ed was killed in a roping accident during roundup at age sixty-three. The Boss Lady, as all the hands called her, lived to be ninety and was interred at the Bandy cemetery beside her Ed.

In the late nineteen thirties, the Daughters of the Texas Republic placed a ranger star granite monument over their grave in recognition of his service with the rangers. No known descendants operate either of the two ranch properties today.

Note: Blondie Wright, an adopted Comanche tribal member, died at Fort Sill, Oklahoma, in April, 1897. He left a full-blood wife, Minnie Lou, and several descendants.